COLD
HEAVEN

BRIAN MOORE

FAWCETT CREST • NEW YORK

A Fawcett Crest Book
Published by Ballantine Books
Copyright © 1983 by Brian Moore

Library of Congress Catalog Card Number: 82-18720

ISBN 0-449-20602-5

This edition published by arrangement with Holt, Rinehart and Winston

Manufactured in the United States of America

First Ballantine Books Edition: September 1984

FOR JEAN, AND FOR MICHAEL

Suddenly I saw the cold and rook-delighting heaven
That seemed as though ice burned and was but the more
ice . . .

—WILLIAM BUTLER YEATS

PART ONE

THE wooden seats of the little pedal boat were angled so that Marie looked up at the sky. There were no clouds. In the vastness above her a gull calligraphed its flight. Marie and Alex pedaled in unison, the revolving paddles making a slapping sound against the waves as the pedal boat treadmilled away from the beach, passing through ranks of bathers to move into the deeper, more solitary waters of the Baie des Anges. Marie slackened her efforts but Alex continued determinedly, steering the *pedalo* straight out into the Mediterranean.

"Let's not go too far," she said.

"I want to get away from the crowd. I'm going to swim."

It was like him to have some plan of his own, to translate idleness into activity even in these few days of vacation. She now noted his every fault. It was as though, having decided to leave him, she had withdrawn his credit. She looked back at the sweep of hotels along the Promenade des Anglais. Today was the day she had hoped to tell him. She had planned to announce it at breakfast and leave, first for New York, then on to Los Angeles to join Daniel. But at breakfast she lacked all courage. Now, with half the day gone, she decided to postpone it until tomorrow.

Far out from shore, the paddles stopped. The *pedalo* rocked on its twin pontoons as Alex eased himself up from his seat. He handed her his sunglasses. "This should do," he said and, rocking the boat even more, dived into the ultramarine waters. She watched him surface. He called out: "Just follow along, okay?" He was not a good swimmer, but thrashed about in an energetic, erratic freestyle. Marie began to pedal again, her hand on the tiller, steering the little boat so that she followed close. Watching him, she knew he could not keep up this pace for long. She saw his flailing arms and for a moment thought of those arms hitting her. He had never hit her. He was not the sort of man who would hit you. He would be hurt, and cold, and possibly vindictive. But he was not violent.

She heard a motorboat, the sound becoming louder. She looked back but did not see a boat behind her. Then she looked to the right where Alex was swimming and saw a big boat with an outboard motor coming right at them, coming very fast. Of course they see us, she thought, alarmed, and then as though she were watching a film, as though this were happening to someone else, she saw that there was a man in the motorboat, a young man wearing a green shirt; he was not at the tiller, he was standing in the middle of the boat with his back to her and as she watched he bent down and picked up a child who had fallen on the floorboards. "Hey?" she called. "Hey?" for he must turn around, the motorboat was coming right at Alex, right at her. But the man in the boat did not hear. He carried the child across to the far side of the boat; the boat was only yards away now. "Alex," she called. "Alex, look out." But Alex flailed on and then the prow of the motorboat, slicing up water like a knife, hit Alex a sickening thump, went over him and smashed into the pontoons of the little pedal boat, upending it, and she found herself in the water, going under, coming up. She looked and saw the motorboat churning off, the pedal boat hanging from its prow like a tangle of branches. She heard the motorboat engine cut to silence, then start up again as the boat veered around in a semicircle and came back to her. Alex? She looked: saw his body near her just under the water. She swam toward him, breaststroke, it was all she knew. He was floating facedown, spread-eagle. She caught hold of his wrist and pulled him toward her. The motorboat came alongside, the man in the green shirt reaching down for her, but "No, no," she called and tried to push Alex toward him. The man caught Alex by the hair of his head and pulled him up, she pushing, Alex falling back twice into the water before the man, with a great effort, lifted him like a sack across the side of the boat, tugging and heaving until Alex disappeared into the boat. The man shouted. *"Un instant, madame, un instant,"* and reappeared, putting a little steel ladder over the side. She climbed up into the motorboat as the man went out onto the prow to disentangle the wreckage of the *pedalo*. A small child was sitting at the back of the boat, staring at Alex's body, which lay facedown on the floorboards. She went to Alex and saw blood from a wound, a gash in the side of his head, blood matting his hair. He was breathing but unconscious. She lifted him up and cradled him in her arms, his blood trickling onto her breasts. She saw the boat owner's bare legs go past her as he went to the rear of the boat to restart the engine. The child began to bawl but the man leaned over, silenced it with an angry slap, then turned to her, his face sick with fear. *"Nous y serons dans un instant,"* he shouted, opening the motor to full throttle. She hugged Alex to her, a rivulet of blood dripping off her forearm onto the floorboards as the boat raced toward the beach.

They were coming in. She could hear the engine slacken speed. The boat owner stood, shouting, waving for attention. Faces of bathers stared up at them as they passed. Then the boat's keel crunched on the pebbled beach and people were all around, pulling the boat up. Alex was a dead weight in her arms. Two young men in red swim trunks climbed into the boat. *"Attendez, mademoiselle,"* one said, as they took Alex from her, lifting him onto a canvas mat that they had spread on the stony beach. They bent over him, one doing mouth-to-mouth resuscitation, people crowding around them, the boat owner talking to her, but she no longer understood his French, she couldn't concentrate, she stumbled on the stony beach, pushing through the circle of onlookers, kneeling down beside Alex. They had put some sort of machine alongside him and two more young men in red trunks came with a stretcher. They attached wires to Alex's wrist. She heard people asking in French what had happened; the boat owner, in his green shirt, holding his little boy in his arms, saying in French that it was the child's fault, the child ran across the boat deck and fell, he was helping the child, he didn't know, he didn't see, and then Marie stopped hearing, for his voice was drowned by the honking sound of a French ambulance, growing louder, then coming to a stop on the promenade above the beach. The pedal-boat concessionaire came up to her and asked for her locker key, offering to go and get her things. She had the key around her wrist. Alex's and her clothes and wallets were in the same locker. One of the lifeguards doing mouth-to-mouth resuscitation stopped, looked up at her, and nodded reassuringly. *"Ça va,"* he said. *"Ça va, mademoiselle."*

"He's all right, then?" she asked.

"You speak English?" the young man said. "Yes, he's okay. His breathing is good."

He was not drowned, he was unconscious from the blow. She thought of that sickening noise as the boat hit him. And then, above the ring of faces peering down at her, she saw a circle of cold blue sky and felt her fear of it, a feeling that guns were trained on her from that vastness, ready to shoot her down. The ring of faces wavered, heads turning to look as two ambulance paramedics in white jackets came down to the beach together with a French policeman who at once began ordering people to move on. She stood up as they lifted Alex onto a larger stretcher, one with steel runners and pillows and a blanket with which they covered him up. They took great care as they moved him. The pedal-boat concessionaire came back with her beach bag and sundress, Alex's shirt, trousers, sandals, and wallet. She shoved everything into the beach bag. The motorboat owner, holding his little boy by the hand, began to make a long, rambling apology, but she nodded to shut him up and walked on, following the paramedics and Alex's stretcher. The policeman came alongside her, asking about the accident, writing down the address of her hotel. She looked at Alex's head. She wondered why they had not bandaged his wound. The paramedics carried the stretcher up a ramp leading from the beach to the Promenade des Anglais, where a new, larger, crowd was collecting. People surrounded her. She saw the paramedics slide the stretcher into a white ambulance. *"Mademoiselle*, get in, please," said the paramedic who spoke English and took her beach bag and put it in and helped her up. She sat on a stretcher bench opposite Alex while the paramedic slid the door shut. The ambulance lights began to flash, the siren started its honking sound as the ambulance moved recklessly out into the oncoming traffic. She had to hold the metal runners beneath the stretcher bench as they went into a crazy swing and took off at high speed, climbing through the streets of Nice. Alex was strapped down on the stretcher. She watched his face. His eyes were shut. The paramedic leaned over him, looked at him, then smiled to reassure her, but she was not reassured. The ambulance rushed through a big square with sidewalk cafés on all sides. She recognized it as a place where she and Alex had had a coffee yesterday. The siren made speech impossible, the ambulance swayed from side to side as the driver wrenched it through lanes of slow-moving traffic. She held on tight, swaying. She saw a clock on a church tower. It was twenty minutes past four.

One of the paramedics took Alex's pulse while the other scrambled to the front of the ambulance and returned with two hand towels and a bottle of pink fluid. He poured fluid on a towel and gave the towel to her. Dutifully, she began to mop the blood from her shoulders and forearms, awkward because she had to hold on to the runner with one hand. It was then that she thought: I can't go into the hospital in a bikini. My sundress and sandals are in the beach bag. The paramedic handed her a second towel to dry herself. He wore a small gold cross on a thin gold chain, the cross lying askew amid the black hair on his chest. Her eye was drawn to the cross. *It is one year since Carmel. One year to the day.* The ambulance, rushing up a narrow street, stalled, hemmed in by traffic, its siren honking in indignation as the driver wrenched the wheel around, then darted through again. She saw a sign on a street lamp: HÔPITAL, and an arrow pointing to the right. They went right. The siren died as they drove into a courtyard and stopped near some doors. The ambulance reversed and backed up to the doors, the paramedics jumped down, helped her down, then slid the stretcher out. Marie fumbled in her beach bag, pulled out her yellow sundress, and put it on over the wet bikini. She found her sandals and as she slipped them on, the paramedics placed the stretcher on a trolley and wheeled it into the emergency entrance of the hospital. She followed, down a corridor, past patients who stared at Alex. A paramedic signaled her to wait. The stretcher was wheeled into a little room where a doctor and a nurse began to examine Alex. She did not see what they did, for the door shut, but a few minutes later the stretcher was wheeled out again. The paramedic signaled her to follow and they went up in an elevator. In the elevator she stood by Alex's head, looking down at his face. Could the blow from the boat have fractured his skull?

The elevator doors opened. The stretcher was wheeled toward a set of double doors that had a red light above them. Again, she was told to wait. They wheeled the stretcher through. The doors shut. She turned and saw a woman in a white coat coming toward her. The woman had a clipboard and a pen. *"Voulez-vous m'accompagner à la chambre de reception?"* the woman asked.

"Do you speak English?" Marie asked. She felt she could not deal with this in French.

"Yes, a little. He is your husband?"

"Yes."

"That is our intensive-care unit. The doctor will speak with you very soon. You have insurance, perhaps, or American Express?"

She said she had American Express. Alex had Blue Shield but she decided not to go into that now. She got her American Express card out of her purse, which was in the beach bag, and the woman admitting clerk took it, put it in a card machine, then gave it back to her. It seemed strange, the idea of a hospital accepting American Express cards. The woman admitting clerk then went with her into the reception room, a sort of waiting room with sofas and French magazines on a table. They sat side by side on a sofa and the clerk asked questions and filled out a form, putting down Alex's name and his home address and occupation and the name and address of their hotel in Nice. The clerk then told her to wait. A few minutes later a nurse came in, an older woman wearing a white headdress. "I speak English," she said in a heavy accent. She also had a clipboard and a form. She asked for Alex's full name and age, and whether he had had any serious illnesses and whether he was taking any medication. She then asked about the accident. She asked the questions in English but Marie noticed that she wrote down the answers in French. When the nurse had finished writing out the form she said, "It won't be long. When I hear something, I let you know."

There were three other people in the waiting room. They sat, quickly flipping the pages of magazines as though searching for some hidden clue. The waiting room looked out onto a court-yard in which there were two dusty palm trees and a bench on which an old man sat. The old man wore a gray flannel dressing gown, striped pajamas, and slippers, and Marie saw that he was weeping. She wondered if he had been given terrible news about his health. She felt sick. She was afraid she might vomit. She went out and asked about the toilets and the nurse at the desk directed her where to go. In the washroom she went to the mirror and saw that her hair was wet and bedraggled and that the wet outlines of her bikini bra and pants showed through her sundress. She stood at the mirror. She did not vomit. Is this a punishment? her mirror face asked. She turned away, alarmed, as though the question had been asked out loud. She went back to reception. When the nurse on duty saw her coming she beck-oned and led Marie into the intensive-care unit. Inside, there were small rooms off a corridor, rooms that had heart-monitor-ing screens above the patients' beds. The nurse told her to wait and then went into one of these rooms, closing the door behind her. After a moment a young doctor came out of the room, re-moving a stethoscope from his ears. He wore a long white coat with ragged sleeves. He asked her something in French and when she did not respond at once, he said, in English, "He was hit by a motorboat, yes? The boat. Did you see it hit him?"

"Yes."

"Did he become conscious at any time after the accident?"

"No," she said. "I don't think so."

"He didn't open his eyes, or speak?"

"No."

"And when was the accident? At what hour?"

"About four, I think. Yes, about four o'clock."

"Thank you. Will you go back to the reception, please."

"But how is he, Doctor?" she said. "Can't I see him?"

"I'm sorry, he's still in coma. He has suffered a severe con-cussion. We are waiting for X ray now."

"Has he anything else, bones broken, anything like that?"

He shook his head. "No, no." He nodded to her and went back into the small room. She heard a sound behind her. A team

9

of three doctors and two nurses came out of one of the rooms across the way. The senior doctor she noticed at once, for he looked like Einstein. He had a comical face, a ragged gray mustache, and ragged gray hair in a halo around his head. He smiled at her, then turned to the nurse accompanying him and asked, *"La prochaine, c'est quoi?"*

"Un accident à la plage," the nurse said. Marie watched as the team went into one of the little rooms. An accident at the beach. So that is Alex's room. She was just about to go and look in to make sure when the nurse from reception came to take her back. She followed the nurse out to reception, went into the waiting room, and sat, looking into the courtyard. The old man who had been weeping was still out there, but now he was playing checkers with another patient, a young girl. As Marie watched, the old man grinned in triumph and made his move, jumping two of his opponent's pieces and taking them off the board. Suddenly, she felt a sense of panic. She was alone in a foreign country. She had learned her French in a school in Montreal. She knew nothing of France. Supposing the doctors wanted to operate? She thought of Reeves Bulmer, who had been on the panel in Marseilles with Alex, earlier in the week. Reeves was a neuropathologist; he would know all there was to know about Alex's condition, if she could find him. But all she knew was that Reeves and Betty had gone on to Paris after the conference. She did not know where they were staying in Paris. She would have to go to the American embassy or consulate for help. There must be a consulate here. What if Alex had brain damage? Sometimes they can't speak, they're in the hospital for ages. She remembered the President's press secretary who had been hit in the head by an assassin's bullet. He was in critical condition for months.

Daniel was the one to call. But she did not know where he was. All she knew was that he was on holiday somewhere in Marin County with Elaine. Besides, could anyone really help her, if what had happened was not coincidence? She looked out at the courtyard, at the old man and the girl in their dressing gowns, setting up for another game of checkers. She thought of the moment, earlier, when Alex and the concessionaire were steadying the little pedal boat in the shallow waters of the beach at Nice, waiting for her to climb in, the moment when she remembered as though a bell tolled a knell, that today was the anniversary of Carmel.

TWO hours later there was still no word from the doctors. The nurse at the reception desk had been replaced by another nurse who told her that Alex was still in a coma and that *"il n'y a pas de bulletin pour le moment."* She advised Marie to go out and get something to eat, but Marie sat on in the waiting room, looking into the courtyard until darkness came and she could see only the outline of the palm trees against the sky. At nine o'clock, a team of doctors came out of the intensive-care unit and said good-bye to each other, shaking hands in the French manner. One of them was the senior doctor she had seen earlier, the older man who looked like Einstein. She saw him go to the reception desk and speak to the nurse, then go back into the unit. The nurse came to the waiting room and looked directly at Marie. It was like a sentence, that look. *"Le Docteur Boulanger vous attend dans son bureau,"* the nurse said and led Marie into the intensive-care unit. There was a small office to the right just inside the double doors. Marie had not noticed it before. There, at a desk amid filing cabinets and samples of blood, stood Dr. Boulanger in his long white coat, his Einsteinian gray hair in aureole, back-lit by the lamp behind him. He came up to her and shook hands. "Good evening," he said. "I speak English, not well, but sufficient, I hope."

Marie nodded. She felt sick with panic. The doctor had large sad eyes that glistened. "I am sorry," he said. "But, I have bad news."

"Oh," she said. She knew, then. It was not brain damage. It was death.

"I am afraid there was not much we could do. He suffered a fracture, not a large fracture, but obviously he did have a very

12

great blow on his head that produced a severe concussion. He was a doctor, wasn't he?''

"Yes. He's a pathologist," Marie said.

"I am very sorry."

She bent her head. She shut her eyes as though to shut out what was happening.

"You were on holiday?" the doctor asked.

"We were at a medical conference in Marseilles. We came on here after it ended."

"Ah, yes, I know. The international conference on atherosclerosis. You are American?"

"Yes."

"Do you have any friends here, someone who can help you?"

"No. It's my first time in France."

"Well, we will contact the American consulate in the morning. They will assist you with arrangements. Oh, I forgot. I regret, but in these cases we have to perform an autopsy. I have some papers for you to sign. Hospital permissions." He sat her down at the desk and gave her a form and a pen. "We will do the autopsy first thing in the morning, so you won't be delayed. Do you want to take the body back to America?"

"I don't know."

"In any case, we will do our best to make things simple." He touched her arm, as though warning her of something. "Would you like to see his body? I think they are moving him now."

She went with him into the corridor. She followed him toward Alex's room. In the doorway, he paused. "One moment," he said. She could see two nurses moving about inside. Dr. Boulanger went in and whispered something and the nurses came out, nodding to her. One of them carried soiled sheets and a pillow. *"Madame?"* Dr. Boulanger said, beckoning to her from the doorway.

When she went in, the bed was empty. There was heartmonitoring equipment over the bed. Two aluminum stands holding plasma and saline bottles were pushed to one side. The room seemed bare as though ready for its next patient. And then, by the door, she saw a trolley. There was no mattress on it and it

13

was covered by a white plastic sheet. Dr. Boulanger went to the trolley and lifted the top end of the sheet. As he did, Marie looked at the other end of the trolley and saw a foot sticking out. There was a plastic hospital identification tag tied onto the big toe. She went toward the stretcher. Alex's face was very white, as though drained of blood. His eyes were closed and they had tied a strip of gauze around his chin to keep his mouth shut. She saw that they had shaved a small area above his left ear to expose a cruel-looking wound, painted in yellow antiseptic, but still bloody, the skin open like lips. The doctor, holding the edge of the sheet, looked at her with sad practiced eyes. "All right?" he said, and when she nodded he drew the sheet up to cover Alex's face. She did not want to leave Alex there alone. She felt as though she were abandoning him. The doctor took her by the arm and led her out. He said they would get a taxi to take her back to her hotel. He said something about the taxi to the night nurse at reception. He then told Marie that she could come to claim the body tomorrow and that they would notify the American consulate and that the consulate would be in touch with her. He said he was very sorry and then he said good-night, shaking hands with her and turning away, going back in under the red light, the doors closing behind him, the doors to that place where Alex lay, alone.

The nurse at reception told her a taxi was on the way. She went to sit again in the reception room in which she had already spent so many hours. She thought of Alex's mother, who must be told, and decided she would telephone her when she got back to the hotel. But, in the taxi, going down the narrow streets, past night-lit cafés and row on row of tightly parked cars, she wondered if she phoned tonight would she have to ask Alex's mother if the body should be cremated here or sent back? It was a terrible thing to have to ask. Marie could not remember Alex ever mentioning a family burial place. Was it in Boston? She realized how little she knew about his life. He did not talk about his past except in terms of fellowships and places where he had studied to become what he was. She knew that his father had been a lawyer who had practiced in Boston and that Alex's mother had not remarried and had some money of her own. She knew that Alex's sister, Barbara, lived in Washington, D.C. She had met Barbara only once, when Barbara passed through Los Angeles with her two small daughters on her way to a Hawaiian vacation. Marie did not know Alex's mother well but had the impression that Mrs. Davenport did not approve of her. She knew that Alex and his mother were not close. She wondered how much his mother would grieve for him. Who would really grieve for Alex? I will, she told him. Despite what I did against you, I will grieve for you. As she told herself this, the cab stopped in front of the Hotel Miramar, a small hotel in a street behind the seafront. Their room was on the top floor. It had a balcony and if you stood at the very end of the balcony you could just see the sea. She paid the taxi and went into the lobby. When she went to the desk for her key, there was a message. It was from an Edouard Duvalier, scribbled on a sheet of ruled paper and stuffed into an envelope that had her name on it. She had read several sentences before she realized it was a note of condolence from the motorboat owner, who did not yet know that Alex was dead. M. Duvalier said he would come to the hospital tomorrow to visit Alex, if she was agreeable. She crumpled up the note, took her key, and went upstairs. She decided she must phone Alex's mother after all. She would not mention cremation, but would ask if his mother wanted him to be buried in Boston. Otherwise, she would arrange for his burial here.

She sat on the bed, opened the beach bag and found Alex's wallet. Inside his wallet he kept a little notebook with addresses and phone numbers. She looked through it: doctors' names, hospital and laboratory numbers. Under M she saw *Mother/Boston*, and a number. She rang the hotel operator. The operator said she would call her back. While she waited, Marie emptied the beach bag and put Alex's shirt, sandals, and trousers in a closet. She put his wallet in the desk drawer. The phone rang. In Boston, it was a woman's voice, but not his mother. The voice said Mrs. Davenport was not in.

"I'm calling from France. Do you know where I can reach her?"

"She's on a cruise. She's in Jamaica or Bermuda. I'm not sure which."

"When will she be back?"

"I don't know. I think a couple of days. I don't know. You see, I'm the cleaning lady."

"Oh. Well, thank you." Marie hung up. I can't tell the cleaning lady to tell Alex's mother that Alex has been killed.

She looked in his notebook for a number for his sister, but did not find one. When she tried to think of the name of the newsletter Barbara's husband worked for, she could not remember it. It was in their address book back in the apartment in New York. She decided to wait till tomorrow to try to contact Barbara. She thought of her father, alone in his house in Brentwood—it was what time on the West Coast, early afternoon? If she called him he might offer to fly over, but what good would that do? The one time she had needed him he'd failed her, the time her mother died. Marie was twelve years old. Her mother, who was only nominally Catholic, had placed Marie as a day pupil in a convent school, a year earlier, when they moved from New York to Montreal. Marie had been in public school in New York. She knew almost nothing about the Catholic faith and at once got in trouble with the nuns. She was punished for disrespect, for talking in chapel, for making rude remarks about saints and penances. She had been publicly reprimanded by the headmistress for skipping evening devotions and her mother had been called in for a talk when Marie defiantly told the nuns that she never went to Sunday Mass. Her father was not even nominally Catholic and so when her mother died Marie asked him to let her change schools. But her father did not grant her request. He listened instead to the nuns, who recommended she now be enrolled as a boarder because, without a mother's guidance, she would need a firm hand. Marie wept and pleaded but her father did not give in. It was convenient for him to enroll her as a boarder. She knew that then. She had not forgiven him then. She had not forgiven him since.

The person she could trust to help her was Daniel. She saw his face, his lopsided grin, his receding hairline, his warm, intelligent brown eyes. If only he could walk in now, small, rumpled, smiling. But she could not reach Daniel. Daniel was somewhere in Marin County with his wife and his teen-age stepdaughter. She did not know where.

She went into the bathroom. At last, she took off her

sundress and bikini. She put on the raincoat she used as a dressing gown while traveling. She thought of the night ahead. She went to Alex's briefcase and found the little bag in which he kept medicines. She took out the last two Dalmane capsules. Alex was very much against sleeping pills, so she rarely took them, even this year when she had begun to have the migraines and the nightmare about Carmel, the nightmare she did not tell to anyone. She wondered if she would have the nightmare and the migraines from now on. *He is dead. I have been punished.*

After she had taken the capsules, she opened the doors to the balcony and stepped out onto its narrow ledge. The balcony looked down on an oval swimming pool lit by underwater lights. A hot gust of wind blew up, causing thousands of tiny corrugations on the pool's still surface. She saw something moving in and out of the shadows along the pool's edge. It was a rat. The rat came into the light and looked down at the water as though it had never seen a swimming pool before. Someone laughed in one of the hotel rooms opposite and the rat slid away into the shadows. Marie heard another round of laughter and thought of Alex floating facedown. She went back into the room, leaving the balcony doors open. It was hot and airless in the room. She took off her raincoat and lay on the bed, naked, pulling a sheet over her. She heard cicadas in the courtyard below. Lying there, she turned her head and looked up at the night sky, oranged by lights from the seafront. *Is it because of what I didn't do? Did they kill him because of that?*

Vengeance or coincidence? Her mind, like a windlass running down a well, fell again into the pit of that ineluctable question.

THE breakfast waiter put his rump against the swinging doors of the kitchen and backed out into the breakfast room, balancing three trays of *cafés complets*. He turned around and went to number 6, a Belgian couple and their daughter, putting in front of each of them a tray containing hot milk, hot coffee, butter pats, jam, marmalade, croissants, and petits pains. *"Bon appétit,"* he told them and turned to see if any other guests had arrived. Number 24 was there, not the young man, just the young lady. He went over. He remembered that, although she was American, she had spoken French to him yesterday.

"Bonjour, madame. Vous avez bien dormie?"

Yes, Marie said, she had slept well.

"Et Monsieur? Il arrive, Monsieur? Je vous apporte deux cafés complets?"

No, she said, just one breakfast. Monsieur would not come this morning.

"Bien, madame. Alors, un café complet," he said, smiling at her as he went back toward the swinging doors of the kitchen. Marie watched him go, his beige tunic, which seemed a size too big for him, hanging loosely over his hips. Yesterday she had chatted with him, while waiting for Alex to join her for breakfast. She remembered he had said his name was Ahmed and that he was a Turk, that he had a family and that they had been two years in France. As she watched him go off now, she thought: He has a wife. I am a widow. The old-fashioned word was frightening. Even now it still seemed possible that Alex would walk in as he did when he came home from a trip, not thinking to kiss or hold her, but asking at once, "Hello. Anything important come up while I was gone?"

She looked at her watch. She did not think the American consulate would open before nine-thirty. After breakfast she would take a taxi to the consulate and speak to someone in authority. She had decided that if she did not reach Alex's mother or sister today, she would have the body cremated and buried in Nice. There would be no service. Alex did not care about such things. Like her, he had no religious feelings. Nor would he want a tombstone. An obituary in *The New York Times,* of course, but that would have to wait.

Ahmed was coming back. Dexterously, he arranged before her the things she did not want to eat: the croissants, the jam, the butter pats. *"Café noir ou café crème, madame?"* he asked, balancing two steaming jugs, one of coffee, one of hot milk.

Black coffee, she said, and as he poured it he asked again, *"Monsieur descend plus tard?"*

No, she said. Monsieur would not come down later. She felt her voice break as she said it but Ahmed did not seem to notice. He departed, smiling, wishing her *"bonne journée."*

She sipped the hot coffee. As she did, one of the desk clerks came into the breakfast room, looked around, then came up to her. "Mrs. Davenport?"

"Yes."

"I have the St. Croix Hospital on the line. They wish to speak to you."

Marie got up and followed him out. He led her to a telephone booth near the reception desk. She picked up the receiver. "Hello?"

"Mrs. Davenport?" A voice in accented English.

"Yes."

"Good morning. Dr. Boulanger asks me to tell you that we have spoken with the American consulate and they are sending someone to pick you up and bring you to the hospital. Our medical director, Dr. Faure, would like to see you. If you will just wait there in the hotel."

"Yes," she said. "Thank you."

After she hung up Marie wished she had asked when the consular person would be coming, but as she had not, she decided she must be ready to leave. She went up to her room. There were maids working in the corridor but the room had not been made up yet. She took her shoulder bag and went back down to the lobby and sat near the door. A few minutes later, she heard her name spoken at the desk by a burly young man who could not be anything but American. He wore a seersucker suit, a white button-down shirt, a red-and-blue striped tie, and large, sensible, black brogues. She got up and went to the desk. When he turned to greet her she saw that he had a florid complexion and a nice smile. "Mrs. Davenport?" He offered her his hand. "I'm Tom Farrelly from the consulate. I have my car outside." As she followed him out, he said, "I'm very sorry about your husband."

She nodded. "Thank you," she said and thought: There are no words to answer sympathy; there is no language for these things.

His car was a bright red Ford compact. As they drove up the hilly streets toward the hospital, he asked her to explain just what had happened at the beach. When she had finished, he asked: "The French police, did they question the motorboat owner? And did they question you, personally?"

"No, they just asked my address. The motorboat owner was with them when I was. I think they spoke to him, I'm not sure." She supposed it was all part of some report he would have to make. There must be official procedures when an American dies abroad. She said: "The hospital told me they'll do an autopsy first thing this morning. Do you have any idea when they'll release the body?"

He seemed to hesitate, before he said, "No, I'm afraid I don't."

"But normally, I mean, what would be the usual thing?"

"Oh, tomorrow, perhaps." He did not seem sure. "Your husband was a doctor. A pathologist, wasn't he?"

"Yes," she said. He asked if they had been on vacation and she told him about the medical conference in Marseilles and that her husband had delivered a paper there.

"Is this your first visit to France?"

"Yes."

"And your husband, was it his first trip?"

"No, he was here once before, at a conference in Lyons."

"When was that?"

"I think about four or five years ago. It was before we were married."

"Did he speak French?"

"A little."

"Do you speak French?"

"Yes, a bit. I learned it in boarding school in Montreal."

"But you're American, aren't you?"

"Yes, we both are."

She saw him turn and look at her. "Sorry," she said. "It's hard to get used to it."

"Of course." But she saw him eye her strangely, this time through the driving mirror. She changed the subject and asked him how long he had been stationed in Nice, and as he began to tell her, they arrived at the hospital. He drove in at the main gate, parked his car in a section reserved for doctors, and led her inside with the air of a man who knew the terrain. He took her to a suite of offices and put her in a waiting room while he went to tell the hospital authorities that they had arrived. Then he came back and sat with her. He told her that they would see three doctors: Dr. Boulanger, who was the doctor who had treated Alex; and also the doctor who was chief of pathology; and Dr. Faure, who was the medical director of the hospital.

"Does that mean they've already done the autopsy?"

"No." He looked at her. "I think I'll let Dr. Faure explain it to you. Tell me, is your French good enough to follow what's said, or do you want me to interpret?"

"No, it's all right. If there's something I don't understand, you can help me out."

"Good. In any event, I know Dr. Boulanger speaks English, and I think Dr. Faure speaks some English as well. We'll manage."

A secretary had come into the waiting room and was approaching them. "Here we go," Tom Farrelly said, standing up. They followed the secretary through a maze of corridors to an office that bore a plaque on its frosted glass door, saying that it was the office of the medical director. When she entered, the first person she saw was Dr. Boulanger. There were two other doctors in the room, the chief of pathology, a tall bald man who, like Boulanger, wore a white hospital coat, and, behind an imposing desk, Dr. Faure, a precise old man dressed in a brown double-breasted business suit with a Legion of Honor boutonniere in his lapel. Marie had the impression that she and Tom Farrelly had interrupted some argument among these doctors. She was introduced and was given a seat. Dr. Faure then peered at Farrelly over his reading glasses and asked in French, "Have you told this lady what has happened?"

"No," Tom said. "I thought I would let you explain."

"François?" Dr. Faure looked over at Dr. Boulanger, who fingered his ragged Einsteinian mustache, then said to Marie, "Madame, I must tell you that your husband's body has disappeared."

"Disappeared?" She felt confused, perhaps she hadn't heard him, perhaps she did not understand. But the word was as clear in French as in English.

"Let me explain," Dr. Boulanger said. "At eight o'clock this morning we had scheduled an autopsy. When the doctor on duty asked for the corpse, the morgue attendant went to the morgue. The identification tag which had been tied to your husband's body was lying on the floor beside the stretcher. We have absolutely no explanation for these events. We at once made a complete search in case, by some extraordinary chance, the body had been mistaken for another. But, as it happens, no bodies had been moved in or out of the morgue during the night. And your husband's was the first body to be sent for this morning. Frankly, as I said, we are completely without explanation. Do you have any idea at all about this? I mean, is there any reason you know of, that anyone would want to steal your husband's body?"

"No, of course not."

"He didn't have any enemies?" the tall bald doctor asked.

"No, no," she said. "It was an accident. He was killed in an accident. We know nobody here, we've never been to France before. Why would anyone want to steal his body? It doesn't make sense."

"That's right," Tom Farrelly said.

"Exactly," the tall bald doctor said. "It makes no sense. In exceptional cases in the past, a corpse has occasionally been

22

mislaid for an hour or so. But it has always been found once we make a search.''

"It could still be mislaid, though," Tom Farrelly said.

"I can assure you," the tall doctor said, "the body is not in the hospital. It has not been mislaid. Someone has taken it.''

Dr. Faure, the medical director, cleared his throat and looked at Marie. "Dr. Pannaud is right," he said. "I am sorry, but we have no explanations. The morgue was locked. It is always kept locked. The key can only be obtained by nurses or doctors known to the personnel in charge of that desk. The door can be opened from the inside, of course. If some outside person planned to steal the body, that person would have to hide inside the morgue. It is completely bizarre.''

Marie felt her throat dry as she spoke. "But what if there was some mistake?" she said to Dr. Boulanger. "What if my husband wasn't dead?''

"There's no question of that," the tall doctor said. "But, let's suppose there *was* some misdiagnosis. Then, why didn't your husband come up and tell us about our mistake? He was a pathologist himself, after all.''

Dr. Boulanger listened to this as to an interruption that irritated him. "Madame," he said to Marie, "listen to me. Your husband was dead. I examined him myself. There were absolutely no vital signs. I made all the tests for brain death.''

"But sometimes, I mean, it happens that people who are pronounced dead aren't really dead. It happens," Tom Farrelly said.

"He was dead," Dr. Boulanger said. He looked at Tom Farrelly and then at Marie. "Madame. I know. Not just because I am a doctor. Anyone who has seen dead persons as often as I have knows. Am I right, Dr. Pannaud?''

The bald doctor nodded. "Dr. Davenport died shortly after seven o'clock last night," he said. "I have looked at the treatment reports, at all the evidence. I completely agree. There is no question of error.''

"So," said Dr. Faure. "The logical hypothesis is that someone removed the body from the morgue and spirited it out of the hospital. In that case, this must be reported to the police. That is, unless Mrs. Davenport has some explanation. And you do not, do you, Mrs. Davenport?''

''No,'' she said. She felt as though she were no longer awake, as though this were a dream so illogical she knew it could not be, and therefore would waken from it. She saw Dr. Faure get up from his desk and whisper something to Tom Farrelly. Then the three doctors shook her hand, one by one, offering their condolences. She heard them continue to speak of the mystery, the puzzle. She spoke too, although, afterward, she did not remember a word she said. Farrelly took her arm and they walked through many corridors, going out at the main entrance, going toward the car parked in the warm Mediterranean sun. ''I don't know what to tell you,'' Farrelly said, as they got into his car. ''I'll take you to your hotel. I imagine the police will send someone to take a statement, probably later on today. And, of course, I'll keep in touch. I suppose you don't have any plans. No, how could you? Have you anyone who might join you over here to help out?''

''No,'' she said. She was silent as they drove back through the streets of Nice. Her mind, whic had fought against the fact of Alex's death, now struggled with the implausible hope that somehow he might still be alive. ''But what if they *did* make a mistake?'' she said, suddenly, as Farrelly's car came to a stop outside the Hotel Miramar. ''There are mistakes. I mean, you said so yourself. I mean, you read about things like that in the newspapers.''

''Then where is he?'' Farrelly said. ''He wasn't dressed. He couldn't have walked out without clothes. It doesn't make sense. I think they must have screwed up somehow and they'll find the body tucked away in some ward in the hospital. That's the only possible explanation.'' He got out of the car and walked her to the hotel doorway. ''Look,'' he said, ''if you need any help for any reason, just give me a call at this number. I'll come, or someone else from the consulate will come if I'm out.'' He gave her his card. ''You look tired,'' he said. ''Maybe you should try to lie down for a while?''

She took his card and tried to smile. It was a habit, smiling, people did it no matter what the circumstances. ''Thank you,'' she said. ''Thank you for your help.''

She watched him drive away in his little red Ford. She went into the lobby, which was filled with tourists waiting for a sightseeing bus. They were Americans. Their familiar accents gave her the sensation of being at home, not here in France, an impression furthered when, waiting for the elevator, she looked through glass doors at the hotel's interior courtyard and the swimming pool. The bougainvillea bushes in the courtyard were like the bougainvillea by her father's swimming pool in Brentwood. Suddenly, frighteningly, she thought: Carmel. Could that be possible? As she got into the elevator she felt herself tremble. Anything is possible, after Carmel.

When she let herself in, she saw that their room had been made up in her absence. She also noticed that the balcony door was open, which surprised her. The room balconies were connected to the swimming pool below by flights of outside stairs. There was a notice on the door saying they should be kept locked *because of danger of thieves,* as the English part of the notice put it. Surely she hadn't left it open? And why hadn't the maid closed it? She at once thought of robbery. When she was a student at UCLA she had shared an off-campus apartment with another girl and it had been broken into, robbed, and vandalized. Now, in panicky haste, she went to the drawer where she had left passports, traveler's checks, money, and tickets. When she opened the drawer her first sensation was of relief. The large travel wallet was still there. But then she remembered Alex's wallet. I put it there last night. I definitely remember putting it there. She scrabbled in the drawer but did not find it, then opened the travel wallet. She saw her passport, a ticket, and some traveler's checks. But there should be two sets of traveler's checks, one signed by her, one signed by Alex. Hers was there. His was not.

She said to herself, Please, please, slow down. Just make sure. She stood for a moment, trying to control the trembling in her limbs. Then, methodically, she went through the travel wallet, item by item. Her return ticket to New York was there. Alex's was missing. And in addition to his traveler's checks, about five hundred dollars in cash was also missing. When she had ascertained these facts she went to the closet and looked inside. They had brought four bags on the trip. His briefcase and one bag were missing. She saw that only a few articles of his clothing were gone. His suits, two pairs of slacks, sweaters, shirts, and socks were still in the closet and drawers. The face of Tom Farrelly came before her. *Then, where is he? He wasn't dressed. He couldn't have walked out without clothes.* He had no clothes, he was wearing swimming trunks. He couldn't walk to the hotel wearing only swimming trunks, could he?

She saw the open balcony door. If someone came in from the balcony while the maid was making up the room, someone who came up from the swimming pool below, the maid might just finish up the room and leave. He could have come up in his swimming trunks, taking his ticket and wallet. It could have happened like that while I was at the hospital this morning. She went into the bathroom. His shaving things were gone. But, in the bathroom, she found something else. One of the fresh hand towels put out by the maid had been used and discarded. There was a strange smell in the bathroom and the bathroom window had been partially opened. She opened the window all the way and looked down. The bathroom faced an airshaft that went down to the ground floor. The rectangle of concrete at the bottom of the airshaft was the dusty repository for scraps of paper and cartons thrown from bathroom windows by careless occupants. But Marie saw something else. At the bottom of the airshaft she saw a pair of old gym shoes caked with what looked like brown mud and, near them, a green hospital scrub suit, a green hospital coat, and a crumpled green scrub cap. She knew those sort of clothes. She had seen Alex wear them in the days when he ran a hospital service. They were the working clothes of the morgue. She shut the window quickly as though to hide that evidence from view. He was alive. He had woken in the morgue, found some autopsy clothing, dressed himself, and walked out as though he were a doctor on duty. Somehow, he had found his way back here, gone through the lobby, out to the pool, and climbed the stairs to the balcony. Maybe the balcony doors were open, or maybe the maid making up the room had let him in. But he had been here, he had changed, packed, taken his passport and money and ticket, and left. Why? Where was he now, why was he hiding himself, even from her?

As she stood in the bathroom asking herself these questions

she heard a loud noise that at first she did not recognize. Rain spattered against the opaque glass pane of the bathroom window. The sound reverberated a second time, directly overhead, seeming to shake the room. It was a knell. Or a coincidence? I know nothing, she told herself, I can prove nothing, I mustn't make assumptions. It's possible that there is some secret in Alex's life, something I never guessed at, something that has made him use this accident to run away from everyone. But as she admitted that hypothesis, her mind rejected it. Alex does not have secrets. I have secrets. What if he is suffering some sort of brain damage and is wandering around Nice, half dazed, no longer the master of his actions? Of course, she thought, of course that must be it. I'll call the hospital and the consulate. We must start a search.

She went into the bedroom to telephone. As she did, she saw again the drawer from which he had taken his passport, money, and airlines ticket. Did it seem like the action of a dazed, concussed man, no longer master of his thoughts, to select those things, pack a bag, conceal the hospital clothes, and walk out of here? Why did he do that? She picked up the receiver, then put it down again. To tell the consulate, to have them notify the hospital and, possibly, the French police, would be an irrevocable step. What if Alex did have some secret mission she knew nothing about, something to do with those antibacteriological warfare tests the Institute was working on. Alex said those tests had nothing to do with his work, but that's just what he would say if he were mixed up in some official secret. At any rate, there were all those security regulations at his office. And as she thought of New York and the Institute, she thought of the missing airlines ticket: Nice to New York. It was a TWA ticket. She took out her own ticket and phoned TWA reservations. The lines were busy. She had to wait. As she did she rehearsed herself and when the reservations clerk came on, she said in a voice she hoped was casual, "Hello, I wanted to check on a reservation. My name is Davenport. My husband and I left New York on flight 762 for Marseilles via Paris on August thirtieth."

"One moment, please."

She waited. The voice said, "Yes, what did you want to know?"

"We were supposed to have reservations back from Nice on flight 567 to New York on September sixth."

"Yes, that's correct."

"Well, I was planning to meet my husband here in Nice. I've been up in Paris for a couple of days and when I got back here today, he's checked out. He's a doctor, he may have had to go home early on an emergency. I wonder if you could check to see if there's been any change in his reservation."

"Yes. Dr. Davenport. We have him on today's flight to New York."

"And when does that leave?"

"The flight leaves at noon."

"Oh," Marie said. "Can you put me on the flight?"

There was a pause. And then: "I'm sorry. I have no space left."

"Put me on standby, then."

"Are you in Nice? You have only about thirty minutes to get to the airport. Even if we had space, I don't think you could get there and clear customs and immigration in time. I'll check to see if we can put you on a later flight. We have one leaving at four P.M. with a stopover in Madrid, arriving at Kennedy at six forty-five P.M. local time."

"No. Please put me on standby. I'm coming out, anyway."

She put the phone down without waiting for an answer and began, desperately, to stuff her clothes into the suitcases, which she pulled from the closet. There was no time to pack, she should leave all this and go; but habit was stronger than sense and she ran about frantically opening drawers, even stuffing Alex's clothes into one of the suitcases. As she finished this helter-skelter packing she called the desk and told them to prepare her bill, to send a porter and call a taxi. She said she was late for a flight and could they help her, please?

A porter came, almost at once, and she hurried ahead of him to take the elevator, running out into the lobby, handing over her American Express card, and running to the front door to ask the hall porter if he had a taxi. The desk clerk caught the spirit of urgency and came out to her with her card and the receipted bill as the porter stuffed the bags into the trunk of a small taxi. She fumbled in her purse for money for a tip for the porter, and told the driver that she was late for a flight, to hurry, please, hurry, the cab darting out into the traffic as though it were a police car in a chase, racing along the seafront expressway in a stream of traffic, and she looked at her watch; it had taken only fourteen minutes so far. The airport was just outside Nice. She might make it. She sat, hunched forward, holding onto the back of the driver's seat, mentally driving with him as the speedometer climbed to 120 kilometers and went on up. As she saw the first airport sign, the traffic thickened maddeningly, slowing to a rush-hour crawl. She took francs from her purse, noting the meter reading, planning ahead for the moment of arrival. She did not even think of Alex; she thought of nothing but the plane. When the taxi entered the airport terminal grounds she rolled down her window to signal for a porter. The taxi stopped in a glut of unloading vehicles and she had luck, a porter saw her and came. She told him the flight number and that she was late, paid the taxi, and leaving the porter to follow with the bags, ran into the terminal and up to the TWA counter. There was a man ahead of her at the counter. "Please," she said, in English, "I'm late for a flight, can you help me?"

A second TWA clerk came from the rear of the counter and waved her to a vacant position.

"I'm on standby for flight 540."

"What name, please?"

"Davenport."

"Mrs. Davenport?"

"Yes."

"I'm sorry," he said. "Nothing opened up."

"But is there no way? My husband's on that flight. Please?"

"I'm sorry. We can put you on a later flight. This flight is sold out. In fact"—he looked at a television screen above his head—"it's boarding on last call, right now."

"What gate?"

"Six. But we have no space."

The porter was waiting behind her. She beckoned him to follow. If she could just get to the boarding area she might at least catch sight of Alex and make sure he was all right. She began to run, the porter, confused, following her, pushing his trolley. She reached the security area, put her purse on the ramp, had it searched, and called to the porter in French, telling him to wait for her, she would be back. Then ran to gate 6. There was a light flashing over the gate, which meant the flight was boarding. The departure lounge was empty. She ran to the boarding gate, where a uniformed TWA official was sorting boarding passes. "Boarding pass, please?" he said. "Are you on standby? I believe the flight is full up."

"I don't have a boarding pass, but I have a ticket and my husband's on this flight. I have to see him for a moment, it's urgent."

"I'm very sorry," he said. "But there won't be time. The flight's just pulling out." He looked down the enclosed ramp where a stewardess stood by the open plane door. Marie ran past the boarding official, ran down the enclosed ramp to the plane, but as she did the door shut with a slam, like the door of a bank vault. The boarding clerk, running after her, caught her arm. "Too late," he said. "Come on. You shouldn't do that."

Through the lounge windows Marie saw the plane begin to move away from the loading area. She said, "Wait," to the official who held her arm. She stared in desperate hope at the row of round plane windows, the faces behind them tiny, like faces in a doll's house. None of them was Alex. But he's there, she thought as the plane slued around moving out. He's there. He's not dead. He's alive.

"If you have a ticket I'll see if I can get you on a later flight," the boarding clerk said.

The plane, taxiing toward the runways, was now out of sight. The sky darkened, filling with a summer cloudburst. As Marie followed the official, going back up the departure ramp, rain fell: heavy, thundershower rain.

UNREAL city: the city in which she had been born, the city her father fled when his business failed, the sky above its monumental buildings tinctured with the flamingo hue of a dying summer's day as a taxi carried her along the East River Drive, turning off into garbage-littered streets, rushing past clicking traffic lights, clattering over ruptured pavement, coming to a lurching stop outside the building on Seventy-ninth Street in which she and Alex had lived for the past eight months.

Henry, the night doorman, came out from behind the glass doors to help unload the baggage. She paid the driver and turned to Henry, in disquiet, for she thought: What does Henry know that I don't, has Alex arrived and is he upstairs? But Henry merely said, "Hello, there, Mrs. Davenport, I'll get a trolley," and loaded the bags onto a high metal trolley, which he trundled into the lobby after her. As she rang for the elevator, Henry asked, "Been on vacation?"

"Yes."

"You picked the right time to be out of the city," Henry told her. The elevator came and they got in. There were no other passengers. "Seventh floor, right?" Henry said, and pressed a button. She thought: Alex's flight would have landed at about one P.M. New York time. It was now after eight. Henry usually came on about six. So he probably didn't see Alex if Alex came in earlier this afternoon. Henry, standing opposite her, took off his uniform cap and wiped the inside leather band with a tissue. "It's been a killer, all right," he said. He mopped his balding brow and announced, "I'm losing my hair. You know why? It's wearing these tight caps. No circulation. We should have a nice light summer-type cap. It's real bad for the hair, sweating in a heavy cap.''

Marie said she supposed that was true. The elevator stopped at the seventh floor and Henry told her, ''You go right ahead.'' He held the door to prevent it from closing. As she went along the corridor she decided she would ask him to leave the bags outside the apartment door. If Alex was inside he might not want anyone to see him. But how do you get a doorman to leave the bags outside? They always bring them in. She searched in her purse and found two dollars. If she tipped Henry before she unlocked the door, that might do it. She could make an excuse about the burglar-alarm system. As she took the money out of her purse, Henry, trundling along behind her, drew level and said: ''Yes, my dad, he went bald real young. And you know something? He always wore a hat. Even in the house, he wore a hat.''

Marie stopped outside 7F and fumbled with her key chain. She said: ''Just leave the bags here, Henry. It always takes me ages to figure these locks out.''

''No hurry,'' Henry said, amiably.

''No, please.'' Marie gave him the two dollars. ''Just take them off the trolley and leave them here. I can manage.''

''No problem, you know,'' Henry said. But he unloaded the bags and placed them near the door. ''Thanks a lot, Mrs. Davenport. Have a nice evening.''

''You too, Henry,'' she said. As he went off with the trolley she pretended to search for the right key. There was a Yale key for the top lock and a Chubb key for the bottom lock. The Chubb key had to be turned twice to the left to begin the deactivation of the alarm system. But if Alex was already in the apartment the alarm would not be set. She waited until she heard Henry go down in the elevator and then tried the Chubb key. When she made the first turn she at once heard the clear low buzz of the alarm system and felt despair. He was not here. She put the Yale key in the top lock, turned and pushed the door inward. If he didn't come home, then where did he go? Wait, wait, she told herself; one thing at a time. Shut off the alarm. Then, get the bags inside. Then, close the door and lock it. Maybe he's been here and has gone out to get some food. Alex would set the alarm even if he only went out for a moment because the apartment belonged to his colleague Hans Werner, who was on a year's sabbatical in London, and Hans had left them in charge of his collection of valuable paintings. Alex worried a lot about theft. Marie hurried to the little alarm box, opened it, put in a third key, and turned it in the lock. This shut off the alarm system. She brought the bags, one by one, into the front hall, then shut and locked the front door. The apartment was hot and airless; the air conditioning had been off all week, the windows were shuttered and locked. She put the lights on, then went into the bedroom and looked in the closet for Alex's bag and briefcase. They were not there. She went into the kitchen. Everything was as she had left it last Sunday when she locked up and went out to Kennedy to meet Alex and fly with him to Marseilles. She checked the kitchen closet in case he had put his suitcase in there. But there was no suitcase in that closet. She went through the living room, which had the tidy dead look of a room that had been cleaned the day she left. If Alex didn't come back here, then where did he go? He had no close friends in New York. He was a Californian: his only connection here was with the Institute. Maybe he went to the Institute. He had a couch in his office and sometimes took naps on it. But if she rang his number at the Institute and he answered, then he might run off again before she could get over there. She went back into the kitchen and opened the refrigerator. There was orange juice and two stale English muffins and some curdled milk. Nothing had been touched. It was then that she noticed the door at the back of the kitchen that led to the service stairs. There was no chain on the door. She tested the door. Both locks had been doublelocked, but she remembered that just before she left for France she had locked that door and put the chain on it. There had been no one here since, no cleaning woman, nobody from the building staff, for she had not left a set of keys with the super. They why was there no chain on the kitchen door?

Alex. Maybe he came in this afternoon by the front door and left by the back door. But, of course, he couldn't have put the chain on inside the back door if he left that way. *He was here.* He may come back. Maybe he'll come up the back stairs and let himself in. Maybe he's gone out to get something to eat? Or to see a doctor? What doctor? Henshey is his internist. Oh, I don't know.

She went back into the living room. It was after one A.M., French time. She felt she could no longer think clearly. If she went to the Institute now, the security people would phone Alex's office before letting her go up there. If she called Dr. Henshey, what would she say to him? It was wiser to say nothing to anyone until she found out what this was all about. Suddenly, she remembered that she had left the bags in the front hall. If Alex comes in by the front door and sees those bags, he might just back out again and disappear. She moved the bags, then decided to turn off all the lights in the apartment and wait in some place where she would hear him come in, no matter which door he used. She picked the master bedroom, switched off all the lights, and lay down in the darkness. If was hot, but she could not put on the air conditioning for fear that it would alert him. She lay on the bed, tense, her mind filled with fears and speculations. Shortly after three A.M. French time, she fell into a heavy, exhausted sleep.

She woke in the heat of mid-morning, confused, not knowing at first where she was or what had happened. When she sat up she remembered the locked doors and the burglar-alarm system. Like a thief she tiptoed through the darkened rooms. There was no sign of him. She turned on the air conditioning, took a shower, and changed. She then went into the living room, picked up the telephone, and rang the Institute, asking for Security. "Hello," she said. "This is Mrs. Davenport, Dr. Davenport's wife. I wonder if my husband picked up his keys last night. Or is he there now, by any chance?"

"Hold on a minute, Mrs. Davenport. Herb, will you check on 65?"

There was a pause. "No, Mrs. Davenport. We have him listed as out of town and his keys are here."

"Thank you. Sorry to bother you."

"No problem, Mrs. Davenport. Have a good day."

The Institute had strict security. Everyone, even the senior people, had to sign in and out each time they picked up their office keys. It had to do with defense contracts, Alex said. So he was not in his office and he had not been in his office. Then where was he? Of course, he could be anywhere: he might be in a hotel, he might not even be in New York, he might have gone back to California. That was home for him, after all. If there was some secret in his life, it could be in California. As is mine, she thought, and in that moment she decided that she must tell Daniel what had happened and, despite the fact that it might wreck everything between herself and Daniel, she must tell him all of it now, must tell him about Carmel and how she believed that it could be connected with this terrible thing that had happened in Nice. Daniel was not like Alex; he was patient, he listened to her, he was not arrogant about being more intelligent than other people. Yet even Daniel might think her mad, if she told him. Who would not think her mad? What if he did not believe her, what if he thought her the victim of some insane delusion? But I have to risk that. I can't go on alone.

And so, sick with apprehension, even though she knew he would not be there, she rang Daniel's private number in Los Angeles. It was his home. It was not serviced by his medical answering service. It rang four times, then Elaine's recorded voice spoke:

"This is 457-4940. We are not at home at the moment but if you will leave your name and message, at the sound of the signal, we will contact you as soon as possible. Thank you."

She waited. She heard the signal beep. She said: "I am in a very urgent situation. Can we meet here or on the Coast as soon as possible. Contact me at my home number."

She did not identify herself. Daniel knew her voice. But as soon as she put the receiver down she realized that not giving her name was no disguise. If Elaine picked up the message, even if she did not recognize Marie's voice, she would know it was not a message from an ordinary patient. She should not have said anything about meeting him. But then, what did it matter? Even if he had not yet told Elaine, none of these things mattered now.

As though in proof, she heard thunder. Maybe it was not thunder, maybe it was some truck noise on Second Avenue. She sat on the sofa facing a van Dongen painting that Alex said was very valuable. The painting blurred. She felt a flashing of light in the lower part of her left eye. It was a migraine aura.

She got up and went to the bathroom to get the capsules. As she did, lightning whitened the room. The capsules were not in the medicine cabinet. She remembered, then, that she had used them in Nice. She went into the bedroom where her suitcases were and scrabbled in one of them to find the little toilet case, which, when she found it, she upended on the carpet. She picked up the bottle of capsules but it was empty. She sat by the bedside phone and closed her left eye as she dialed the drugstore. She asked for Hal, and when he came to the phone she explained and asked if he could send up some capsules right away.

"Hold on a minute, Mrs. Davenport," Hal said. He put the phone down and while she waited she opened her left eye. About half of the eye's vision was gone. "Mrs. Davenport, I'm sorry, but our delivery boy is out on a call just now. I'd say within the hour is the best we could do on a delivery. Maybe you could come down and pick them up?"

She said all right, she would do that. She felt it was better to risk blindness in the street than to wait here for an hour. She stood up, found her purse, and walked slowly out into the front hall, where she checked to make sure she had her keys. The box in the hall that housed the alarm system winked its little red light, reminding her to set the controls, but she did not feel able to go through the complicated process of unlocking the box, inserting a key that had to be turned twice, relocking the box, then hurrying out the front door and locking the lower Chubb lock, which set the alarm on alert. If you did not do this last part quickly, the alarm went off and rang until you came back in and started all over again. So she ignored the little red warning light and simply locked the upper Yale lock as she left. You might just as well leave the door open, Alex used to complain.

Waiting in the corridor for the elevator, Marie felt dizzy, but consoled herself that she had no headache. When the elevator came there was no one else in it. She was grateful for that, but when she came out into the bright lobby with its wing chairs and bowls of cut flowers, she became nervous at the sight of John, the doorman on duty, a tall, talkative fellow who liked to make jokes. What would she say if John asked whether her husband was back yet? She walked unsteadily toward the front door. In her anxiety about facing John she felt a tightness in her chest as though she were short of breath.

"Hi, Mrs. Davenport. So you beat the rush, right?"

"What?" What was he talking about?

"Labor Day weekend," John said, grinning. "By tomorrow or the next day, people will be coming back into the city like Long Island was on fire. You were smart to get home early. Want a cab?"

"No, thanks, I'm just going down the block," she said, moving past him into the street, where a light shower had made the pavements steam. She walked carefully along Seventy-ninth Street, stifling the urge to take shelter in a doorway, filled with her familiar fear of the open, the invisible guns trained on her from on high, following her every step. She turned into Second Avenue and passed a store window in which mannequins in winter clothes were grouped around old-fashioned full-length mirrors. Through one of these mirrors her image passed as on a television screen, and at sight of it she did not, at first, realize that the girl in the light summer dress, her hair falling like a long dark veil on either side of her face, was herself. Second Avenue was deserted as though the city had been evacuated and the empty buildings and sidewalks awaited enemy attack. Ahead of her a light clicked green. A lurch of taxis passed, and then, somewhere in the direction of the East River, she heard the unbearable squeal of a speeding ambulance, a sound that until now had meant someone else's troubles, but which brought back the French ambulance racing through the streets of Nice, swaying so that she must hold on to the steel rungs under the seat opposite the stretcher. The unbearable sound diminished. The street was quiet again, the only sound in her ears the loose flop of her sandals on the pavement. When she reached Kane's Drugs, she thought, I don't have to worry about Hal asking about the trip. I didn't tell Hal we were going away because Alex said you should never let the neighborhood know you were out of town, it was an invitation to thieves. Kane's was deserted, with only one customer, an old Oriental man waiting at the counter for a prescription to be filled. Hal looked down from his dispensing desk.

"Hi, there. So you made it."

She nodded and smiled. When she looked up at him, the blind-level rose almost to the top of her left eye.

"I have your prescription right here." He told her the price and she thanked him and paid.

"Do you have a glass of water? I'd like to take two capsules now."

"Sure thing."

But when he came back with a little paper cup full of water and she put out her hand to take it, the aura left her eye. Vision in both eyes was completely normal. Was it coincidence or something else? And then she heard a rumble of thunder, like old malicious laughter. She took the capsules anyway. It would have been rude to Hal not to. She said good-bye to Hal and went out into the street. It had begun to rain again, a shower that grew heavy, forcing her to take shelter in the doorway of a store a block away from Kane's. As she stood in the doorway looking up Second Avenue she saw a bus coming and people waiting for it at a bus stop, two women sharing an umbrella, and behind them a young man wearing sneakers, chino pants, and a navy tennis shirt, shielding himself from the rain by holding a newspaper over his head. There was about him something instantly familiar, a hunching of shoulders that made her heart jump. *Alex.* She could not see his face but she knew. She ran out into the pelting rain, running along the pavement just as the bus came to a stop up ahead, the two women folding their umbrella and getting on and she calling out, "Alex, Alex." But he did not hear and got on behind the women. She waved, hoping the bus driver would see her and wait, but the bus door shut and the bus pulled away from the curb. She waved up at the windows, but the windows were so sluicing wet she doubted the passengers inside could see out. She turned, stared after the bus, and, wild with excitement and the fear of losing him, ran recklessly into the street, waving for a taxi; a taxi passed, ignoring her it seemed, then suddenly pulled into the curb. She ran and got in, dripping wet, saying, out of breath, "That bus, the bus up ahead, can you catch it?"

"The bus." The cab driver was Puerto Rican. He grinned. "You want to take a bus?"

"There's someone on it," she said, breathlessly, as though

that explained everything. The cab started, then jammed on its brakes at a red light. The bus had just gone through the intersection. What should she do, should she tell the cab driver to go ahead of the bus, pay off the cab at a bus stop, and wait until the bus caught up, then get on the bus? But what if Alex gets off the bus at the very next stop? If he saw me and is hiding from me, he'll run away again. She sat forward in the cab seat, tense as though she would faint. The driver looked at her through his rearview mirror. "You want to catch up with the bus, right?"

"Yes, but I don't know where this person will get off."

"I can follow the bus, right? If they get off, you can catch them."

"Yes," she said. It *was* Alex, wasn't it? Had he come back and slipped in and out of the apartment while she was in Kane's? It was Alex. Suddenly, she was sure. "Yes," she said. "Follow the bus and if you stop behind it at each stop, I can see if the person gets off."

The rain had slackened. As the taxi caught up with the bus, she saw the bus pull in at a bus stop. She watched, anxious and uncertain, for there was traffic ahead of her. Alex did not get off. The bus pulled out again, the taxi moving in behind it, and in this way, stopping and starting, followed the bus downtown, until it reached Forty-second Street, where, when it had unloaded some descending passengers and the new passengers were getting on, Alex suddenly jumped down into the street at the last moment, turned and walked away along Forty-second Street. Marie had money ready. She pushed it at the driver, saying, "Keep the change," and got out of the cab, saw Alex in the crowd ahead, and ran after him. He was walking at a normal pace, and so, running past other people, she came up behind him, drew level, and saw that he was not Alex. He was the same young man she had seen get on the bus at Seventy-ninth Street but he was not Alex.

She stopped walking, then walked again, moving aimlessly toward Grand Central Station. She had been sure it was Alex. She had been sure but now was sure of nothing. She paused in the street, feeling dizzy. She wondered if the dizziness was because she did not remember when she had last eaten. She went into the first coffee shop she came to and sat at the counter.

When the waitress put a menu and a glass of water in front of her, she tried to think of food. "Eggs, please," she said to the waitress.

"What kind eggs?"

"Scrambled."

"Toast and coffee?"

"Thank you," she said. Everything around her went on as it had always gone on. Toast and coffee. Scrambled eggs. These unreal events were happening in this real, reassuringly ordinary world, a world where people ate three meals a day and slept each night because if they did not eat and sleep they would sicken and die. She remembered as one remembers something that happened in another time, that the stewardesses on the plane had kept offering her a snack or dinner, but that she had eaten nothing. In fact, she did not remember eating anything since the accident. She picked up the glass of water and sipped it. It tasted brackish so she switched to the cup of black coffee the waitress had put in front of her. It, too, tasted brackish. She put sugar and cream in it but at the second swallow felt that she would be sick, so got up hurriedly and went to the bathroom, which, in this coffee shop, was a small room with one toilet and a sink. She stood in the room, holding on to the sink until her nausea passed. She still felt light-headed, so told herself again that she must try to eat something and went back to the counter to sit staring at scrambled eggs. When the waitress came by to inquire if everything was all right, Marie asked for a small glass of milk.

Milk was brought. Milk was something she had always been able to drink, even when she felt unwell. But she did not pick up the glass. She looked at the milk and the eggs and the toast and thought that if she touched any of these things she would be sick. The waitress went by again, noticed the uneaten food, but said nothing. It was New York, after all. New Yorkers were not like Californians. They minded their own business. Well, some of them. There was a boy sitting further down the counter, looking her over. She knew his sort. He was fat and cocky, yet unsure, looking for a chance, any chance, to get into conversation. If she was not going to eat anything she should ask for her check and leave. She looked again at the milk and, taking up the glass, sipped it. It tasted brackish like the other liquids. She put the glass down and, when the waitress went by, said, "May I have a check, please?"

The waitress made out the check, put it on the counter, and said, "Have a nice day."

"Thank you. You too."

When the waitress had moved away, Marie opened her purse. As she did the fat boy's voice came at her from the side, swift as a mugger's grab.

"Excuse me. But would you happen to be a model?"

She pretended deafness. She found money and tried to calculate the tip.

"You look like a model."

She did not turn her eyes on him but, hoping to end it, shook her head.

"No? You know why I thought you were a model, apart from your looks? It's because you ordered that food but you ate like a bird. That's what models do. Are you on a diet, maybe?"

She decided on a dollar tip, put a dollar under the plate, and shut her purse.

"You're not leaving? Wait. Are you, maybe, in the movies?"

She got up, not looking at him. Dizziness came. Humiliated, she held on to the countertop, waiting for it to pass.

"You're certainly pretty enough to be in the movies. You know what I mean? Some of the movie stars nowadays are real dogs."

The dizziness passed. She went to the cash register. She did not believe he was the sort who would follow but she wished the cashier would hurry. When she got her change she went into the street, where the rain had stopped, leaving the sun in solitary command of an empty blue sky. She turned toward Third Avenue. He had come out of the coffee shop and was slinking up behind her. "I hope you won't be mad at the suggestion," his voice said. "I know it's early, but maybe you'd let me buy you a drink."

She shook her head and went on walking.

"Ah, come on. Give me a break. I'm a nice guy. I think

you're really cute. Come on, what about just fifteen minutes? Just one drink, okay?''

If you kept walking, a plague like this would finally desist. She looked up at the sky. Guns were leveled from that blue brightness, following her every step. If only they would fire and hit him instead.

"Thank you for your courtesy." His voice was now sarcastic. "Thanks a lot. Cunt." She went on. He no longer followed. She continued on over to Third Avenue simply from habit. From Third she could take an uptown bus. What will happen now? If Alex has run away, will the American consulate in Nice report his disappearance to the authorities here? Will the French police investigate? But there was no crime. I mean, Alex has committed no crime. She reached Third and turned uptown, forgetting about taking a bus, going up the rain-blotched avenue toward the apartment in which she and Alex had lived for the past eight months, an apartment she had never thought of as home. Their furniture, such as it was, was in a Bekins warehouse in Los Angeles. It seemed to her that her whole life had disappeared with Alex. There was no one here, no one anywhere, who would believe her story. Not even Daniel. It was probably too early to hope that Daniel would get her message and call back, which was why she walked block after block, killing time. She had found that movement distracted her from the tension of waiting. She thought of Alex, alone, wounded, perhaps suffering some sort of brain damage. She had no plan now, without him. She was waiting for news of Alex, hoping for a sight of Alex, hoping it had all been some terrible hospital mistake. But if it was a hospital mistake, then why was he hiding, why did he run away without leaving her any message?

At last, hot and weary, she reached Seventy-ninth Street and turned east. As she came up the block toward the apartment, John, the doorman, saw her coming. He had been standing out on the sidewalk and now he preceded her in, holding the door open for her. "How about that weather? Look at that sky. Never know we'd had a thunderstorm, would you?''

I would, she thought, but smiled and nodded as though she agreed. In the lobby the elevator waited, its door open. When it stopped at her floor there was no one in the corridor, but Mrs. Prell's door was ajar, and as Marie drew near to it, Mrs. Prell staged her familiar stratagem of coming out dressed for the street, as if she were going down to the corner on some errand; poor lonely Mrs. Prell, who waited behind her door until she heard passing footsteps, then came out to talk about the weather, her grandchildren, the crime rate, or the price of food, with the relentless discursiveness of the true solitary for whom such encounters are the high point of a silent day, conversations that did not end even after you said good-bye to her and she to you, for then she would have one last thought, which led to another until, to escape, you must pretend to hear the phone ringing back in your apartment or remember an imaginary appointment for which you were already late.

But now as Mrs. Prell emerged and carefully locked her door, she seemed disappointed to see Marie. Her withered face peered over her shoulder, bereft of its usual conciliatory smile. For once, she waited for Marie to speak.

"Hello, Mrs. Prell."

"Oh, hi there. It's raining out?"

"It was. It's sunny now."

"So, you had a nice vacation," Mrs. Prell said, after a second atypical pause.

How does she know we were on vacation? And what can I say?

"You missed some heat," Mrs. Prell informed her.

"Has it been hot?"

"Murder. You just came back today?"

"Last night."

"Ah, ha." Mrs. Prell nodded as though she were thinking of something else. "Your husband, he's feeling okay?"

Why does she ask that? Never mind, she's probably just making conversation. But what do I answer?

"My husband?"

"He's not sick, is he?"

"Sick?"

Mrs. Prell shrugged as if she had said too much. "Well, I've got to go now," Mrs. Prell said, sounding not at all like her usual garrulous self.

"Thank you."

Marie watched Mrs. Prell go off down the corridor, hurrying, she who never hurried, going off to tell someone? Tell them what? Why did she ask if Alex is sick?

A new feeling of unease overcame her. She hurried to the door of her apartment, put her key in the lock, turned and pushed. But the door did not open. She bent down and put the second key in the lower lock, which at once gave off the quiet buzz of the alarm's alert signal. She turned the key. The door opened and she hurried to the alarm box, opened it, put in the third key and turned it, shutting off the alarm. Then thought: But I didn't set the alarm when I went out, did I? She was not sure. She went into the living room and despite the fact that the air conditioning was now on she smelled a dead musty smell. She went and sat on the sofa. I must try to remember. Did I or did I not set the alarm? She looked again at the van Dongen painting. She remembered Alex saying that Magda Werner had bought these paintings as a hedge against inflation because she did not trust currency. Magda's parents had come out of Rumania in 1940 with diamonds sewn under their skin and as a little girl Magda had spent seven years in a Siberian gulag. Marie remembered being reassured by this grim story: it seemed to prove that other people could survive terrible things. Did I or did I not set the alarm? Suddenly, she thought: What if Daniel has picked up my message? What if he phoned back while I was out? She picked up the phone in the living room and dialed her answering service. She asked if there had been a message from Dr. Daniel Bailey.

"Just a moment, please," said a girl's voice. She thought this girl's name was Doris but was not sure. All of the operators on the service sounded alike.

"No, Mrs. Davenport, nothing for you."

"Thank you." But it seemed strange that there was nothing at all. "You mean there's no message from Dr. Bailey?"

"No. No messages."

"You mean no messages at all for us?"

"Right."

"But we've been away for days. Are you sure?"

"I just came on duty, Mrs. Davenport. Hold on, I'll check again."

Marie waited. There must have been messages.

"No, nothing. Maybe they've already been picked up?"

"Thank you." She replaced the receiver. Picked up by Alex? She thought again of the burglar-alarm system. She did not remember setting it before she went out. In fact, she was sure of it. Alex has a duplicate set of alarm keys. I've been away for more than an hour. He could easily have been here. If he came here, I put my bags in the closet and made the bed before I went out. He might not have noticed that the air conditioning was on. He might not know that I had been here. Oh, I can't think straight. She walked distractedly through the rooms. She looked again in Alex's closet, but everything was as it had been before they went off to France. She went into the bedroom that they had converted into a study for Alex. She sat at his desk in front of the orderly clutter of his pencils, his microscope, his slides, his notebooks. She pulled on the handle of the metal desk drawer, but the desk was locked and she did not know where he kept the key. Above the desk was a cork notice board and in one corner of it she saw, affixed with a red push pin, a faded snapshot of Alex's parents, taken when they were young. They were standing on the boardwalk of an amusement arcade in Old Orchard Beach, Maine. Alex's father, long dead, wore a large-brimmed Borsalino hat that made him look like an old-fashioned political terrorist; his mother wore a cardigan that came to her knees. They held hands and smiled at the camera, but as Marie looked at her mother-in-law's photograph, the photograph's eyes seemed to accuse her: This is your fault, the eyes said. You have deceived Alex: you are the cause of this terrible thing. You are deceiving me. Why have you not telephoned me? Where is my son?

There was a filing cabinet in the corner of the room. Marie went to it and opened it. She looked at files on research grants, files on government medical programs, records of international medical meetings, files on funding. Alex's work was done at the Institute: he used this office only on those evenings he devoted to writing grant applications for further funds. He complained about this endless scrounging for money, but accepted the drudgery of it; night after night he had worked at this desk. It was ambition, she knew, but it was more than that, for Alex was obsessed by his ideas: he lived his life as if the breakthrough would one day occur, as though Davenport would be a name like Fleming or Salk or Pasteur and the world a different place because of it. To slow down the process of human aging. That was what she told people when they asked what sort of research he did. His terms were different, words that hung in the air when he and his colleagues talked, words like *lipoproteins* and *platelets, tryglicerides* and *atherosclerosis*, words that emphasized what she had learned in the first year of her marriage, that she was a stranger to the largest part of his life. She shut the filing cabinet. There were no secrets here. She was the one with secrets. She went into the bathroom. There was a dead musty smell in the bathroom. She did not remember noticing it earlier when she showered and changed. She tried to track it down, but could not. It was just a smell in the bathroom, a slightly sweet unpleasant smell. It told her nothing. She went through to the bedroom once more. She sat on the edge of the bed, sniffing, trying to locate the smell. As she did she saw that something was written on the notepad by the telephone. She picked up the pad. It was Alex's writing, a pencil-jotting in his small, neat hand.

MONDAY. LOBOS MOTOR INN.

Lobos Motor Inn. As she read those words she caught her breath. To see that name written by Alex was like being told he knew about Daniel. *Monday. Lobos Motor Inn.* It must have been a message from Daniel to me, a message he telephoned in to the service earlier, while I was out. Alex came here while I was out. He phoned the service and picked up this message.

In panic, she dialed the answering service. "Hello. This is Mrs. Davenport. I asked you a few minutes ago if there were any messages and you said there weren't any. You said maybe they'd been picked up already. Is there any way you could check on that? There's a message I've been waiting for. Maybe my husband picked it up, but he's not here now. It's very urgent."

"Hold on a minute, I'll ask the other girls."

She sat, feeling her heart thump as she heard the operator ask the question in that unknown telephone room. "Okay, just a minute," the operator said to her, "here's Doris."

"Hello, Mrs. Davenport. Yes, Dr. Davenport picked up a message about a half-hour ago."

"Maybe it was a message from a Dr. Bailey. Do you remember if it was?"

"No, sorry, I don't. I just know it was a message for you."

"For me?"

"Yes. Wait. I didn't take it off my pad yet. Let's see. It was: *Meet Monday Point Lobos Motor Inn. Call if you can't make it.* They didn't leave a name. And right after that, Dr. Davenport rang and asked who had called. I guess he was in the apartment but didn't pick up the phone."

"And you gave him the message?"

"Yes. I just read it off to him. Okay?"

"Yes, thank you. Thanks, Doris."

Marie put the telephone back on its cradle and stared again at Alex's handwriting. He came here while I was out at the drugstore. He picked up this message but he wouldn't know who it was from. *Meet Monday Point Lobos Motor Inn. Call if you can't make it.* It was a message from Daniel. He's the only person who knows the Point Lobos Motor Inn. She picked up the phone and dialed directory assistance and got the number in Carmel.

"Point Lobos Motor Inn, can I help you?"

"Yes, I'm calling long-distance. Do you have a reservation for a Dr. Bailey for Monday night?"

"One moment, please. Yes, we have."

"I see." Suddenly, she decided to go to Carmel. She must talk to Daniel. Alex might be on his way there, too. It couldn't be coincidence, all of this. Daniel had chosen Carmel of all places; that inn of all places. Daniel, who knew nothing about what had happened to her there. "Hello," she said. "Can I make a reservation for tomorrow night?"

"Single or double?"

"Double, I guess. Look, I'm going to take a flight out of

New York later this afternoon. I'll spend the night in San Francisco and drive down tomorrow morning. All right?''

"Fine. We hold reservations until six P.M. What's the name, please?''

"Davenport, Marie Davenport.''

"All right then, one double room. And thank you for calling.''

She replaced the receiver, then dialed an airline. She got a reservation on a flight leaving for San Francisco at seven P.M. She reserved a room in a San Francisco airport hotel and arranged for a rental car to be picked up the next morning. She did these things with the practice of one who has done them before. She repacked her suitcase. The musty smell still lingered in the bathroom. After that, she went to the kitchen and forced herself to drink frozen orange juice and eat some crackers she took from a tin in the pantry. But all of these preparations could not kill enough time. At five, having told herself that she must do something until it was time to take a taxi to the airport, she went down the hall and stood, looking at the books. She had placed them inconspicuously on the lowest shelf of the bookcase and one day, when Alex noticed them, she lied, saying they had belonged to her mother. There was a biography of Catherine Labouré, a book on the happenings at Beauraing, and a paperback entitled *A Woman Clothed by the Sun*. They had about them the soiled used look of their last resting place, secondhand bookshops to which come books whose style and subject are no longer in vogue. Of course, her mother would never have bought such books. Her mother paid lip service to religion but did not practice it. As a result Marie had rarely been taken to Mass and had never received religious instruction until she attended that convent school in Montreal. Until then she had not realized that she had never been confirmed in the Church. When she asked her mother about it, her mother said, simply, "I forgot. We can get you confirmed now, if you like.'' But, of course, it never happened. Her mother died soon afterward. So Marie had never known this religion into which she had been baptized. That was the irony, that was the mystery. She turned away from the bookcase. That is what I don't understand.

As she went back up the corridor, the red light of the burglar-alarm system shone from the box in the hall. She went into the living room and bedroom and turned off the air conditioning. She locked and set the burglar-alarm system as she went out. The Werners would not be back until spring. If she did not know how long she would be in California, if she did not know when she would come back here, she should tell the building staff that there was no one staying in the apartment. But what if Alex showed up tomorrow? It was safer to say nothing.

In the lobby, John was no longer on duty. It was the relief man, Bob, who came to carry her suitcase. "Get you a cab, Mrs. Davenport?"

"Please," she said. She did not tell him she was going to the airport. Normally, she would have said it because cab drivers liked airport trips. She watched Bob put her bag down just outside the front door and go into the middle of the street, waving, his whistle in his mouth. It was still light. The sky was clear and clean and filled with menace, and when the cab came she hurried into it as to a shelter. On the airplane, as in a taxi, she felt insulated from that naked, hostile sky. On the plane, its jet contrails streaking across America, she would be returning to Carmel, going back to that place she had sworn she would never visit again. It could not be coincidence that Daniel had selected Carmel for this meeting. They were, all three of them, puppets. They had become puppets last Friday when she and Alex pedaled that little boat out into the Baie des Anges.

FIVE years ago, as a promissory act, the McDuffies had begun to fly first class. Since then, Sara's novel had brought her a certain fame and recently they had accumulated some amusing horror stories of her escapes from the importunities of fans. As a result, nowadays when they made flight reservations they asked for bulkhead seats, which screened them off from the view of other passengers. It was understood, however, that if Tom chanced on any interesting acquaintances traveling on the same flight, he would persuade Sara to leave her hiding place for champagne and gossip.

But on this flight, an evening flight to San Francisco, Tom thought it doubtful that they would run into anyone they knew. Shortly after the plane was airborne and the seat-belt sign was switched off, he got up and inspected his fellow passengers in the first-class section, returning to his seat to announce, "Nobody."

"Bliss," said Sara, as though she meant it.

After dinner Sara put on a sleep mask while Tom watched the movie. When the movie was over, he tried to doze, but after a time got up and walked back into the tourist section of the plane, passing families sprawled in fretful tableaux, compulsive talkers hunched on the armrests of each other's seats, sleepers in dark rows, shrouded in airlines blankets. He looked at and dismissed faces in his reflexive scan for a pretty girl. In the midsection of the tourist compartment he edged his way past a line that was waiting for the toilets and, when he reached the rear of the plane, crossed over and came back up the opposite aisle. In the second-to-last row of this aisle a girl sat at a window seat, not reading, but staring ahead. The moment he came on her from behind he had a feeling that he knew her, and as he drew level he commanded his brain to deliver an identity. But no answer came. He hesitated in the aisle and, turning, looked down at her, willing her to look at him, ready to smile, hoping she would declare herself. But as he did, she seemed to glance in his direction and then, as though avoiding him, turned to look out of her window at the metallic night sky. He went on, but knew that he had met her. He knew, too, that it had been a recent encounter.

Marie saw Tom McDuffie, recognized him, knew that he was an acquaintance of Alex's, and turned from him, avoiding him. She was not sure if he had recognized her. When he passed her in the aisle she had been sitting tormented in reverie. If I had not fallen in love with Daniel would none of this have happened? Is there a connection between that and Carmel and the accident and the nightmares and all of us going back there now? Is it a way of punishing us for being in love, for the fact that from the minute I met Daniel I knew I had made a mistake in my marriage? I had no idea of what love was until then. I was in love with Daniel, I am in love with him, and because of that I was able to rebel against them, I was able to refuse them. Would I have had the will to fight them for a whole year if I had not been in love? I don't know. I rebelled against all that long ago in school, but that was different, wasn't it? I asked once in Confession in school why it was that I felt as I did. The priest said faith is a gift, some are given it, others must pray to be granted it. He told me to pray. But I did not pray. I did not pray for the gift of a belief I didn't need. Perhaps they did not forgive me then, as they do not forgive me now. But if I give in to them, I know I will never have a normal life again, a life with Daniel. And, because of that, I had a right to refuse them.

Just before the seat-belt signs came on and the plane began its descent into San Francisco, Tom McDuffie again walked down the aisle and looked at the girl whose name he could not remember. And this time it came to him. He went back to his seat and said to Sara, who was awake and making up her face, "Guess who's back in tourist? The wife of that doctor we met at the Showles' house in Stanford."

"Which doctor?"

"Davenport. Alex Davenport. The heart guy."

"Is he with her?" Sara was interested, he could tell.

"Not that I saw. But, the seat beside her was empty, so, come to think of it, he could be."

"He's supposed to be brilliant," Sara said. "Van Kamp told me his research is outstanding."

"And she was quite nice too," Tom said.

"We should say hello, then," Sara decided. "Or did you speak to her already?"

"No."

"But she saw you?"

"I think so."

"Well, we'll just say hello when we get off the plane," Sara said.

"I remember her first name," he said. "It's Marie."

After they got off, they both kept an eye out for Marie Davenport. "There she is," Tom said. "Over there."

"Do you see him?"

"No, she's alone."

"Let's see if we can catch her," Sara said, and at once both McDuffies began to stride purposefully in pursuit, narrowing the gap between them and their quarry until, suddenly, Marie Davenport turned in at a door marked Women.

"Damn," Tom said. "Do you want to go in?"

"Oh, let's forget it. Maybe we'll see her in the baggage area."

But they did not. Marie had seen them when she came off the plane and had hurried ahead, hoping they would not follow. When she suspected that they were gaining on her she went into the ladies' room and locked herself in a toilet until she was certain that they would have left the airport.

When at last she reclaimed her bag and went outside, the evening was cool, almost cold. She took a bus to the airport hotel where she had arranged to spend the night. She had not slept on the plane, and now as she undressed in the anonymity of the hotel room she felt heavy and exhausted. She pulled aside the covers, lay down, and fell into sleep without even switching off the light. She woke at six A.M. San Francisco time, showered, dressed, and by eight o'clock was in a rental car driving south.

Shortly before ten she turned off the freeway onto a road that led out to the Monterey Peninsula. She bypassed the resort town of Carmel to drive further south, down a coastal road built by convicts, into that lonely region known as the Carmel Highlands. Here, gray-green hills eased down to empty beaches, past arroyos over which sea gulls wheeled and screamed. Here, only a passing car and a few half-hidden habitations announced man's presence in a wilderness of mountain, rocky cliffs, and shore. She drove until, at a turn in the road, she saw a familiar, solitary sign.

POINT LOBOS MOTOR INN
Motel—Dining Room

She drove past the sign, going in at the entrance and along a semicircular driveway ringed with a row of neat two-story units, the units grouped around a larger building, which was the office and dining room. The place was new, built on a freshly cleared slope overlooking a great stand of land that drove out into the Pacific. Marie parked in front of the main building, took her bag out of the car, and went into the motel office, where the room clerk gave her a guest card to sign and put her credit card through a stamping machine. As he reached for the unit key, he took a note from the cubbyhole and read it. "I have a message for you," he said. "Dr. Bailey will be arriving tomorrow evening. Okay?"

"When did you get the message?"

"This morning."

Should she ring him? Where was he? The thought of having to spend a day and a half here waiting for Daniel put her into a panic, a panic that made her want to turn around and drive back to San Francisco. But at that moment the clerk picked up her bag and asked her to follow him and, confused, in despair, she followed. He led her to one of the units and unlocked the door of the upper unit. He informed her about mealtimes, showed her how the television worked, and left. It was not coincidence that she was here. She looked around the room as if for some sign. But this was a perfectly ordinary motel, unsinister, Californian. The Point Lobos Motor Inn was simply a place that happened to be near that other place. There were no secrets in these neat new rooms; there was no hidden purpose behind the sign she could see from her window, a sign lettered on a redwood marker, the lettering announcing Cliff Walk. And yet as she looked at that sign she felt that she was being summoned. She left the room, locked the door, and went down the outdoor staircase to the graveled driveway. Like a somnambulist she turned toward the redwood sign. As she did, there came into her vision three monarch butterflies, hovering like tiny kites, moving ahead of her toward the cliffs and sea. The butterflies were not innocent. They had come to the grounds of the inn to lead her on and now they glided ahead of her, enticing her as she stepped out onto the narrow path that led ostensibly toward the beach below. Halfway down, this path forked, one trail continuing to the sea and the sands, the other winding upward, until it rounded a headland where the inn was out of sight. As they had done a year ago, the butterflies veered in the direction of the upward path and again she followed them as though mesmerized by their lazy graceful flight. And so she climbed up toward the headland, rounding it, and came to that other place, and as she did, the butterflies, their mission completed, settled on some grass near the path's edge, wings folded, tiny bodies motionless, as though they slept.

Ahead of her, twenty feet below the cliff walk, a second shelf of cliff thrust out into the ocean. It was shaped in a rough rectangle and resembled the great gray deck of an aircraft carrier. Ultramarine seas, greening in from darker depths, broke on its seaward edge, a thin spill of water sluicing over its rocky prow. Directly below Marie the main expanse of cliff was untouched by this wave spill. It was smooth, sun-warmed, its only ornament small tufts of mossy grass stuck here and there in half-hidden rock fissures. When she looked down at this cliff, her eyes were drawn inexorably to a jumble of rocks directly below the place where she stood. These rocks were grouped as though they composed the opening to a cave, and out of them sprouted the dark green foliage and twisted witch shapes of two Monterey cypress trees. The noon sun sat high in an empty sky. There were no gulls. There was no sound save the dull crash of sea on rock. She stood completely immobile, staring at the twisted trees, waiting for them to move. She felt a shiver of fear as though she confronted the lineaments of a dread, yet familiar face.

But this day, this clear cloudless day, seemed empty of any movement save the meeting of land and water, the natural confrontation of elements in a serene, familiar world. Yet Marie stood tense as one who faces a firing squad. A minute passed, so slowly that it seemed time had stopped. Her tension lessened. Her body began to relax. It would not happen. She thought of the butterflies, but perhaps the butterflies were irrelevant: perhaps they had always been irrelevant.

But if it was not to happen, then why had these extraordinary events conspired to bring her here? If it was not to happen, then what was the next step? As a diviner holds the forked rod, ready to follow the slightest indication, she found herself turning away from the cliff's edge and continuing along the upper headland path, passing yet another sign that said Cliff Walk. She had not gone this far last time, and now as she went on, she came to a new vista. Below, to her left, she could see the convict road winding toward Big Sur. Further down that road, half hidden in a stand of eucalyptus trees, she saw first a red tiled roof and then a long white building. As she went on she realized that there were three buildings, not one. One was a structure like a monastery or school, one seemed to be a sort of barn, and the third was a white building with two towers, one domed, both towers surmounted by small crosses. Marie recognized it as a church built in the Californian Spanish-mission style. It drew her on. She abandoned the cliff walk and went through a grassy field, going down toward the convict road. As she reached the road, a pickup truck approached from the direction of Big Sur, racing by in a cloud of dust. She walked along the road until she came to an opened set of gates, which led to an avenue lined by eucalyptus trees and up to the mission-style buildings. All was hot and still and dusty in the noon heat. A solitary car was parked in a parking lot. There was a hand-painted sign in the driveway, a sign at which she stared in sudden alarmed excitement.

SISTERS OF MARY IMMACULATE
Gift Shop

She stood for a moment, rereading the words. There could be no doubt. All had been planned. In fear, but compelled, she entered this enemy place, walking up the avenue toward the main entrance to the building. Its doors were padlocked. To her left was a side entrance marked Gift Shop. Welcome. She went up a few steps and entered a small room, like an anteroom, its rough whitewashed adobe walls lined with dark wooden display cases containing teddy bears made of plush and dolls dressed in brightly colored clothes fashioned from cloth remnants. In a special case there was a large doll, wearing a heavy silver crown, a rosary of white beads in its right hand and an Infant cradled in the crook of its left arm. The Infant doll was naked but wore a similar silver crown. The large doll was dressed in a garment of silk, sewn with gold lace. Smaller replicas of this Mother-and-Infant doll were at the bottom of the display case. There were two tourists in the shop, a woman and her teen-age daughter, who were standing at the counter selecting postcards from a circular postcard rack. When they had made their choice and paid, the old nun in charge of the shop put the postcards in a cheap brown envelope.

"It's about an hour's drive to Big Sur, right?" the woman asked the old nun.

"It is, yes."

The tourists left. The old nun sat down on the stool behind the counter, put on her reading glasses, and picked up one of the teddy bears, which she was in the process of fashioning. The old nun was dressed in a habit familiar to Marie, a gray and white habit of the sort nuns wore before the new dress code came into effect. Outside, the engine of the tourists' car came to life. The car drove off, leaving a silence.

Here, in the terrain of her enemy, Marie waited for some signal, something that would tell her what would be asked of her. In the main mission building an electric bell shrilled and then the church bell began its slow toll. The old nun made the Sign of the Cross and said a silent prayer. Marie remembered from her schooldays that this was the noon prayer, the Angelus. When the old nun recommenced sewing, Marie abandoned her pretense of looking in the display cases and approached the counter.

"Excuse me, Sister, but doesn't your Order have a school in Montreal?"

The old nun looked up and smiled. "We do, yes. We do, indeed." Like some of the old nuns in Montreal she had a faint Irish accent.

"I went to school there."

"You did not!" If the old nun had been told that she had won the Irish sweepstakes, she could not have sounded more delighted.

"Yes. On Jeanne Mance Street."

"The very place." The old nun nodded her head. "Well, now, imagine that. Our Order has only two schools, one in Canada and one in Chile, and I'd say you're the first person to come in here and tell us she was a pupil. Oh, Reverend Mother will be pleased when I tell her. She used to teach there. That would be before your time, I'd imagine." The old nun paused, then looked quizzically at Marie over her spectacles. "How did you get here? I heard no car."

"I walked down from the Point Lobos Motor Inn."

"Ah, the new place. They say it's very nice. Are you from Canada, then?"

"No, I'm American."

The old nun, still sewing, turned the teddy bear over. Marie watched fingers swift with practice stitch a black snout on the teddy bear's face. What would happen now? Something must happen.

"Do all the nuns make these toys?"

"Ah, no, just a few of us. It's a sideline, you might say."

"Is it a big convent?"

"There's just eighteen of us now, although we were forty-five once upon a time." The old nun peered again over her spectacles. "Would you like to see the house? You could come back later. Our Superior is from Montreal, as I said. I'm sure she'd enjoy talking to you."

So this was the next move. She looked at the old nun. Was this old woman aware that her casual invitation might not be the result of her own free will? She watched the practiced fingers fashion an ear and swiftly stitch it to the teddy bear's head. Of course not.

"When should I come?" Marie asked.

"About five, if you can manage it. I close the shop at five and the garden nuns come in from their work then. Our community hour is from five-thirty to six-thirty."

"At five, then," Marie said. "I'll come here to the shop."

"Lovely. And, in the meantime, if you'd like to have a look at our chapel, go past the main building and you'll see it behind the trees. It was built by monks from Mexico. It's a lot older than the convent. What's your name, dear? I didn't get your name."

"Marie. Marie Davenport."

"I'm Sister Catherine. We'll see you at five, then."

Outside, all was still. To her left, red bougainvillea spilled dry petals on a bed of wilting impatiens. Sun and bright color, heat and quiet. It reminded Marie of a graveyard. *And, in the meantime, if you'd like to have a look at our chapel.* Was it, like the invitation to return at five, not a casual remark but a move she must make if she were to see Alex again? She turned and walked past the main building with its barred, narrow, Spanish-style windows, its long covered veranda, its red stucco-tiled roof. Ahead and to her left she saw a high adobe wall and, as she came closer, an open set of iron gates. Inside the gates was a very large vegetable garden, row on cultivated row, and in the garden five nuns bent over picking lettuce. The nuns wore the same gray old-fashioned habits as Sister Catherine, their veils slanted forward over their foreheads like visors. They did not see Marie, and as she looked at them it was as though, in their medieval clothing, working under this harsh high sun, they were a representation of reality rather than reality itself, peasants at harvest in a Breughel painting rather than real nuns at work in a convent garden. And yet this scene was contemporary. There was an old Ford pickup truck on a path at the rear of the garden. The nuns used yellow plastic containers to stack the lettuce they had picked.

Marie moved on. Behind a row of eucalyptus trees were the two towers she had first sighted from the headland. Now she saw that the larger one was of Moorish design and contained a church bell. The chapel, as the nun had said, was much older than the convent buildings, a sandstone edifice with a flagstone courtyard, a stone bench and a row of graves along the side wall. She passed by the first grave marker and read: *Fray Juanito Matute, 1898.* The front doors of the chapel were open. She stood, looking in. It was a church, and a church was a place she would not enter, a place where there must lurk a priest, waiting to hear her tell what she was determined not to tell.

But, as she stood looking into this particular church, she told herself it must be different. There would be no priest inside this place. It was the private chapel of an Order of nuns. Nothing would be risked by going in. The old nun had said to visit it. Perhaps it was the next move.

And so she entered the vestibule, passing a holy water font and an offertory box. The church was empty and was smaller than it had seemed from outside. She walked up the center aisle to the Communion rail. Beyond the rail was the main altar, backed by a wooden triptych of a crucifixion scene, wood-carved statues of Our Lady and St. John, attendant on the crucified Christ. This altarpiece and the adjoining statues and carvings in the chapel were crudely executed, probably by Indians, and garishly painted in the Spanish-mission style.

Marie had not been in a church in many years and had not prayed since she was a little girl in convent school. She walked into this place like a tourist, staring up at the altar, then turning into a side aisle where she came upon another altar, in which she saw a statue, a larger replica of the doll in the convent gift shop. This statue was about four feet high, dressed in a heavy robe of gold cloth, both Virgin and Infant adorned with crowns of real silver. In the Virgin's left hand was a large mother-of-pearl rosary. Below this altar, under glass, Marie saw a framed, printed notice.

Our Lady of Monterey

On an expedition to the Monterey Peninsula in 1780, the Archbishop of Merida sent this statue in care of the Franciscan monks to be conquistadora of this new land. On arrival the monks placed it in a temporary altar and later installed it in the mission built in this place.

In 1799 Captain Portillo gave the statue a silver crown in thanks for the miraculous relief of his vessels when they were almost shipwrecked on the cliffs near this chapel. An invocation to Our Lady of Monterey produced a sudden, total calming of the elements for several minutes during which the vessels were enabled to come about and the crews and vessels were saved.

When the mission was abandoned after secularization, the statue was cared for by local Indians in their homes. After the Sisters of Mary Immaculate established their convent here in 1921, the statue was found in the home of one of the surviving Indian families. It was restored to its original chapel in 1937.

On the cliffs near this chapel. The cliffs on which stand the jumbled rocks, the twisted cypress trees. *A sudden, total calming of the elements for several minutes during which the vessels were enabled to come about.* The printed words danced in her mind. The butterflies glided before her, moving along the ribbon path of the cliff walk, the walk that had led her over the headland and down to this convent, to that old nun, to her further instructions in this ghastly game of hide-and-seek.

She looked up at the face of the statue, at the round painted doll cheeks, the vacuous eyes, the wig of false black hair beneath the silver crown. It was impossible to believe that this statue had been fashioned in Mexico two hundred years ago, impossible to imagine its being carried over the sands of Monterey by cowled Franciscan monks, attended by armed Spanish sailors. For this statue was as empty of mystery, as unsuitable for veneration, as a doll on sale in a department store. And yet as she looked up at its face, it came to her that this very doll could be the reason for what had happened to Alex in Nice. Stupid doll eyes stared back at her, filling her with new disquiet, a sense that she was not alone here. She had never before felt any sense of presence in a church. As a child, when she had been forced to go to Mass, she had felt only boredom and resentment. At the convent school in Montreal she had waited for the day when she would leave all these rituals behind and live, like her father, in a world where prayers and Mass and worship would have no meaning, no relevance. But now, in this church, she feared the doll's stupid eyes as she feared the naked sky, thunder, and the jumbled rocks and the twisted cypress trees. There was a presence here.

She turned back to the main altar. As she passed it, she noticed a glass panel behind the tabernacle. She had seen one like it, years ago, when Mother Imelda, the headmistress of her school, took some of the senior girls to visit the convent of an enclosed Order of nuns. Marie had never forgotten that visit. It began with the class filing into a convent parlor, where there was a grille behind which were the unseen Colletines, nuns who had taken a vow to remain isolated from the world for the rest of their lives. Beside the grille was a wooden turntable built into the wall. The unseen nuns put chocolates on it and spun it around so that the schoolgirls in the parlor could help themselves. The chocolates had been a gift to the Colletines. The Colletines did not eat chocolates. They spent their lives in prayer and in the adoration of God, said Mother Imelda who afterward led the class into a small chapel and showed them a one-way mirror above the altar. The nuns' chapel was on the other side of the altar, hidden behind that mirror, Mother said. The Colletines knelt unseen in their hidden chapel. They could watch the priest say Mass but themselves could not be seen. In that hidden chapel, invisible to others, even to the priest who said Mass, they prayed most of the waking hours of their lives. Marie remembered how the thought of those nuns, life prisoners to prayer, had frightened and angered her, filling her with a rage against this religion that asked such inhuman sacrifices.

Now, her heart beating faster with the memory of that fear, she faced a similar glass panel and realized why this chapel seemed smaller inside than out. This was the public part. Behind that glass panel was a second, hidden chapel on the opposite side of the altar. And, listening, she thought she heard a faint sound, the sound of the hidden nuns at prayer. She turned away, walked quickly down the main aisle, through the vestibule, and out into the midday stillness, hurrying past the walled garden and the padlocked main building, past the gift shop and the empty visitors' parking lot. When she reached the avenue of eucalyptus trees leading to the main road, she began to run as though the road ahead were freedom. Nothing was coinciden-tal: she knew that. And while she ran, escaping, she knew there was no escape. She had been told what she must do next. She must come back at five.

SOMEWHERE within the main building an electric bell shrilled, announcing the hour. Sister Catherine rose from her stool, covered the postcard rack with a cotton dustcloth, and took a steel cashbox from under the counter. She then drew the wooden shutters of the window and preceded Marie to the gift-shop door, leaving the teddy bears and dolls shadowed in their display cases. As Marie looked back in that instant before the old nun shut the door, the large Virgin doll seemed haloed in a strange crepuscular light. The old nun turned the key in the door and they went together across the parking lot toward the main entrance to the convent, which Marie noticed was no longer padlocked. The old nun's gray habit was patched and repaired, its nap worn shiny with use, its long hem dragging the dust as though Sister Catherine had shrunk in the years she had worn it. As they went in at the entrance and down the corridor, two nuns walking ahead of them turned with bows and smiles. They were elderly, but in their manner reminded Marie of very young children who might at any moment erupt into shy fits of giggling. Sister Catherine did not introduce Marie but followed them into a large room where six other nuns were already assembled, sitting in high-backed chairs in a loose semicircle. "This is our community room," Sister Catherine told Marie. "Reverend Mother will be along any minute." The nuns in the room offered tentative smiles of greeting but seemed unwilling to be introduced before the arrival of the Superior. The room was very clean, but shabby because of the worn condition of the furniture. There was an ugly cactus plant in one corner and a large old Singer sewing machine in another. On one wall were two shelves of books, a collection of devotional works and a shelf of detective stories. A wooden crucifix hung over the door and a colored photograph of the Pope adorned the mantelpiece. There was no television set.

A nun entered, a stout brisk woman in her fifties. The other nuns rose and bowed to her in a gesture of respect. Reverend Mother acknowledged the bow, then came toward the visitor. "Welcome to our house," she said. She spoke in an accent which Marie recognized as French-Canadian.

"Mother, this is Marie Davenport," Sister Catherine said. "Marie, this is Mother Paul. Marie was in our shop today and she tells me she was a pupil at our school in Canada."

"And when were you there, Marie?"

"Eleven years ago," she said, smiling uneasily at the attentive smiling face of Reverend Mother.

"Sister Benedictus would have been headmistress then?"

"Yes, she was."

"She and I were postulants together in Montreal." Reverend Mother resettled her coif on her head in an absent-minded gesture. "I remember throwing snowballs at her in the convent yard. You can't imagine. After all these years out here, I still miss the snow."

The other nuns, sitting in their semicircle, smiled through this exchange. "But you must meet the Sisters," Reverend Mother said and, taking Marie by the arm, led her around the room, introducing the nuns by the odd-sounding names they had been given when they abandoned their own families to become part of this community.

"I saw you today," one old nun told Marie. "You passed by when we were at work in the garden. You were coming from our chapel and you were in a great hurry."

She seemed too old and frail to have been one of those nuns in the garden. "You were picking lettuce?" Marie asked.

"I was."

"About half of us work outside," Mother Paul said. "We live off our garden, or try to." She led Marie to a worn sofa and sat down beside her. "Are you a Canadian, Marie?"

Marie had intended to answer only what was necessary. Here in the enemy's terrain, she must be totally on guard. But these nuns seemed just like the nuns she knew in her school days, their lives the opposite of any life she would wish for herself, their minds full of superstition and pious nonsense, their opinions not worthy of serious attention, their questions naïve as their faith. And so, forgetting her fears in her old contempt for the foolish ways of such women, she found herself telling them that she had been born in New York but that her father had moved to Montreal to start a new business there. She said she was ten years old at the time. She took a childish delight in telling them that the only reason she had gone to their school was because it was two blocks away from her new home and her mother had found it convenient to send her there. She said that she had been enrolled, at first, as a day pupil.

"A day pupil?" Sister Gonzaga asked, her old head doddering, her bloodless lips trembling as though she wept. "Did she say a day pupil? I thought it was a boarding school."

"It's both." Mother Paul said. "Isn't it, Marie?"

"Yes. I was a boarder there for my last three years. After my mother died."

The nuns, at mention of her mother's death, bowed their heads in sympathy. "And is your father still in Montreal?"

"No. He moved to Los Angeles after the funeral. That was when he enrolled me as a boarder. I joined him later in Los Angeles, after my graduation. Then I went to college in Los Angeles. To UCLA."

"And what did you study there?"

"English."

"English. Do you teach?"

"No. I did graduate work for my doctorate. But I got married, so I didn't finish." Her tension increased when she said the word *married*.

"Oh, this *is* an inquisition," Mother Paul said, smiling, and again adjusting her coif, which had slipped sideways. "We must stop asking you so many questions. I'm sorry."

"No, no," Marie said. For if the questions had some hidden purpose then they might lead her to the next step. And so she told them she had been married four years, and that her husband was a pathologist. In answer to a question from Sister Catherine, she said that she was spending two years in New York, where her husband was on a visiting fellowship.

"So you're back here on vacation," Sister Placidus said. "And is your husband here too?"

The question hung in the air. She looked around the semicircle of smiling sisterly faces. What did they know? "No," she said. "But I'm hoping he'll join me."

"So you haven't been back to our school since you graduated?" It was Mother Paul who asked the question.

"No."

"You'd find it very changed, I believe. Enrollment is down. Half the school has been closed off and the convent is almost empty. We don't have the vocations nowadays."

The semicircle of old heads nodded in agreement. "It's the same in other orders," Sister Placidus said.

"Few nuns and fewer funds," Sister Gonzaga told Marie. "In Chile, our nursery school has shut down for good."

"Maybe you can tell us, Marie," Sister Placidus asked. "What's happening? Why are there no girls who want to be nuns today? Did you, yourself, ever think of becoming a nun?"

She stared at the old foolish face in fear. Was it just an innocent question or was it something very dangerous? Mother Paul noticed her hesitation.

"Oh, Placidus," Mother Paul said, reprovingly.

Sister Annunciata, a stout nun who had been silent, now began with the rushed delivery of a very shy person who has decided to speak out. "There are plenty of vocations, plenty, it's just that they're all contemplative vocations. People don't want to be nursing or teaching sisters nowadays, they want to be shut away from the world. Isn't that right, Gonzaga?"

"Alone, adoring God," Sister Gonzaga said. *"Solus ad solum."*

"Yes, yes." Sister Annunciata nodded her head vigorously. "To worship God through prayer, to give yourself up totally to Him. It's amazing, isn't it, that the hardest vocation to carry out is the one that's popular today. We see it here, we do indeed. We could fill this convent with contemplative nuns if we had the funds."

Marie remembered the glass panel behind the altar of the convent chapel. Where were the contemplative nuns at this moment? Suddenly, she felt sure that this conversation had a hidden purpose. "But you're not a contemplative Order?" she asked.

There was a silence in the community room, a tiny yet unmistakable hesitation. The nuns looked to Reverend Mother. "Not now, no," Reverend Mother said. "We did have a contemplative branch in Chicago but it had to close down for lack of funds. Some of those nuns are with us now. Speaking of which . . ." She reached into her sleeve and drew out a man's pocket watch on a leather thong. "If you'll just excuse me for a moment." Rising, she left the room.

"Gone to clear out the chapel," Sister Catherine said. The other nuns smiled.

"Mother St. Jude is with us," Sister Annunciata informed Marie. "She was Superior of that contemplative branch Mother Paul was telling you about. She's a living saint."

"She is, indeed," Sister Catherine said. "It's when people meet her that you hear talk of vocations. If only we had the money."

"We need a miracle," Sister Gonzaga said.

A miracle? Marie felt her body grow tense. It's only a word, a manner of speaking, she warned herself. It has no importance.

"Something like the loaves and fishes," Placidus said. "But with dollars and cents."

Sister Gonzaga laughed a wheezy laugh. "I'd settle for loaves and fishes. I like fish. I could live off it."

"Mother St. Jude would live off nothing, if we let her," Sister Catherine announced. She turned her head with a starchy rustle of her stiff coif. "Speaking of which, here they come."

Reverend Mother reentered the community room, followed by seven nuns in single file, their hands muffed in the deep sleeves of their habits. They glided in silently, the first of them a stout plain girl, younger than Marie, the last a tall old woman, with dark-skinned Mexican or Indian features, who at once drew Marie's attention, for she had about her an air that set her off from the others, her movements almost catatonic, her manner that of someone listening to a conversation although no words were said. And it was to this nun that Mother Paul turned first, saying, "This is our visitor, Marie Davenport, who was at our school in Montreal. This is Mother St. Jude.'' The tall old nun bowed her head in acknowledgment and then Reverend Mother introduced the other six contemplatives, who fidgeted, embarrassed, as if the recital of their names was a sin of pride for which they must later do penance. The youngest, the stout plain girl introduced last, was called Sister Anna. She alone of the contemplatives looked for an instant into Marie's eyes before lowering her gaze again in the headbent humble attitude of the others. Then, the contemplatives, with the exception of Mother St. Jude, sat down on a row of straight-backed chairs lined against the wall. The other nuns, seemingly pleased by the contemplatives' arrival, at once became talkative, retelling for their silent sisters the details of Marie's visit. Marie, half listening, found herself watching the mysterious Mother St. Jude, who stood looking out of the window as though she were alone in the room. Watching her, Marie realized that her seemingly catatonic movements could be part of an act of silent prayer. Mother Paul noticed Marie's interest in the old nun and said briskly, ''Mother St. Jude. Please sit.''

The tall old woman turned at once to her younger Superior, made a bow of reverence, and went to a vacant chair. Somewhere in the convent Marie heard a clock strike the half-hour. Were they waiting for her to leave? She stood, saying awkwardly, ''Well, thank you for having me. I'd better go now.''

''We'll be taking supper in a few minutes,'' Mother Paul said. ''Won't you join us?''

It's just a gesture, Marie told herself. She remembered from her school days that the nuns of the Order, no matter how humble their resources, would always offer hospitality to a stranger. But she could not be sure. It could be a command. As she hesitated, she felt a sudden power in the room, a power that drew her gaze toward the tall old nun, and as she turned to Mother St. Jude she realized that the noncontemplative nuns were observing her. Then Mother St. Jude raised her bowed head and looked Marie full in the face, her dark luminous eyes intense, her expression one of overwhelming reverence joined to a complete and enveloping love. It was as though, in Marie, she saw one she had waited for all her life and now, praying for her wish to be granted, she gazed in supplication.

There was a moment of silence while they stared into each other's eyes. Then Marie heard her voice say, "Yes." The old nun at once dropped her gaze, bowing her head in her former posture of humility.

"Good," said Reverend Mother. "Then, let us go in."

The refectory was a large bare room with a wooden lectern in its center and narrow wooden tables lining the walls. There were places for many more than the nuns who went in. Supper was a slice of homemade bread and a bowl of vegetable soup. After Marie had been served, the nuns filed past the tureen, each ladling her portion. Mother St. Jude was the last to serve herself. She took only a tiny portion, leaving most of the vegetables. Mother Paul, who was talking to Marie at the time, turned back to the table, picked up the ladle, and silently filled Mother St. Jude's bowl.

"Oh, Mother, that's far too much for me," the old nun protested. Mother Paul shook her head. All sat. Grace was said. The simple meal was eaten in silence. When it was over, Mother Paul gave thanks. The nuns made the Sign of the Cross, then stood. Mother Paul asked Marie, "Have you seen our chapel?"

"Yes. I was there this morning." She did not know if it was the right thing to say. She did not want to go back to the chapel, but in this game of hide-and-seek, with Alex's life at stake, every casual remark could be a further clue. Should she go with them? She had said that she had already seen the chapel. Was that a wrong decision?

"Then, if you will excuse us," Mother Paul said. "Oh, Sister Catherine. Will you show Marie the way out? I hope we'll meet again, Marie. Come and visit us. How long will you be in Carmel?"

"I—I don't know yet." She thanked Reverend Mother for supper. The nuns, forming a double line, began to file out of the refectory, saying their farewells to her as they passed. The last two nuns in the procession were Mother St. Jude and the youngest nun, Sister Anna. As the tall figure of Mother St. Jude drew level, it halted, and Mother St. Jude turned toward Marie. At once she felt the extraordinary, compelling warmth of those dark, luminous eyes. "Come back," Mother St. Jude said in a whisper. "God bless you."

Mother St. Jude and Sister Anna moved on out into the corridor. Alone with Marie in the refectory, Sister Catherine smiled in wonder. "Wasn't that something!" She saw that Marie did not understand. "Speaking to you. Oh, Mother St. Jude is terribly shy, she never speaks unless she's spoken to. Do you know that's the first time I ever saw her really look at someone."

"Oh?"

"Yes, indeed." Sister Catherine began walking her toward the convent's front hall. "That was the old way in convents. I remember when I was a novice, you never spoke unless you were spoken to. You were never supposed to make a noise, even opening or shutting doors. When the cloister bell rang, you had to drop what you were doing and go at once. You were supposed to guard your eyes, never to look at another person directly. There must never be anything worldly in your actions. Yes, those were the old rules. I remember them, but Mother St. Jude still lives by them. She is the most humble person I ever met. She has no self. Do you know what I mean, Marie?"

"Yes," Marie said. A week ago she would not have understood. She would have thought of these nuns with the contempt she felt for their religion, her mother's superstitious faith, with its priests and penances and indulgences and its denials of the importance of this world for an illusionary life hereafter. But now it seemed to her that this innocent-seeming remark was a warning, a warning that she must give up her own sense of self, that sense that had made her always rebel against them and their religion, that had made her refuse to do what they demanded of her. As she drove down the convent driveway she looked up toward the fields that led to the headland. She felt ill, yet strangely excited. She heard again the light, innocent voices of the old nuns talking of vocations and the lack of religious funds, a conversation far from innocent when she connected it with what had been asked of her. She had been waiting for a sign from these nuns, but perhaps she had not been brought here for that. She had been brought here so that it could be revealed to her, at last, why she was being ordered to testify.

She drove out of the convent gates onto the road. She turned right, going back toward the Point Lobos Motor Inn. Of course she could be wrong. Perhaps it was paranoid to think those things about the nuns. It could be coincidence that the Sisters of Mary Immaculate had a convent in this place. It could all be in my mind. My mind, which I no longer trust.

At the Point Lobos Motor Inn there were very few visitors' cars. She drove to her unit, parked, then walked up the outside staircase. When she unlocked her door she saw a pink message slip on the carpet.

WHILE YOU WERE OUT
Mrs. Davenport. Call unit 21.

It must be Daniel. Her heart beat in sudden excitement. He must have made it today, after all. She looked at the telephone by the bed, its little message light blinking red. She ran to it and picked up the receiver.

"Mrs. Davenport here. Is there a phone message for me?"

"Yes. We put a slip under your door. You're to call unit 21. Want me to ring for you?"

"Yes, please."

She waited. The phone rang four times in unit 21 before it was picked up. A hoarse male voice answered, "Yes?"

At once, she hung up. She acted instinctively, for even in her panic, she knew she must not say or do the wrong thing. She must be careful, very careful. She stood up, trying to control a sudden trembling. She took her key and went out of the room.

Number 21 was the only unit in the motel that faced directly on the headland and the cliff walk. As Marie walked toward it, she wondered if that could be significant. She warned herself to walk slowly and behave in a calm manner. Everything is relevant, she told herself. Everything will be made clear. She paused for a moment at the foot of the wooden flight of steps leading to number 21, which, like her own room, was the top half of a double unit. She told herself again that she must be calm, but a fearful excitement filled her. She went up and knocked on the door. She heard footsteps. Someone unlocked from inside.

When the door opened and Marie saw her husband standing in the narrow hallway of the room, her overwhelming impulse was to hold him. But as she went toward him he backed into the room, avoiding her, saying in a hoarse voice, "Wait."

"Yes," she said. She told herself that she must do what he wanted. Whatever had made him run from her must be dealt with very carefully. She watched him as he shut and locked the door. He was wearing chino slacks, a long-sleeved checked shirt, and brown loafers. He also wore a canvas tennis hat to conceal the wound in his skull and the area where his head had been shaved. She saw too what she had not seen when she looked at him on the stretcher in the intensive-care unit in France. There was an ugly, contused, bluish bruise on his right cheek.

"Sit over there," he told her. "I'll sit on the bed."

She did as he said. He went past her and sat on the bed. The moment she entered the room she had noticed his eyes and now, as he passed her, she looked again. His eyes were opaque. They glistened dully, as though they were covered by a thin film of oil. She remembered Dr. Boulanger in the French hospital, his gray, patient face, looking first at Tom Farrelly, then at her. "Madame, I know. Not just because I am a doctor. Anyone who has seen dead persons as often as I have knows."

She paused on her way to the room's only chair, and turned toward Alex. "Why won't you let me kiss you?"

"Sit there." He spoke with no inflection, as though he had learned the words by rote. "Look," he said. "There's something wrong with me. I don't want you to touch me. Don't worry. I'm getting better. I'll be all right."

The chair faced the window. She turned it around so that it would face the bed. "Don't," his voice said. "Don't stare at me."

She did as she was told. She resettled the chair and sat, facing the window. In the summer sky a bloody orb of sun fell, second by second, into a distant sea. She looked up at the headland around which the butterflies had led her to that spur of cliff.

"Promise me something," his hoarse voice said.

"I promise." She stared at the red sky.

"Don't ask questions."

"All right." But how could she not ask questions?

"I'll ask the questions," he said.

"Yes. All right."

"Did you leave that message for me to come here?"

She felt herself go tense. "A message?"

"On the service in New York. To come here."

Daniel's message. "Yes," she said. "I left it."

"Why?"

"You ran away," she said. "I thought you might want a place where you could hide." It sickened her that she could lie so easily. But in this year of her affair with Daniel she had learned these skills.

"Did you speak to anyone in New York?" he asked.

"No."

"Did you ring my mother or Babs?"

"No."

"Do you have a car?"

"Yes. I rented one."

"Good. I don't think I can drive. I took a taxi from San Francisco."

"Alex, have you seen a doctor?"

"I told you. Don't ask questions. I haven't seen anyone. I don't want anyone to know about this. Do you understand?"

What did he mean? He had done nothing wrong. He was the victim of a terrible accident, that was all. Or the victim of her refusal to obey. When she thought of that and of what he must have suffered these last days, she felt like crying. "No," she said. "I don't understand. Alex, you must see a doctor."

He did not answer. She heard him move on the bed. In the abrupt Pacific sunset the red sky turned black. In the room all objects became silhouettes. "It was an accident, wasn't it?" he said. "We went out from the beach in that little pedal-boat thing."

"Yes."

"I remember that I got out of the boat and that I was swimming and you were pedaling the boat along behind me. There was a motorboat coming, I saw it but I thought it was all right. I thought if they don't see me in the water, they certainly must see our pedal boat. It came right at us, right at you in the

73

pedal boat. That is why I wonder if it was an accident. It was as if they were trying to kill us."

Despite her promise, she turned around in the chair.

"Don't," his voice said. "Turn away, please."

She did as she was told. She saw the face of the motorboat owner, sick with fear and guilt, saw the boat owner's little boy crying from his father's slap. The boat owner was not acting, was he? He was afraid, he was sick at what he'd done. "It was a man with a young child," she said. "The child fell in the front part of the boat and the man left the tiller to go and pick the child up. He didn't even know he had hit you. The motorboat hit you and went over you and then smashed into our *pedalo*."

"Were you hurt?"

"No." She pretended to bend down to adjust her shoe, risking a quick look at him. He was sitting on the edge of the bed, his back to her, his head bent forward as though he were about to fall over.

"So they took me to the hospital," he said. "Was I conscious?"

"No."

"And what did they do?"

"I don't know. They took X rays. They said you'd fractured your skull. They said you'd suffered a severe concussion. You were in the intensive-care unit for several hours."

"Did you see me?"

"Not then. Afterwards."

"Where?"

"In a room in the intensive-care unit."

"And what did they tell you then?"

"That was when the doctor told me you'd suffered a severe concussion and that you had a skull fracture. He said there was nothing they could do."

"Did he say if I'd regained consciousness?"

"No, he didn't."

"And how long was it after the accident that he told you I was dead?"

"I'm not sure. I think about three hours."

In the shadow-filled room she saw him stir, then lie down on the bed, stretching out, his face against the pillows. The tennis hat spilled off his head. Was he in pain?

"Why won't you see a doctor?"

He did not reply. She saw the white tonsure where they had shaved around the wound. There was no dressing on the wound.

"What did they say?" His voice was suddenly loud. "What did they tell you, afterwards? Who told you I was missing?"

"The doctors, three doctors at the hospital. There was a man from the American consulate who went with me. The doctors said they had no explanation. They asked if you had any enemies."

"Why did they ask that? Did they think that man in the boat was out to kill me, was that it?"

"No, no," she said. "I don't know why they asked, really."

"And what did you say, when they asked that?"

"I said you had no enemies. You don't, do you?"

"What else did they say?"

"They said they had reviewed all the medical evidence and that there was no question of them having made a mistake. They said you were dead and this was the case of a dead body having been stolen and that they would have to report it to the police."

"And did they?"

"I suppose so. I don't know."

"Was there anything in the French newspapers?"

"I don't know. I don't think so."

"But what did you think?" he asked. "I mean when you heard my body was missing."

"I hoped you were still alive."

"Why?"

"Why?" His question was like a wound. "Why not?" she said. "Do you think I want you dead?"

"I didn't mean that. I meant you'd been told I was dead and you'd seen me dead. Why did you think I was still alive?"

"When I went back to the hotel room I saw a hospital scrub suit lying at the bottom of the airshaft. And your air ticket and money and bag were missing."

"Did you tell them that, the consulate people or the hospital?"

"No. I didn't have time. I phoned TWA about your ticket and found you were on a flight to New York. I tried to get on that flight, but I couldn't. Alex, why did you leave the hospital like that, without telling anyone? What happened? If you tell me that I won't ask you any other questions."

She heard him move. The lamp came on. Blinding light erased the shadows of the room. He sat up on the bed, gazing at her, his filmed eyes opaque, the ugly wound in his head like two lips, discolored by yellow disinfectant. "Why do you want to know?" his harsh voice asked.

"Because it's important."

"Why is it important?"

But, of course, she was afraid to tell him why. Was it a mistake by the French doctors or was it because of her? Alex would know if the doctors had made a mistake; he was a pathologist, he was an expert witness on his own condition. But if they simply made a mistake, why did he slip out like that, why did he hide from everyone, even from her? "Just tell me," she said. "Did you wake up, or what? Did they make a mistake?"

He gazed at her with those lightless eyes, eyes that aroused her most secret fear. "All right, I'll tell you," he said. "I woke up in a dark room and I knew from the smell that it was a morgue freezer room. I was lying on a trolley with no pad under me, wrapped in a plastic sheet, my hands and legs tied together with gauze, a strip of gauze around my chin. I thought I was having a dream, a dream about work, in which I was the corpse. But when I sat up and got the gauze off and switched on a light I knew it couldn't be a dream. It was real. I remembered that I'd been swimming. That was all I remembered. But I knew I had been counted out, that's why I was there. Morgues have a button inside the freezer room which you can use to let yourself out in case you get locked in accidentally. I found the button and went into the pathologists' locker room. There was no one about. I dressed in scrub clothes and cap. Even found old shoes. There are usually old work shoes in those locker rooms. When I went upstairs I saw that it was just before dawn. I walked past the desk. Nobody stopped me. They thought I was some staff man going off duty.''

"But why did you do that? Why didn't you tell them what had happened?''

His dulled eyes avoided hers. "You asked about the hospital. I told you about the hospital.''

"No, you didn't tell me. I asked you if they made a mistake.''

"What are you talking about?'' Suddenly his voice was loud again. "Of course they made a mistake.''

"Then why run away? It was their fault, not yours. And why didn't you get in touch with me? If you were afraid of the treatment at the hospital we could have gone to another.''

"I told you. Stop asking questions.''

"But I just want to know why you didn't come to me.''

"I was afraid.'' He leaned forward and put his hands over his face.

"But why?''

"I don't know. I suppose I wasn't thinking straight. I felt someone was trying to kill me. I felt I had to get out of France at once. When I got to New York, I don't remember what I did. I know I was in our apartment. I remember finding your message on the service. I felt I had to come here.''

"Why?''

"I told you. I don't know.''

"Alex, you must get help. Anyone can see that you're ill.''

"No. I have to work it out myself. You'd better get that straight.''

"But how can you?''

"I mustn't see a doctor. I mustn't let anyone know what happened to me.''

"That doesn't make sense.''

"It does. Don't you see? For the rest of my life I wouldn't be known for my work or for anything else. I'd just be a goddamn medical freak.''

"Why a freak?''

"Oh, shut up.'' His voice filled with rage. "You wouldn't understand. You've got to trust me, you've got to do what I say. If you won't trust me, then get out. I don't need you.''

"I do trust you, let me help you. This isn't your fault."

"What do you mean it isn't my fault? What are you talking about? What do you mean, fault?"

She was silent. She had said she trusted him, but did she? Was he still making his own decisions? "Nothing," she said. "I just meant you had an accident. I just meant that you need help if you're going to get better."

"I am getting better. It'll be all right. If you say nothing about this, it will be as if it never happened." He twisted spasmodically in the bed. She saw that he was taking his pulse. "Marie?" It was the first time he had said her name.

"Yes."

"Go back to your own room."

"Why? Let me stay with you."

"No." His voice was hysterical. "You can come back in a while. Go on, go now. I'll call you later."

She told herself she must not anger him, she must do what he wanted her to do. She rose and went to the door, looking down at him as he lay back on the bed checking his pulse.

"Is that door self-locking?" he asked. He tried to sit up, but lay back again. "Check that it's locked."

She went to the door. She saw the doorknob was in the locked position. She unlocked it and went out, closing it behind her, pretending to check it. "It's locked," she called back through the shut door. She listened, then went down the wooden steps to the gravel driveway. At first it seemed that there was no moon, but as she walked toward her own unit a full moon slid out from behind a black cloud, a bright high noon of night, casting its steely radiance on the buildings and parked cars. Again she felt the menace of the naked sky. She hurried to her own unit, running up the steps, unlocking the door with shaking hand.

She went in as one goes to shelter and sat, facing the window, trembling. What did he mean someone was trying to kill him? Would they still kill him unless she agreed to testify? She saw his filmed eyes, heard the fear in his voice, his lunatic concern that the freakishness of what had happened would interfere with his plans, his career. And even now, afraid for him, she felt her old anger at his selfish single-mindedness.

78

She sat and looked out at the moon-filled night. She did not know how long she sat before the telephone rang. It would be him asking her to come back to the room. She picked up the receiver.

"Hello, Marie?"

"Yes," she said. "Daniel?" Her heart lifted. It was as though, hearing his voice, she could see him, see that lopsided smile, his rumpled clothes, feel his nearness. She heard music and noise at the other end of the phone. He must be in some public place, some bar.

"I guess they've been ringing the wrong room," he said. "I almost gave up. I was getting no answer. Then I rang back a second time and they connected me. Anyway, how are you?"

"I'm all right," she said. "How did you know I was here?"

"I didn't. I called your New York number and your service told me my message had been picked up. So I called here in case you'd already arrived. Where's Alex? Is he in New York?"

She did not answer. "What time will you be here tomorrow?" she said.

"Late afternoon, I hope. I'm still up in Marin."

"Then you haven't told Elaine yet?"

"No. We had a sort of crisis this afternoon. Betsy went out riding and fell and Elaine was worried sick. I decided I'll tell them later, when things have calmed down. Listen, what's this urgent situation you mentioned in your message?"

"It will keep until you get here," she said. "Daniel, why did you pick this place? Why this place?"

"Why not? It was the first place we were together. And I thought we could meet there and have a little time together before we went on to L.A. Marie, what's wrong? Have you told Alex, is that it?"

"No, I haven't told him."

"Why did you come back early from France? I thought you weren't due till Tuesday?"

"I'll tell you later," she said.

"Is Alex still in France?"

"We'll talk about it tomorrow."

"There *is* something wrong. Tell me."

79

She hesitated. If only I could. Daniel was the opposite of Alex: he listened. He knew at once from her tone of voice that something terrible had happened. Daniel will worry about me. He is worried now.

She looked out of the window. Alex's light is off. Daniel has been ringing that room and getting no answer.

"Marie, are you there?"

"Yes, Daniel. I'll see you tomorrow."

"All right. Tomorrow. I love you."

"Good night," she said. "I love you." She hung up. Why was the light off? Was he asleep? Or was it something else? She went out, locking the door, remembering that she had not locked Alex's door. He will be angry if I walk in and he realizes I lied to him about locking his door. I'll have to risk that. If he's asleep I'll slip in and sit by his bedside. She hurried across the moonlit driveway, past the other units, and up the wooden steps. She moved quietly, hoping he would not hear her. When she reached the top of the steps she saw that his light had come on again. She felt a wave of relief. She decided to pretend she did not know about the unlocked door. She knocked. She listened. There was no sound inside. She knocked again, then knocked a third time. When she still heard no sound, she turned the handle and went in.

He was lying in the bed under the lit bedlamp, his eyes open. "Alex?" she said. He did not answer. She went toward the bed and, with the certainty Dr. Boulanger had spoken of, saw that he was dead. His mouth was open. His eyes were open. He was not breathing. She bent over him and touched his skin. The skin was still warm. She took his wrist and felt for his pulse, but her own hand shook so that she could not locate the vein. She took a pocket mirror from her handbag and put it to his mouth. She had seen someone do that once in a movie. The mirror did not cloud. She lay down on the bed beside her dead husband and in fear and guilt and desperate affection laid her cheek against the dead flesh of his cheek, put her arms around his dead body and held him. She did not weep. It seemed to her that what she felt was beyond tears. She lay beside him, awkwardly, and after a few minutes sat up and looked at his white face, his bruised cheek, the naked ugly wound in his skull. With its mouth open the corpse had an inhuman look. She tried to push the jaw shut, but it fell open again. She closed the eyelids although it made her shiver to do it. She left the corpse and walked across the room to the window. She sat in the only chair and looked out at the silver sea, the mysterious moon, the dark shape of the headland. Alex is dead. He is dead because of me. Daniel will come tomorrow but it will make no difference. Nothing will ever be the same. They have done this to Alex to punish me. They did not kill me in that accident because they still plan to use me. They killed Alex. They killed him to warn me.

She looked out of the window at the dark shape of the headland. I thought I had free will. I thought I had the right to ignore what happened to me. But what use is it to talk about rights when they have shown that there is no right or wrong, when everything I thought was superstition and false might be true, but not true in the way those nuns believe it to be true. Oh, I have news for you, Mother St. Jude. God is something you could never understand, something we call God but it may not be God at all. Something evil. And yet I am to blame. I blame my pride, my selfishness, for even after the accident, if I had done what was asked of me, perhaps Alex would have been spared.

She looked again at the sprawled figure on the bed, a figure that was no longer Alex, but dead flesh. She saw what seemed to be a notebook lying on the bedtable and got up at once with the irrational hope that he might have written her a last message. On top of the notebook was his wristwatch, a ballpoint pen, and a thermometer. She put these things aside and, taking the notebook, went back to the chair. She opened the notebook. On the first page were notations in his small precise hand. She read the first page, then read it again.

4. *10 hrs ½ hr. 70 deg. Pulse 52.*
   Stoppage 2 hrs?
   No urine output. Pulse 48 at 1806. 56 at 1710.
   Temp. 78.
5. *No urine output. No food or fluids.*
   Stoppage 1 hr at approx. 1300.
   Temp. 80. Pulse 54 at 1500.

> 6. *0800 hrs. Stoppage while pulse taking. 20 mins?*
> *Pulse 56. No urine output. Foods, fluids rejected.*
> *Stoppage ½ hr? at circa 1400. Temp. 87.*
> *Pulse 58. N.B. vision impaired. Anxiety increase.*
> *Aphasia when confronted unawares. Memory lapse?*
> *Sense of smell. No detectable odor. Putrefaction?*

Anxiety increase. Aphasia when confronted unawares. Aphasia was the loss of the ability to speak, wasn't it? She put the notebook down. He died without knowing what has been going on for the past year, without knowing that I was planning to leave him this week. A mercy, or the cruelest betrayal? I don't know. I suppose I should tell someone that he is dead. I'll have to tell his mother and sister. There's no sense in ringing them tonight, is there? Does anything make sense anymore, does anything matter anymore? She looked again at the notes. *6. 0800 hrs. Stoppage while pulse taking. 20 mins? Pulse 56.* Pulse taking. He had been taking his pulse when he made her leave the room. What *did* happen to him? Was it really connected with out there, with the headland in the dark? Now, no one would ever know. She supposed there would be an autopsy. She would have to make up some story, she would have to tell people something. She would say that it had been a hospital mistake and that his sanity had been affected, that he had run away, crossed to New York, and then come on to this lonely place and had sent her a message to meet him here. And had died tonight, shortly after she and he had met again in this room. Would people believe it? She supposed they would. It would be the sort of story that would get in the newspapers, but it would be the sort of story the newspapers understood. Unlike the other, the unreal true story, which no one would understand. If she told that, people would say she was mad. She would just have to wait for the next move. In the meantime she would tell the made-up story and people would believe it. The true story was impossible. Besides, if she told the true story, she would be letting them win. And I will not let them win. Not now.

She sat for some time, her head bent, no longer looking out at the dark headland. Should I wait until morning to tell the motel that my husband is dead? Until midmorning, say, when Daniel will already be on his way here. I could tell them that I fell asleep in my chair and did not discover that he was dead until I woke. She turned and looked at the bed. It would be easy to believe he was just sprawled there, alseep. She looked at the bed again. The corpse was not in the same position. It seemed to have moved. She sat still, still as she had been out there on the headland when she looked down at the jumbled rocks, the twisted cypress trees.

The body moved. It turned stiffly in the bed and she saw its left hand take hold of its right wrist as if feeling for a pulse. After a moment the hands separated and the left hand groped along the bedtable and took up the wristwatch. Again, he took his pulse. She watched, then saw him sit up and grope unsteadily for the notebook she had taken away. She saw him look around the room, look at her, then past her, as though he did not see her.

"Do you want your notebook?" she said.

"Where is it?"

She brought it to him. He looked at her through filmed eyes as though trying to remember something. He took the notebook and wrote in it, then put the thermometer in his mouth and lay back, exhausted.

"How long?" she asked.

He looked in her direction but did not speak. His lips remained closed on the thermometer.

"How long this time? An hour, or more than an hour?"

He did not seem to hear her. She picked up his notebook. He had written:

7. *Fourth stoppage. Pulse 56. 45 mins?*

She put the book down again, where he could reach it. He took out the thermometer, looked at it, then wrote in the book. *Temp. 80.* He put the book back on the bedtable, lay back, and closed his eyes. She could hear his harsh, painful breathing. She went to the chair and sat. At first she heard no sound but the sound of his breathing. Then a faint rumble. Was it thunder? A scrim of dark clouds obscured the bright moon, like a ghostly illustration of the twisted shapes of cypress trees. The thunder came again, loud now, warning her that the world was not the real world she had known all her life. She sat in this room like a murderer with her victim. But, unlike a murderer, she had been given a second chance.

SHORTLY before dawn she fell asleep in her chair and when she wakened it was after nine. Alex's bed was empty. She heard water running in the bathroom and a moment later he came out. "Hi," he said. His voice was less hoarse. He went to the window and looked down at the beach. "I'm much better," he said. "Don't I look better?"

"Yes, you do." He looked ill but euphoric. There was even some color in his face. He turned and went back to the bed, taking up his notebook. She noticed a tremor in his hands and for some reason this affected her, making her want to weep with relief, as though the tremor were a sign of fragile, struggling life. She noticed that he was unshaven. "You could do with a shave," she told him.

"Could I?" He seemed delighted to hear it. He got up at once and went to the dressing-table mirror, peering at the mirror, fingering his chin. "Yes," he said. "Yes." Then looked around as if he had lost something.

"What's wrong, Alex?"

"I don't know." He seemed puzzled. "It must have been the concussion. That's sometimes an aftermath of concussion, temporary, partial loss of memory. Nothing to be alarmed about."

"What don't you remember?"

"Did I bring a bag?"

"Yes, I saw one in the closet. You didn't unpack."

"Is there a razor and stuff?"

"I'll look," she said. "Why don't you lie down? You mustn't tire yourself. Let me unpack your bag, okay?"

He nodded and lay back on the pillows. She opened his suitcase. Everthing had been stuffed in in a muddle. It was not like him: he was very neat. She found his razor and toilet case. "I'll put it in the bathroom," she said. "But you don't have to shave now. What about some breakfast? You haven't eaten anything, have you?"

"Breakfast." He reached for the notebook and flipped through its pages. "I don't know," he said, as to himself. "I'm having some minor memory lapse or dysfunction. I don't remember when I last ate."

"Let me get you something. I'll bring it up from the dining room. What would you like?"

"Like?" He turned away from her and sat, face averted. He sat too long, as though trying to collect his thoughts. Then he said, "Coffee. Toast. Juice."

"Eggs?"

"No, I . . ." He did not finish the sentence. But he looked up at her with eyes which, in sudden joy, she saw were no longer filmed.

"It's all right," she told him. "You're going to be all right. I'll get your breakfast now."

"Good." He nodded his head. "Good," he said again.

"You don't have to lock the door," she said. "I'll be right back."

"I'll shave."

"All right."

She took her purse and left, going down the steps and across to the main building. The only customers in the dining room were four elderly tourists who were finishing breakfast. She asked the waitress if she could have the food on a tray. "It's for my husband. He's not feeling well."

"Toast will take a minute."

"Fine."

She went over to the dining-room window and looked out at the sea. She remembered herself and Daniel having dinner here, last year. But then, as a mist rolled up the beach, she thought, instead, of her first meeting with Alex. It had been on a beach near Los Angeles, at a university picnic in aid of the antinuclear movement. She was a UCLA student at the time and he a fellow at the UCLA medical center. After beer and hot

86

dogs and a speech by a liberal senator, most of the picnickers were drowsy, but she and Alex, who had been introduced over lunch, went for a walk on the sands. A mist came in, a mist like this one, enveloping them, isolating them. They walked and talked for more than an hour and when they got back to the picnic Alex offered to drive her home. She made her excuses to the people she had come with and that evening she and he had dinner together in Westwood. She was going around with someone else at the time but all of that changed when Alex decided he was in love with her. She stared now at the sea mist coming in and felt a familiar twinge of guilt. He was the one who was in love. I didn't really care about finishing graduate school. I didn't know what I wanted to do. When I wrote that paper on Baudelaire, Professor Haines said: "Obviously Miss Gillan is a hedonist." I laughed and thought, Well that's no crime. But after I married Alex, I remembered what Haines had said. Did I marry just to have an easy life? If so, I have paid for it.

The waitress came with the tray. Marie signed the bill, took the tray, and went out into the growing mist. As she opened the door of the unit, she heard the shower going in the bathroom. "Breakfast," she called. "Alex, breakfast's ready." The shower stopped and a moment later he came from the bathroom, naked, toweling himself. She noticed, with relief, a redness in his skin as he rubbed it vigorously. He wrapped one of the towels around his waist, smiled at her, and sat at the table. "You've shaved," she said. "Let me kiss you."

But he put his hand up, halting her. "Wait," he said. "I'll tell you when."

Obedient, she went to sit on the bed, watching as he picked up the glass of orange juice and sipped it as carefully as someone tasting medicine. He swirled the juice around in his mouth. "Yes, I am feeling better," he said. He drank a larger swallow of the juice, put the glass down, and sat with his head bent, as though waiting. "Good," he said again. "No nausea. Very good." He looked up at her and smiled, a smile made sinister by his bruised cheek and the ugly open wound in his skull. The wound seemed wet.

"Your head," she said. "Shouldn't you have some sort of dressing on it?"

"Why? Is it bleeding?" He put his fingers up and touched the wound.

"A little, I think. Was it before?"

"No." He felt again and looked at a droplet of blood on his fingertips. "Good," he said. He got up, went into the bathroom, examined the wound, washed it and dried it carefully. "Yes, it should have a dressing," he said. "I must get one." He sat down and drank the rest of the orange juice. "Maybe what I needed was you," he said. "I certainly feel a lot better since you showed up."

She watched him bite tentatively on a piece of toast. "How did you find this place?" he asked. "And why are we in California, not New York? That's one of the things I don't remember."

"I told you," she said. "I thought you might need a place to stay, away from New York, away from everyone."

"But why this place? Why Carmel? We don't know Carmel, do we?"

"I was here once," she said. "I remembered that it was a quiet place."

"When were you here?"

"Before I knew you." The lie came easily. Lies now seemed half-truths. She watched him chew on a piece of toast, saw the slight reddening of the dead skin as the hidden blood beneath it moved in his veins. She knew he was not safe: far from it. Unless she did what she had been told to do, he would not continue to improve. This was a reprieve, not an acquittal.

"When were we supposed to come home from France?"

"Today. You were to go back to work at the Institute tomorrow."

"We'll have to phone my office," he said. "I'll think of some excuse. We'll have to stay here a few more days. Nobody knows we're here, right?"

"Nobody."

Suddenly, he gagged on the toast. He coughed and quickly drank black coffee.

"Are you all right?"

"I'm fine." He put down the coffee cup and went to the bathroom, pausing to pick up the thermometer and wristwatch before closing the bathroom door. She looked at the mist, which lay like a blanket just above the waves. She thought of Daniel's message, which had been responsible for bringing both her and Alex to this place. All of this had been willed. We have all been placed here like pieces on a chessboard. She looked into the drear and rolling mists and remembered: This is just a reprieve. She heard Alex move around in the bathroom and then the door opened and he came out again. He seemed pleased with himself. He came to her and put his arms around her. He was still naked except for the bathroom towel around his waist. "Now you can kiss me," he said. She felt the warmth of his body. His cracked lips touched hers. She held him and kissed him and for a moment it was as though he had returned to her, as though nothing had happened, as though she had never planned to leave him.

"How's your temperature?" she asked him. "You took your temperature, didn't you?"

"Normal." He sounded jubilant. "Normal, by God. And my pulse is fine and my pupils are normal and everything else seems perfect. I'm all right. Whatever went wrong is okay now. It's a miracle."

"A miracle?" she said. "That doesn't sound like you. Do you think there ever could be such a thing?"

He released her and went to the closet, where she had put his clothes. "A miracle?" he said. "Well, I suppose a miracle is something that happens for which there's no possible rational explanation. If you accept that definition, what happened to me is a miracle."

"What *did* happen to you?" she asked.

He put on underpants and pants and took out a sports shirt before answering. "I don't know," he said. "I know some of my symptoms but I don't believe them. Maybe I made a mistake. Maybe I wasn't really capable of evaluating my condition."

"What symptoms?"

He did not answer. He pulled the sports shirt over his head, careful not to let it touch his wound. He said: "The thing I remember most about the last couple of days is how I felt afraid."

"Afraid of what?"

"I don't know. I had a feeling that someone was going to

harm me. I felt I had to get out of France. I had to hide from everybody.''

''Even from me?''

''No, not really. I don't remember. I know that I wanted to be alone to find out what was happening.''

''And did you?''

He hesitated. He buttoned up his shirt. ''No. And maybe I never will.''

''Does that worry you?''

''Not now. It might, later on. I hope not.''

''But what about your skull fracture? Surely that should be treated?''

''There's no special treatment for a skull fracture. It will heal on its own. What I want is to be well enough to get back to work. Marie?'' He turned to her. ''This is going to stay between us, isn't it? Promise me you won't tell anybody.''

''But why must it be such a secret?''

He came to her and put his arms around her as though to win her over. ''I told you, I don't want to go through life as a medical freak, like somebody in the *Guinness Book of Records.*'' He grinned. ''Please, Marie?''

She nodded. He kissed her cheek. She kissed him back, a Judas kiss, for this could not remain a secret. The other world would not give him back his life for nothing. It must be paid for.

He released her, then went to the bed, where he slipped his feet into loafers and took up the ruled notebook. She watched him write something in the book. When he had finished he shut the book as though it were a final act and sat, meditative, looking out of the window. As he did, the mist lifted up like a great sail, revealing a blue sky above it. ''It's clearing,'' he said. ''Let's go for a walk.''

''Are you sure?''

''Yes. The exercise will do me good.''

''Take a sweater, then.'' She got up, went to his closet, found a navy crewneck, and brought it to him. As he put it on she looked around for the room key. ''The key?'' she asked and saw that his face was blank. He looked at the bedtable, then at the circular table by the window.

"I forgot where I put it. I keep forgetting things. Wait. Is it under the pillow?"

It was. She put it in her purse. "All right, then," she said. She took his arm as though she were his nurse.

"Wait." He went to the closet and put on the foolish tennis hat. "Mustn't forget this. I look like the Frankenstein monster without it."

As they went down the wooden steps, he leaned heavily on her arm. She asked him, "How did you manage on the plane from France?"

"I told them I was airsick. I told them I'd had an accident, and they got me a wheelchair. In New York, too. I went through customs in a wheelchair. It's funny. A lot of it went blank. I did things like a robot."

Like a robot. The phrase disturbed her. They had reached the graveled driveway. Ahead of her she was the sign marked Cliff Walk. She stood, a sudden alarm rising within her. Was this willed by Alex, or by someone else? Would he go toward the headland?

As she stood, waiting, he turned in the opposite direction. "Let's walk down to the road," he said.

"Yes, let's." But his step was unsteady and after they had gone about fifty yards he stopped and shut his eyes. "Dizziness."

"Let's go back, then."

"No, no, I'll be all right. The air's doing me good."

A middle-aged maid, wearing a white smock, came out of one of the motel units, pulling after her a cart filled with bedding and cleaning equipment. She looked at Alex, then at Marie, then looked again at Alex. "Morning," she said.

"Good morning," Marie said.

"You folks checking out today?"

"No, not today."

The maid looked again at Alex. "Take care, now." She pushed her cart along the driveway, going back toward the main building. They walked on. "Take care," Alex said. "I must look pretty strange."

"It's that bruise on your face. Will it take long to heal?"

"Not now," he said. "It will turn yellow soon and then it won't be so noticeable."

They were approaching the road. As he walked, his movements seemed to become stronger. Suddenly, he released himself from her arm. Then, as though memorizing a lesson, he announced, "We went to the atherosclerosis conference in Marseilles. I gave a paper on platelets. Hobson was there and he gave a paper on the Ewing experiments at Stanford. Reeves Bulmer and I were on a panel together. After the meeting you and I went to Nice for a few days' vacation. We stayed in a hotel called the Miramar. Now, were we on our own, or were the Bulmers with us?"

"You don't remember?"

"It's just temporary. We were alone, weren't we?"

"Yes."

"Then nobody knows about the accident, apart from the consulate and the hospital?"

"Not as far as I know."

They had reached the road. He paused, as if considering which way to go. She realized that if he went to the right, the road would lead to the convent of the Sisters of Mary Immaculate. Her anxiety returned. This walk could still be willed by some other force. Her alarm grew acute as he turned right. "You mustn't walk too far," she said. "You mustn't tire yourself."

"I know. But I feel fine. I feel different. I feel as if, suddenly, I'm a different person."

"Different?"

"Yes. You'd like me better if I were different, wouldn't you?"

"What do you mean?"

"Something was wrong with you last year. Something I don't understand."

Her eyes searched his face. What did he mean, was he talking about her and Daniel? "What do you think was wrong with me?" she asked him.

"You were strange in some way."

"I'm surprised you noticed." Suddenly, she felt not fear, but a familiar resentment at his selfishness, his assumption that his career transcended anything else in their lives, his sending her off to service the car or deal with the superintendent and the plumber, or asking her to pack his suitcase for his trips because: "I'm too busy." She thought of his coming home at ten o'clock at night, not having telephoned to say he'd be late, coming in and calling out in the hall, "Marie, what's for supper?"

"Yes," he said. "I noticed, all right. It's my fault, I suppose. I was away far too much."

"Yes, you were." Her anger came up like a flame, but she damped it. Everything had changed. Those things didn't matter anymore. What mattered now was that they were walking toward the convent.

"I'm sorry." He took her arm. "I promise you it will be different from now on."

"Don't think about it. Just think about getting better."

He looked at her. "All right, I will. But I am better, much better. That damn hospital, I'll never know what really went on there. Trouble is I wasn't well enough to evaluate what was happening to me. I was afraid to let someone else do it. I was afraid I'd become known as a sort of Lazarus."

A sort of Lazarus. She looked at the road before her. She had been told that this road was built just fifty years ago. Before that, the region south of Carmel had been reachable only by sea. It was a road into a wilderness, but a road that now led to something more dangerous than any wilderness, a danger that lurked, perhaps in the light, foolish voices of the nuns in the convent up ahead. She looked back at the Point Lobos Motor Inn, at the orderly arrangement of motel units, at a sheet fluttering on a balcony, at an ice-cream truck parked outside the dining room. It was a scene utterly prosaic, utterly familiar. She was walking away from this scene, walking down a road that led into a wilderness with a man who said he was a sort of Lazarus, who unknown to himself had been raised from the dead because another extraordinary world desired that this place of wilderness become unique and celebrated. And remembering that, she told herself again that the other world waited for her surrender. Alex's life depended on it. She must go now, give in now.

Yet, knowing this, resenting it, she thought of one final delaying move. "Let's go back to the inn," she told him. "Let's celebrate your recovery by having lunch in the dining room. We'll get a table overlooking the sea."

THE WAITRESS waited. Alex read the menu, then read it again. Marie looked out at the sea. "Soup," Alex said. "Chicken soup."

"And what else?"

"Just soup."

"And the seafood salad for you," the waitress said confirming the order.

"Yes, thanks," Marie said. When the waitress had gone, she looked at Alex. "Are you sure you're all right?"

"I'm fine." He stared at the sea. A heaviness seemed to have come upon him. "I haven't really eaten anything for the past two days," he said. "'I've got to be careful."

"I didn't mean that. It's something else, isn't it?"

"Yes," he said. "I was all right until you suggested we come back here for lunch. I was all right. But now I feel afraid again. I can't think straight. I feel panicky. I thought I was over it, but I'm not."

"Do you want to go back to your room?"

"No. I'll try the soup."

He sat, turned slightly away from her, looking out of the window at the beach. But she guessed he was not really looking at the beach. He was not looking at anything. She noticed that his hands had again begun to tremble. She reached across the table. His fingers felt cold. After a moment, he took his hand away. They sat, in silence, until the food came. Very tentatively he spooned his soup and drank a mouthful. He swallowed, then looked at her. "It's all right," he said. "It went down."

"Good." She looked at her own food but did not eat it. She watched him spoon and drink another three mouthfuls. Then he gagged. He put down his spoon and stood up, unsteadily. "Alex, are you all right?"

"I think I'll go back to my room. Finish your lunch."

But, of course, she did not. She paid and came after him as he walked unsteadily along the driveway, past the other units. When she caught up with him and took his arm, he leaned on

94

her like an old man. "Are we going in the right direction?" he asked. His voice was hoarse.

"Yes. Do you feel dizzy?"

"Nausea. It will pass."

She helped him up the wooden steps and, when they were inside the room, sat him on the bed and took off his loafers. He lay back, closing his eyes. "Draw the blind," he said. "Please."

She lowered the venetian blinds. She could still see him clearly in the shuttered light of the room. He lay, eyes closed, mouth open, looking as he had looked last night when she watched over him. Fear came on her. She looked at her watch. It was after one. She should not have tried to delay by having lunch. She should not have waited, she should have gone at once. Maybe her time had run out? She watched as Alex jerked, suddenly, convulsively. She said: "Alex?" He did not answer. She put her hand on his brow. It felt very cold. As she touched him, his eyes opened and stared blankly, as though he had lost his sight. She took her purse and ran out of the room.

PART TWO

"WOULD Father Niles care for some peach cobbler?" Mrs. Peters wanted to know, but Ned Niles shook his head, smiled, and patted his flat stomach. "I have to draw the line somewhere," he told Monsignor Cassidy. "Otherwise I'll be out to here. All this wonderful food."

"Perhaps just some fruit then?" Mrs. Peters suggested.

"That would be good," Ned Niles said.

"Just fruit and coffee," Monsignor told the housekeeper, although, had he been lunching alone, he would have had a little peach cobbler to finish off. Ned had said he jogged every day, back in Worcester. Went five miles on a track. Ned had always been ascetic, Monsignor remembered.

"What time would you like dinner tonight?" Mrs. Peters asked when she brought the fruit.

"We're going over to Monterey," Monsignor told her. "We should be back around six. Let's say seven-thirty."

Mrs. Peters left. Monsignor offered Ned some papaya and strawberries. What he had in mind for his guest this afternoon was nine holes of golf. Ned had mentioned that he played golf. Trouble was, although he and Ned were first cousins, Monsignor knew very little about Ned except that he had worked in inner-city parishes in Boston and now ran a small religious publishing program under a special dispensation from his bishop. Monsignor had already been an ordained priest when Ned was in his first year as a seminarian and so there was not much they could reminisce about. Still, if Ned did play golf, the Pebble Beach course would knock his eye out. And now, as he poured coffee, Monsignor said, "Guess who was playing two holes ahead of me the other day? Arnold Palmer. In a foursome with Gerry Ford.''

"I'm looking forward," Ned Niles said. He had said this about everything, so far. "That's where they have the Crosby Pro-Am, isn't it?"

"That's right," Monsignor said. "We call it the Bob Hope special. You've probably seen it on TV. Matter of fact, Bob's a friend. Very generous with his time. He did a big benefit for Catholic Charities last year."

"Is he Catholic?"

"His wife is," Monsignor said. "A lovely woman. Dolores."

Ned Niles hulled a strawberry and ate it. "Quite a life you have, Barney. Championship golf course, celebrities, beautiful climate, rich parish, well-run school, good curate. And this refectory is like a resort hotel."

"Well, it's not all roses, believe me. It has some special problems." Although he knew, and Ned knew, that compared with Worcester, Massachusetts, it was paradise. Still he doubted if Ned would be happy here. A place like Our Lady of Carmel did have its tricky side. Monsignor doubted that, after years of working in inner-city parishes, Ned would have the tact needed to deal with parishioners in the fifty percent bracket.

Mrs. Peters appeared in the doorway. "Sorry to disturb you, Monsignor, but there's a lady waiting to see you."

"Where's Father Cowan?"

"He had to go down to the school. Some mix-up in the schedules, he said."

"You see," Monsignor said. "No bed of roses. Even on my day off."

"I know," Ned said. "And the telephone. I notice it kept you busy this morning."

"Indeed," Monsignor said. "Well, excuse me, I'll just see what this lady wants."

Monsignor Cassidy, unlike Ned Niles, did not jog and was glad of a golf cart on the links. Now, as he went down the tiled Spanish corridor to the vistors' parlor, he reflected that it was always thin people like Ned who went on about gaining weight.

Monsignor was, as his Irish grandmother would have put it, a fine figure of a man, on the heavy side, but then who wasn't a tad overweight at fifty-seven? This morning he was a colorful figure in green madras slacks, purple Izod tennis shirt, and white golfing shoes. His hair was white, neatly combed, and very thick and full. He had a delicate skin that did not take a tan but blushed a permanent pink from exposure to the California sun.

Monsignor remembered that Mrs. Peters had not mentioned the caller's name, so it was not likely to be Mrs. Shean or one of his other regular interrupters. He might mention to Ned Niles that the rich were often lonely and were ruthless about taking up your time. But, when he went into the parlor, the young woman who stood up to greet him was not anyone he knew. She was tall and not bad-looking with dark hair parted in the center of her head, falling in long tresses to her shoulders. He noticed a wedding ring. Her yellow summer dress was very light, almost translucent, outlining her figure against the golden glow from the parlor window.

"Monsignor? Are you Monsignor Cassidy?"

"Yes, I am. You're Mrs. . . . ?"

But she did not give her name. "I'm sorry to disturb you," she said. "You don't know me. I live in New York. I've come a long way. There's something I have to tell you."

"Sit down, please," Monsignor said. He realized she was very nervous. "From New York," he said. "I see." He did not see. What did she mean she'd come a long way? Did she mean she'd come from New York to see him?

She sat and he sat facing her. "I don't know how to begin," she said.

"Take your time." Although he hoped this wouldn't take long. He planned to be on the golf course by two-thirty, a little ahead of those who would be lunching at the lodge.

"First of all," she said, "I don't think you're going to be-lieve me. I don't blame you. It's something I wouldn't believe if it were told to me. Yet, it's the truth."

Educated, Monsignor noted. He couldn't make her out. She was upset and seemed almost hostile, yet if he was any judge she wasn't a crazy. He'd had experience with those. Well, you never know. Hear what she has to say. "Yes, yes," he said. "Just tell it to me in your own words. Take your time."

"First of all," she said. "I'm not a Catholic. I was brought up as a Catholic until I was twelve, but then my mother died and I stopped pretending to believe. I never really did believe in it. My father isn't Catholic and once I got out of Catholic school at sixteen, I never went into a church again."

Monsignor nodded. What age would she be now? About twenty-five, he guessed.

"That's very important," she said. "The fact that I don't believe in an afterlife or religion or any of that. My husband isn't a Catholic either."

"I see," Monsignor said. He hoped this wasn't some prelude to a diatribe against the Church.

"So, I'm here against my will," the young woman said. "I resent having to come here, but I have no choice. I've been forced to come."

"Forced? I don't understand. Who forced you?"

She hesitated, then said, "If you'll just bear with me for a moment."

"Of course." It was one twenty-five already. How long, Oh Lord, how long?

"A year ago last week," she said. "I came to Carmel. I spent the night in a place called the Point Lobos Motor Inn."

"On Cabrillo Highway."

"That's right. I'd driven up from Los Angeles to Monterey to be with a man. When I got there, it wasn't possible for me to stay at his hotel so I drove south again and picked this motor inn at random. The man came to me there and we spent the night together. I was married at the time. I still am."

She stopped, and flushed, as though caught unawares by her own confession. "You'll have to excuse me," she said. "This is hard to explain."

"Take your time."

"Well, the next morning, the man I was with had to go back to Monterey and I had to go back to Los Angeles. We had breakfast together and after he left I felt lonely. I decided to go for a walk along the cliffs before starting the drive home. Do you know those cliffs?"

"Yes, I think so," Monsignor said. "They're near the state park."

"Well, when I was walking along this cliff walk, some butterflies flew in front of me and I found myself following them." She shook her head as if to correct herself. "I don't know," she said, "maybe the butterflies had nothing to do with it. Anyway, I followed them until they settled on some bushes near a point on the headland. I found myself looking down at a big shelf of rock which was sticking out into the sea about twenty feet below the path." She paused, looked at Monsignor, and said, "I'll try to describe it, the rock, I mean. It's important. The rock itself had a completely flat top like the deck of a big ship. But just below me there was a small clump of rocks like the opening of a cave, and outside this cave were two of those Monterey cypress trees." She looked past Monsignor, looked out of the window, remembering. "And then I felt something very strange," she said. "It was a sort of silence, as if the sea wasn't moving, as though everything was still. Then the branches of the cypresses rustled and shook and someone came out through the trees below me. It was a young girl: she couldn't have been more than sixteen. It was a cloudy day, did I say that? There was no sun at all. And yet she was surrounded by a little golden path of light."

"A halo of sorts?" Monsignor offered.

"No, more like a stage light. It was phony-looking. And she was wearing a white veil and a long white dress and her feet were bare. She looked up at me and joined her hands like this." The young woman faced Monsignor, her hands in an attitude of prayer. "And then she said: 'Marie, I am your Mother. I am the Virgin Immaculate.' "

"Your name is Marie?" Monsignor said. Of course her name is Marie. It would be.

"Yes. But I want to explain that until she said she was the Virgin, I hadn't thought of that at all. Even then it seemed ridiculous. She was far too young. But afterwards I read that many of the apparitions of the Virgin are young. Almost children."

"You've read about such things, have you?" Monsignor asked and saw her give him a look, as though she despised him. "Only afterwards," she said, angrily. "I told you I didn't believe it was the Virgin Mary. I don't believe in miracles and I don't believe in the Virgin Mary. I read all that stuff after I saw the apparition.''

"And then what happened?"

"Then it said, 'This rock must be a place of pilgrimage.' And it opened its arms as if it wanted to reach up to me and said, 'Marie. You will tell the priests.' "

"A place of pilgrimage?" Monsignor said. "I wonder what she meant by that. Did she mean it would become a shrine?''

"I don't know what it meant. I still thought it was some trick. I looked to see if the light around the figure was made by a hidden spotlight. But then something happened which couldn't have been a trick."

"And what was that?"

"Lightning. It lit up the whole sky behind the apparition. And, as it did, the light around the figure began to fade. And as I watched, the figure itself began to fade away in front of my eyes until I was looking at bare rock. And then the thunder came, very loud.''

"What did you do then?" Monsignor asked. He thought of Ned Niles. Ned would be interested in this.

"Nothing. I felt afraid of the thing, the apparition. I didn't want anything to do with it. I'd just spent the night with a man I was in love with. I was thinking of leaving my husband for him. I had my own life and, as I said, I don't believe in Catholicism. I decided I'd do nothing. I went back to the Point Lobos Inn, packed my bag, and drove home to Los Angeles. And I told nobody."

"Nobody?" Monsignor asked. Frankly, he found it hard to believe that she didn't tell a single soul.

"Well, I couldn't tell my husband, could I? I wasn't supposed to be there. Besides, he'd never believe me. And the man I'm in love with, I haven't told him either. He's a doctor, the same as my husband—and he's like my husband, he thinks religion is all nonsense. I was afraid he would believe I was mad. Besides, I thought, if I tell people about this, there'll be publicity and it will all come out, our affair and all the rest of it."

"And then what happened?" Monsignor asked. "Was there a second apparition?"

"No. But I started having nightmares about what I'd seen. I'd go to sleep and about midnight I would dream I was standing on the cliff, and the apparition would appear and say the words over and over until I woke up screaming. And I began to have migraines. I never had migraine headaches before. I get them now. Especially when I hear thunder."

"Thunder," Monsignor said. "There was thunder at the time of the apparition. Is it possible, do you think, that the apparition itself was some sort of nightmare?"

"I wish it were," the young woman said. "Sometimes I wish someone would tell me I'm mad. It would be better than this."

"You said your husband is a doctor?"

"Yes."

"But you haven't been to see a doctor, have you?"

"I saw a doctor about my migraines, but I didn't tell him anything about this."

"Perhaps you should see a specialist. It's possible that these nightmares and migraines are related to some illness."

"No," she said, angrily. "Look, I'm telling you, this isn't a fantasy. It happened. I have proof. That's why I've come here."

"What proof? What's your last name, by the way?"

She hesitated. "Davenport."

"And you say you have proof?"

"Yes. It's something that happened a few days ago. Just one year after the apparition appeared to me. Exactly one year to the day. Something happened to someone I know. Something that makes me believe I'm being punished for not telling what I saw."

"May I ask what that was?"

Again, he saw her hesitate. "Something bad, an accident happened to this person I know. The person nearly died. And now I believe that unless I do what I'm doing now—come here to tell you—that it will happen to this person again."

"Something that happened to someone. What was that?" Monsignor's voice was gentle.

"I don't want to say."

Monsignor felt in his shirt pocket and pulled out a pack of

105

low-tar cigarettes. He offered them, and when she shook her head, he asked. "Do you mind?"

"No, no."

"Well, now, let's see." Monsignor found his Zippo and lit up. He wanted to get the details straight for Ned. He remembered that Ned had written an article on mariology. "So this apparition told you that it was your mother and that it was the Virgin Immaculate and that it wanted that rock out there on the headland to become a place of pilgrimage. And that you must tell the priests. Right, so far?"

"Yes, Monsignor." He noticed it was the first time she had addressed him by title.

"And you said earlier that you've come a long way to tell me this. Do you mean from Los Angeles or from New York?"

"From New York. About four months after it happened, we moved to New York."

"And you've come because you're afraid that something bad is going to happen again to someone you know."

She nodded.

"So, although you say you don't believe in religion, you do believe that this apparition was the Virgin Mary?"

"I didn't say that." Again, she was angry. "I don't know what it was. I believe—I think I have some proof now—that it wasn't a trick or a hallucination."

Monsignor found an ashtray and stubbed out his cigarette. He had been hoping to get through the afternoon without lighting up. It was force of habit that made him do it: tension, really. He looked again at Marie Davenport. How was he going to handle this? "Mrs. Davenport," he said. "You say that you have some proof that this wasn't just imagination, that something bad happened to this friend of yours. Can you tell me what that was?"

"I'm sorry, but I want to keep my friend out of this. It's bad enough that I'll be mixed up in it. That's what I've been trying to avoid for a whole year. I suppose that's not possible anymore. For there *will* be publicity, won't there?"

Monsignor did not answer. He said, "Are you planning to go back to New York soon? Now that you've been to see me and done your duty, so to speak."

"I don't know." Suddenly, she seemed about to weep. "I don't know what to do. I was told to tell the priests. I've told you. Now maybe they'll let me alone. Or will there be an investigation?"

"It's a bit early to say." Monsignor smiled, a reassuring pastoral smile. "I mean, it would depend on whether people better versed in these matters than I am decided that an investigation was warranted. You know, Mrs. Davenport, or, indeed, you may not know, but there are dozens of these reports every year. And very, very few of them reach the stage of an official investigation. In this case, I'd say it's not too likely. After all, there was only one apparition. Tell me. Have you gone back to that place since? Did you go back this time?"

"Yes. I went there yesterday."

"And nothing happened?"

"No."

"Well, as I said, you've only seen this apparition once. If, later on, there's another appearance, to you or to some other person, your testimony could be asked for."

He saw that seemed to please her. "So, there mightn't be any investigation, is that what you're saying?"

"In all probability, there won't be."

"But how will you know? I mean who will you ask about this?"

"I'll keep you informed," Monsignor said. "I mean, I'll take your home address and phone number and if something is required, I'll be in touch. But, as you said yourself, you're not a practicing Catholic and you have your own private reasons for preferring that what happened not be made public. My advice to you is to go home and try to forget about it. After all, finally, you've done what you believe you were asked to do. So you mustn't feel guilty anymore. Perhaps the headaches and so on won't bother you now." He rose. "Go in peace, as the saying goes."

"Thank you." She stood up, uncertainly.

Monsignor took out his pocket reminder and pencil. "Now, it's Mrs. Marie Davenport, correct? And what's your home address and phone number?"

She gave it to him, a Manhattan address, East Side. Monsignor had spent four years at Fordham in younger days. "Good," he said. "I'm sure it will be a great relief to you to get this off your mind. Whether it was a dream or an apparition or whatever, I imagine it must have been very disturbing. And thank you for coming all this way to tell me about it."

He led her from the visitors' parlor to the main door. She had not said a word since giving him the address. As he opened the door to let her out, he saw that sea mists were moving in across the Carmel Valley. He had hoped for sunshine on the course. "Nice to have met you," he said, and offered her his hand. He almost said, "Have a nice day," but caught himself in time. There were so many occasions in parish work when that phrase was definitely out of order.

"Is that all, then?" she asked.

"Now, don't worry." He smiled at her. "It's in my hands. Good-bye, Mrs. Davenport. Have a good trip back to New York."

He watched her go down the path. She walked quickly, as though she were late for some appointment. He decided to take the Volvo station wagon, a gift from a parishioner. More room for the clubs in the Volvo. He looked again and saw that she was running now, racing across the parking lot to her car. What was her hurry? Sea mists came in, rolling toward her like clouds of smoke. He shut the door. He went back to the dining room and Father Niles.

IMPATIENT in a stream of tourist cars cruising slowly through the streets of Carmel, Marie at last escaped the town and began to speed down the highway, her mind seesawing between what was happening to Alex and her encounter with God's improbable functionary in his green madras slacks and purple tennis shirt. To have scrupled against and feared this meeting for a whole year now seemed, like all overwhelming fears, foolish and unreasonable. It had been unreasonable to think that she would be believed, unreasonable to think that her coming forward would result in an immediate clamor of publicity. Why should he believe her, why should anyone believe her? It had happened only once, a year ago. And she had not told him the part about France. God's golfer had treated her gently and politely, as though she were some foolish ill woman in need of medical treatment. He had no intention of investigating. Most likely, he would not even bother to report it to his superiors. But, if that was the only outcome of her visit, would Alex's sufferings cease? As she drove on, recklessly speeding past slower cars on the winding coast road, she remembered some of those others she had read about, Bernadette Soubirous, the children at Beauraing, the sheperd at Guadeloupe; they had been disbelieved when they first told their stories. All had returned to the scene to be given some further sign, to convince the doubting priests. The priests always doubted: it was part of the pattern.

And so, agitated and afraid of what she might find, she drove into the Point Lobos Motor Inn, which suddenly seemed to have been emptied of guests. She parked the car below Alex's unit and ran up the steps. The door was locked. She had not locked it when she left. She knocked and called his name, fear rising in her when he did not answer. She turned away, thinking to go to the office and ask for a key, but, as she did, the lock clicked and the door opened. Alex stared out. He was wearing the clothes he had put on earlier. His face was paper pale, the purple bruise on his cheek like some botched tattoo. "What are you doing here?" he asked.

"Are you all right, Alex? While you were having a nap, I went off to do something."

He interrupted her. "How did you get here? Who told you I was here?"

"We had lunch together. Don't you remember?"

He stared past her, his vacant eyes searching the driveway. He said, "Is that your car down there?"

"Yes."

He turned again to face her, looking at her as though he stood lost on the edge of some wild place, a person with no sense of who he was or why he was here. She knew that he was not alive, as she was alive. He had been granted life, but it was a simulated life, a life in limbo. The man she knew, Alex Cates Davenport, her husband, who played tennis and chess, who had climbed a mountain in Norway and won Lazer races in the Juan de Fucca Straits, who hated detective stories and liked silly British stage comedies, who was greedy for pistachio ice cream and claimed that bananas gave him indigestion, that man, in short, tagged in her mind by the hundred small things she knew about him, had disappeared in the hour she was absent in Carmel. It was as though his soul had fled his body. She told herself that there is no such thing as a soul. But something, some animus, was gone from him, perhaps forever. Tears came to her eyes. She took his hand as she would take the hand of a blind person and led him back into his room, led him to the bed and made him sit on it. Then she closed the room door and came back to him. "You've forgotten, haven't you, Alex?"

"Forgotten what?" Uneasy, his eyes searched her face.

"You remember you had an accident?"

"Yes." But she knew he was lying.

"You know who I am, don't you?"

"You're—" He hesitated, then said, "I know. You're Marie."

"Yes. I'm Marie. And you don't remember things now, but you will. You've had an accident. You have a head injury. But you're going to be all right. Do you understand?"

He nodded. He leaned back on the pillows. "I'm afraid," he said.

"Afraid of what?"

"I don't know. I don't remember. I'm afraid because I don't remember."

"But you will remember. Just rest now."

She took off his loafers and put a blanket over him. "Try to sleep."

"Are we in California?"

"Yes."

"My name is Alex?"

"Yes, Alex."

"Alex." He said the name again as if trying it out. He turned toward the wall. She heard him whisper, "Alex."

"Davenport," she said. "Alex Davenport."

"Davenport."

"Yes, that's right. Try to sleep. Would you like a sleeping pill?"

"No."

She sat in the only chair, turning it so that it faced the bed. She noticed that his body had begun to tremble; a slight, continuous tremor. Suddenly, his shoulders twitched and then he lay very still. Alarmed, she got up and went to him. He was sleeping, his breathing regular, the tremor gone. She returned to her chair. It was no longer misty outside. In the heavens, the sun ruled a majestically slow-moiling sea. Daniel would be here soon. At least he would be able to examine Alex and find out what those notebook notations really meant. Or would he? She looked at the bed, at her husband struck down, then resurrected like Lazarus, her husband, who had been restored to her then taken away, who lay there now, his mind blank, robbed of some animus that could be his soul. Was this a new punishment, a warning that she should have told that priest about France, that she could not choose what to tell and what not to tell? She thought of the power that had caused these things to happen. If it was omnipotent, then why had she been able to hold out against it for the past year? Again, her mind fell into the pit of that question.

ALEX SLEPT until four. He woke, asked for water, drank a few mouthfuls, then went back to sleep. He slept so soundly that she decided to shower and change in the other unit, where her clothes were. Daniel would be here soon. She went out, not locking the door, and walked quickly to the unit, where she showered, then carefully did her hair and makeup. As she went down to the driveway, she heard the sound of a car behind her. She looked back. A green BMW had stopped by the office door. A man got out, rumpled, in an old sweater and floppy brown corduroy trousers, his thinning hair blowing up in aureole at the back of his head. Her heart lifted in happiness, the happiness of seeing him again. He had not seen her, and now she ran back to join him. He was getting his bag from the trunk of the car. He looked at her. She saw his face twist into that lopsided grin. His brown eyes mirrored her joy. She ran to him and he held her. "Are you all right?" he asked.

"Yes."

"Have you got a room?"

"Yes."

He went to her, his arm around her as she led him to her room. "So," he said. "What is this urgent situation? You don't know how worried I've been. What's up?"

"I'll tell you in a minute. How are you?"

"Great. I've done it."

She looked at him with foreboding. "Done what?"

"I've told Elaine. It's all out in the open now. I've left."

"What did she say?"

"Oh, she's very upset, of course. But listen, tell me about you. What's this urgent situation?"

They had reached the motel unit. She unlocked the door. "First of all," she said, "you're not going to believe me. I don't blame you. It's something I wouldn't believe if it were told to me. Yet it's the truth." They were, she realized, the same words she had said to that fat old priest.

112

He took her hand as they went in. "Go on," he said. "I love you, you know. I'll believe you."

And so she told him, beginning with the accident, and her hours of waiting in the French hospital and the doctor calling her in to tell her that Alex was dead. And when she came to that, Daniel held her in his arms. "So, that's it," he said. "Poor Alex."

"No. No, wait, I've not finished." And she went on until she came to the part about finding out that Alex was on the plane to New York, and how she had followed him. "So it was a hospital foul-up," Daniel said. "Did you find him? Where is he?"

"He's here. He's in another unit in this motel."

"Here? Why?"

She told him why. She told about Alex's amnesia and his shifts from being well to deathly ill.

"My God, why haven't you taken him to a hospital?"

"He won't let me. He's afraid he'll be treated as a medical freak."

"But that's nonsense. What about France, wasn't there some police inquiry, some consular inquiry? What happened there?"

"I don't know. We left without anyone knowing we'd left. And nobody knows we're here except you."

"You mean to tell me he's here and he's in that state, yet nobody's even examined him?"

"I told you. He won't let me call a doctor."

"But that's stupid. He doesn't know what he's doing; he's probably badly concussed, he may have suffered a brain injury. I don't understand you, Marie; how could you do such a thing? We'll have to get him to a hospital right away. Where is he? What room?"

"I'll show you," she said, and they went out, hurrying toward the headland and Alex's unit. For the first time since the accident someone was helping her. Daniel was a surgeon; he would find out what was physically wrong with Alex. "Promise me you'll be careful," she said. "It doesn't make sense, but we've got to humor him."

He nodded. She unlocked the door and they went in. Alex seemed to be asleep in the bed. She stood back, letting Daniel go forward and switch on the bed light. Alex did not wake. She saw Daniel bend over and look at the wound on Alex's head, then take his wrist and check his pulse. Alex still slept. When Daniel had finished, he came over to her. "I'm just going to get my stethoscope and stuff," he whispered. "I'll be right back." She heard his footsteps running down the outside staircase. She went to the window, and looked out at the headland and the sea. The sun set as she watched, its crimson rim dipping under the horizon, the light changing, second by second, from a dull orange to the first faint violet shades of night. She went to the bed and looked at Alex. He slept, his features calm, his breathing regular. In the dying light his face had a rosy, natural look. Had she been wrong not to get help as soon as she found him? What if, after all, this was just some hospital mistake? But as she asked herself these questions she felt compelled to turn and look again at the rapidly darkening sky. Far from shore the steely breakers rolled in, in tumbling white walls of water. Into her mind came the stupid doll face of the statue she had seen in the chapel of the Sisters of Mary Immaculate. The words of the printed notice beneath the statue filled her ears as though someone spoke them aloud. *An invocation to Our Lady of Monterey produced a sudden, total calming of the elements for several minutes during which the vessels were enabled to come about and the crews and vessels were saved.* Invocation or medical treatment? She was again in the pit of that question.

She heard Daniel come back up the staircase. He came in, his hair tousled, smiling at her; a messenger from the normal world. He went to the bed, putting his stethoscope around his neck, taking out a thermometer, shaking it. "Well, Alex," he said. "Wake up now. We're going to take a look at you." Alex opened his eyes and looked at Daniel. Marie knew from his look that he did not know who Daniel was. Daniel put the thermometer in Alex's mouth, then undid his shirt and began to examine his chest. She watched them together, watched Daniel continue the examination, noticed the quiet way in which he spoke to Alex, first looking into his eyes, examining his pupils, then getting him to sit on the edge of the bed and cross his knees while he tested his reflexes. She heard him ask Alex, "Do you remember what happened to you?"

"Yes," Alex said. "I had an accident."

"What sort of an accident?"

Alex did not answer.

"How old are you, Alex?"

Alex bowed his head.

"All right now," Daniel said. "Lie down again. Do you have a headache?"

"No."

"That's fine. Just take it easy."

She watched as Daniel tucked a blanket around Alex and switched off the bed light. Then he came to her in the dark, taking her hand, going with her onto the outside landing. Above them an insipid moon drifted in and out of a veil of hazy cloud. "He doesn't know who he is," she said.

"That could be the result of the concussion. He did know earlier, you said."

"Yes. He seems to drift in and out of it."

"Well, his reflexes, temperature, heartbeat, those things are all normal. The thing to do is get him into a hospital, take X rays, run some tests. I think our best bet is Moffitt in San Francisco. It's only a couple of hours away, it's part of the U.C. system, and a good hospital. I know people there."

"San Francisco," she said. "But you'll have to go back to Los Angeles, won't you?"

"Yes, tomorrow. I'm operating on Wednesday and Thursday. I'll take you to San Francisco, check him in, then go to L.A. and try to get back up to San Francisco by Friday."

"Can't we take him to a hospital in Los Angeles? That way we won't be separated."

He shook his head. "I'd rather not risk it. It's too far. I want to get him into a hospital tonight. Let's see. You've got to pack and check out. I'll get him ready here and take him in my car. You can follow. You have a car?"

"Yes, a rental. I'll turn it in at Carmel and we can drive to San Francisco together."

"Fine," he said. He took her in his arms and kissed her. "Marie," he said, "it's going to be all right. Remember, no matter how bad things look to you now, we're going to be together. From now on, we'll be together."

"Yes," she said. She did not allow herself to think about that. It was dangerous to think.

"All right, go ahead and check out. I'll pack for him and get him ready. Meet you here."

She did what he said, hurrying along the gravel driveway, packing, phoning the car-rental office, then paying the bill for both units. She put her bag in the rental car and drove to Alex's unit. As she got out of the car she heard her name called. "Marie?"

Daniel had switched on the porch light and was standing at the top of the steps, outside Alex's room. "Catch," he called and threw down a set of car keys, which she missed as they fell jangling on the gravel by her feet. "Bring my car around, will you?" he called. "We're ready."

When she returned, driving Daniel's BMW, the two men were waiting for her at the foot of the steps. Daniel had his arm around Alex as he led him to the BMW. He sat him in the front seat, buckled the seat belt, then said, "Wait here with him. I'll get his bag." She waited. Alex did not look at her. He sat staring ahead at the lane of light made by the car's headlights. Daniel ran down the steps with Alex's bag. She heard the trunk slam. He came to her. "I'll follow you into Carmel," he said. "I don't know the town."

"The car-rental place is on Lopitas Avenue," she told him. "I just rang them and they're open till nine."

"Good. Where's your car?"

"Back there. The yellow one."

He nodded and she went to start her car. As she drove out of the Point Lobos Motor Inn she looked in the rearview mirror and saw the BMW just behind her, Alex seemingly asleep in the passenger seat. She swung her car out onto the coastal road, going away from the convent and the headland. Was this what was wanted of her, to go away from here? If Daniel was a puppet in this drama, then her leaving was preordained. But, somehow, it did not seem right. She thought of the shepherd at Guadeloupe, told to return to the mountain where he had seen the apparition, told that further proof was needed. She thought of the impossible roses the shepherd found growing in that winter place, of the Lady who tied the roses up in his cloak,

116

those roses that the shepherd would spill irrefutably at the foot of the bishop's chair. What further proof must I put at that Monsignor's feet? This cannot be part of their plan. It will anger them, my leaving like this. And what hospital can save Alex from a power that controls life and death?

"WHAT will we say about the accident?"

Daniel, staring ahead in the night at the insect-warren sameness of South San Francisco, suddenly voiced this question in the silence. Beside him, Alex slept as he had slept since Carmel. But Marie leaned forward from the backseat to make sure Alex was not awake before she answered. "Do we have to say anything?"

"Yes, of course. It's going to sound pretty strange if you tell the people at Moffitt that this happened in France—when?—four days ago."

"Why don't we say he fell in Carmel? We could say he fell while walking along the cliff path."

"But supposing there's already an inquiry going on back in France."

"Well, they're not going to know about that here, are they? Please, Daniel. Let's just say he fell."

He turned to look at her. "But I don't understand," he said. "Why this secrecy? You haven't done anything wrong, you're the victims of an awful hospital foul-up. Alex was probably in shock of some kind, that's why he disappeared and came home without telling anyone."

"I told you, Alex will be in a rage if this becomes a story in the newspapers. He's convinced it will interfere with his research funding. Don't ask me why. But he insists that if the media gets hold of this story he'll be known not as a scientist, but as a medical freak."

She saw Daniel look at Alex asleep in the seat beside him. "It was a hospital error. Why would he be known as a freak?"

"I don't know. I told you he made notations on his temperaure and so on. There were some real abnormalities. He wrote them in his notebook. It was on the bedside table with the rest of his stuff. You must have seen it when you packed for him?''

"A notebook? No, I didn't. What do you mean, abnormalities?''

"I mean his pulse stopped, his heart stopped—oh, I don't know. It doesn't make sense.''

He looked at her, his brown eyes puzzled. "It certainly doesn't. What do you mean, his heart stopped?''

And she was afraid. What could she tell him, without telling all of it? "Look,'' she said. "I'm trying to help him and to help us, as well. We don't want a lot of publicity, do we? I want him to get better so that I'll be able to leave him and come to you. If all this gets in the newspapers it will only complicate things.''

"But if we're to find out what went wrong we need all the facts,'' Daniel said. "Don't you see that?''

She looked at him. What could she say? He was so reasonable, so sensible. He was the opposite of Alex. Alex always did what suited him and to hell with other people. She looked down at Alex now. A zombie. I want to be with Daniel and I'm tied to this zombie. Angry and ashamed, she stared at Alex's face. As she did, he opened his eyes. "Alex,'' she said, softly, leaning toward him.

"What did you say?'' Daniel, maneuvering past another car in the fast lane, did not turn his gaze from the road.

"Alex,'' she said, again. "Are you awake, Alex?'' She saw Daniel give a startled, sideways look at his passenger.

"Yes,'' Alex said.

"Have you been awake long?''

"Long?''

"Alex,'' Daniel said. "Alex do you know where we are?''

"Yes. We're driving toward San Francisco. We just passed a sign for Daly City.''

"Do you know who I am?''

Alex turned his head, as though surprised by the question. "Yes, Daniel. But I don't know what you're doing here.''

"We're taking you to a hospital,'' Daniel said.

"I don't want to go to a hospital.'' With an effort Alex sat up straight. "Marie's right. We don't want any publicity, do we?''

"It's not just a matter of publicity, Alex," Daniel said. "You should be in a hospital. An hour ago you didn't even know your own name."

"That was temporary." Alex sounded calm and cold, very much his normal self. "I was concussed. These things happen, as you know. But I'm recovering. I'm greatly improved. Isn't that right, Marie?"

"Yes," she said. If he heard what we said, did he hear what I said about leaving him? She looked up into the rearview mirror and met Daniel's eyes in it, his face a mirror of her guilt.

"So, let's not talk about a hospital," Alex said.

"I'm going to put you into Moffitt and run some tests on you and take some X rays," Daniel said. "There won't be any publicity. We'll say you had a fall. I know people at Moffitt. Carter's on staff there. And I know Dick Watanabe, he's a senior resident. Come on, Alex. You know you can't ignore something like this."

"Say I fell." Alex seemed to be turning this idea over in his mind. She watched him as he said it. He can't have been awake when I mentioned that earlier. When did he wake? When?

"Yes," Daniel said. "We'll just say you had a fall in Carmel. We'll fudge it, if that's what you want. By the way, what were those notations you took on your condition?"

"Notations?" Alex leaned back in his seat and closed his eyes. He was silent for a moment. Then he said: "All right. We'll run some tests in Moffitt. I'll sign myself in."

"Good." Daniel looked at her in the rearview mirror, shaking his head slightly, warning her to silence. Alex seemed to be going back to sleep. What had he heard? In silence she sat, watching Alex's sleeping face as the car came off the expressway and began its switchback climb through the hilly streets of San Francisco.

"BEAUTIFUL, isn't it?" said the old lady. She sat beside Marie, her liver-spotted hands clasping the head of her cane, as though by doing so she was able to remain upright. Her head moved in the dodder of age; her bright summer clothes seemed as incongruous on her wasted body as a top hat and frockcoat on a chimney sweep. She turned now, her wrinkled face grimacing in a mile that showed large, too-perfect teeth. "I love it," she said. "The Golden Gate Bridge, the lights. Over there is Marin County. Over there." She nodded her head in the direction of the windows. "My husband was born in Marin," she said. "They asked me about a private room for him on one of the upper floors, so he could see the bridge and the view. But I thought it doesn't matter. His sight is not so good anymore." She looked out of the window at the glitter of myriad lights far below the hospital, which was on the highest point of the city. "Are you just visiting someone?" she asked Marie, then answered her question. "No, no I'm wrong. Visiting hours are over. You're waiting for news, are you?"

"Yes." Marie looked out into the dark, at the bay, the city lights. She thought of that other hospital in France, where she had looked out at a courtyard with dusty palm trees at an old man in a dressing gown who sat and wept.

"No news is good news," said the old lady. "I'm waiting for my grandson. He works nights in a French restaurant. He's coming after work soon to drive me home. Do you have a car? After ten, the buses only come up here once an hour."

"Yes, I have a car," Marie said. She looked across the expanse of the waiting area. She saw an elevator come down. Daniel got out of it. He was with his friend Dick Watanabe, the Japanese resident. They stood by the elevators chatting animatedly, as if they had just met by accident, Daniel did not look over to where she waited. She had been here for almost two hours. What were they talking about? What had they done with Alex?

"It's a very good hospital," the old lady told her. "The Chinese come here. I mean when they don't go to the Chinese hospital, they come here. They're very clever, the Chinese. But one of the nurses here told me you mustn't ever give them a glass of cold water. They think cold water is bad for them. They think you're trying to kill them. Imagine." Again, she gave her toothy smile. "There's a Chinese doctor, over there." She nodded toward the elevators.

"He's Japanese," Marie said. "Japanese American."

"Oh. Is he your doctor?"

Marie nodded. She watched Watanabe shake hands with

Daniel, then go back into a waiting elevator. Daniel turned, looking for her. She stood up. "Good-bye," she said to the old lady. "It was nice talking to you."

"Take care, dear."

As she crossed the waiting area, going toward Daniel, she wondered again where they would spend the night. She and Alex usually stayed at the Fairmont, but that was expensive. She might be here for weeks; it would be wise to find a cheaper hotel. She was surprised at herself for thinking about a hotel instead of thinking about Alex. When Daniel came to her, he took her arm in a gesture that was like a covert embrace. "Sorry," he said. "It took a while."

"How is he?"

"He's asleep now. I had a quick look at the X rays. He has a small fracture on the left side of his head; it may not be serious. We'll just have to watch him and see how he comes along. I've arranged for a private room tomorrow but tonight we're putting him in an observation ward where they can keep a close eye on his progress."

"What do you think?"

"I don't know. I phoned my friend Carter and he's promised to try to get one of the top neurologists to have a look at him sometime tomorrow."

"But how was he?" she said. "I mean, Alex. What sort of mood is he in?"

"Hard to say. When Dick Watanabe and I talked to him earlier he seemed quite coherent. But quiet. Maybe a bit depressed."

"Do you think he heard what we said?"

"In the car?"

"Yes."

"I don't know." Daniel pushed open the front doors and they went out into the moonlight, walking toward a hospital parking structure. "Do you feel badly about that?" he asked.

"Of course I do. Don't you?"

"I don't know. No, I'd rather we got it over with. I'd rather he knew."

"Well, I wouldn't," she said. "Not until he gets a bit better. It's just too much for him to handle now."

"I suppose you're right."

In silence they got into Daniel's car and drove down vertiginous streets. "Where are we going?" she asked.

"What about the Mark Hopkins? I usually stay there."

"No, I don't want to meet someone I know. Besides, if I have to stay here for a while, I'll need a cheaper hotel."

They settled on a hotel called the Shropshire, near Union Square, a place both of them had heard of but neither of them knew. It turned out to be a small, old-fashioned hotel, its Victorian lobby painted in a light green color which at once depressed her. Daniel took a double room in his name and a bellhop brought their bags up. As they went into the room she saw that the bellhop was carrying Alex's briefcase along with the other bags. When the bellhop left, she went to the briefcase. "Do you remember if you saw a notebook in this?" she asked Daniel.

"What sort of notebook?"

"The one I was telling you about. A graph-lined one."

"I didn't put anything in that."

She opened the briefcase. The notebook wasn't there. Was it in the bag she had given to the nurse when Alex was admitted to the hospital? Or had it been left behind in the Point Lobos Motor Inn? Suddenly, she felt uneasy. The notebook had been a sort of proof, a written confirmation that those things had happened. "Are you sure you didn't leave any stuff behind?" she asked Daniel.

"Not that I know of. I think I took everything. Why is this notebook so important?"

She did not answer. She went to the window and looked out at night-lit rectangles of stores and office buildings. Behind her, she heard Daniel pick up the telephone, call Moffitt Hospital, and leave his name and telephone number in case of emergency. She was reminded of Alex. Doctors always did that when they arrived at a new place. They were never out of touch. She thought of the first time she had met Daniel, thirteen months ago. She wondered what her life would have been like now if Alex had not changed his mind about going to that party in the San Fernando Valley. It was a party given by an ambitious vascular surgeon for other doctors who might put business his way, and at first Alex told her to send regrets, then changed his mind because he heard there was someone coming whom he wanted to see again. That someone was Daniel. And so, on a hot night, on a crowded terrace, under decorative lights with the loud noise of a mariachi band in the background she was introduced to Dr. Daniel Bailey and his wife, Elaine. She did not like his wife, a loud stout girl, but remembered the rush of pleasure she felt at the sight of Daniel. He was attractive, but did not know it, rumpled, untidy, not tall and handsome like Alex. In fact, he was Alex's opposite. He did not try to impress her with his knowledge or his importance. Unlike other doctors he did not seem accustomed to laying down the law. She found him shy, but he could make her laugh. He told quiet jokes, watching her, with a lopsided grin. He made her feel pretty, made her feel she was the person he most wanted to talk to at the party. He danced with her five times that evening. Unlike Alex, he was not a good dancer, but unlike Alex, he had fun dancing. Nobody noticed that they danced five times. It was that sort of medical party, with lots of shoptalk and mingling and many trips to the bar. She knew, as soon as she danced with him, what was happening to her. It was something that had not happened before, not with this intensity. Afterward, she did not remember what they talked about. What she did remember was that his wife had chatted to her during dinner and that she had offered to send Elaine Bailey the schedule of new plays at the Mark Taper Forum. She remembered it because, when the party was over and they were all four of them waiting for the parking jockeys to bring up their cars, Elaine said to Daniel, "Give Marie our address, will you? She's promised to send us the Taper schedule." She noticed that he looked at her, shyly, strangely, as he gave her his card, as though he wanted to say something but did not dare. She put the card in her purse, then, suddenly, said to him, "I'm in the phone book. I have my own number under my name, Marie Davenport."

He looked at her again. "I enjoyed meeting you," he said. Afterward in the car, when Alex drove her home, she kept seeing Daniel Bailey's face, his lopsided grin, seeing the admiration in his eyes. She found she was not listening to what Alex was saying. That night, she lay in bed in a state of excitement.

The next day she went around with him in her mind. She did not leave the house. She did not think he would call. She wanted him to call. He did not call that day or the day after. On the third day, when she had not heard from him, she asked Alex, "Would you like to have those people, the Baileys, over for dinner?"

"Why?"

"Because I liked them."

"I thought you were bored with doctors and doctors' wives?"

"They're different."

"Have them on a Saturday, then. I don't have time for dinner parties during the week."

That evening, she called Elaine Bailey and asked if they would be free for dinner that Saturday. "I'll have to check with Daniel, he's got a very heavy schedule. Just a moment."

She heard Elaine's voice speaking to someone, but not what was said. And then, with a start of pleasure, she heard his voice. "Yes, say yes. We can make it. Great."

And she knew.

Now, in this hotel room in San Francisco, she heard his voice on the telephone, the only voice she wanted to hear. When he had finished, she heard him put down the receiver and then felt his arms around her. "I've missed you," he said. "Remember, the last time we were together, you were waiting for me at the Hilton when my taxi got in from Kennedy."

"Yes," she said. He means we went to bed at once. We always went to bed at once when he flew in from Los Angeles to see me. She remembered that they had stayed in bed and phoned the Asian Pearl Restaurant to send in Chinese food. "It was July fifteenth," she said. "The day before your birthday."

"Doesn't it seem a long time ago?" He kissed the nape of her neck. A long time, weeks and weeks, but longer than ordinary time because time has been different since France. She saw again the lifted sheet, the drained face, eyes closed, the strip of gauze tied around the chin. That is the difference. Before that, nothing stopped me, not even the nightmares and the migraines. He was my shield. Love casteth out fear. Again, she

125

felt him kiss the nape of her neck. Now, it no longer casts it out. Not since France.

She looked out of the window at the downtown building backlit by an orange sky. She moved away from his embracing arms and went to the dresser mirror, picking up her hairbrush. She began to comb her hair. Into her mind came the unit in Carmel. She thought of the mirror she had put to Alex's lips, the mirror that did not cloud.

"Are you feeling down?" Daniel asked.

"A bit. Maybe we should go out someplace."

"Are you hungry?"

"A little." She was not.

"Okay, then." He put on a tweed jacket and knotted a woolen scarf around his neck. "It's after eleven so we may have to settle for a drink and a sandwich. There's a place two streets over from here."

"Fine," she said. Now that they were going out she felt she could kiss him. She went to him and kissed him. He held her tight.

"If only I didn't have to go back to L.A.," he said. "But there's no one who can take over for me."

"What time will you go?"

"Before noon."

"Will you be able to talk to the neurologist before you leave?"

"Depends. I doubt if Carter will be able to fix up an appointment for Alex that early. Anyway, you'll be speaking to the neurologist yourself. And I'll call him from L.A."

It was cold in the street, a damp San Francisco chill that sent them hurrying along the two blocks to the restaurant. When they went in, they were met by a blast of music and a chorus of voices singing an Irish ballad. The place was a sort of New York Irish pub, with a blackboard menu posted over the dining area, an Irish trio playing noisily on a dais, waiters in long green aprons, and a large crowd standing three-deep at the bar under old photographs of Dublin streets. "I didn't remember they had music," Daniel said. "Maybe we should go someplace else?"

"No, this is fine," she said. She welcomed the noise and the

126

distraction. They found a seat side by side on a small banquette and ordered beer and corned-beef sandwiches. As she sat down some young men turned from the bar to look her over. She thought of the days before her marriage, days of singles bars, where boys looked you over and tried to pick you up. It was as though she were remembering another life. She glanced up at the musicians, young men in white Irish sweaters and green corduroy trousers, one with a flute, one with a fiddle, and the third a curly redhead, belting out a song:

> "While going the road to sweet Athy,
>   Hurroo! hurroo!
> While going the road to sweet Athy,
>   Hurroo! hurroo!
> While going the road to sweet Athy,
> A stick in my hand and a drop in my eye,
> A doleful damsel I heard cry:
> Och, Johnny I hardly knew ye!
> With drums and guns and guns and drums
> The enemy nearly slew ye;
> My darling dear you look so queer,
> Och, Johnny I hardly knew ye!"

As the singer finished the chorus, he roared out a reprise, the crowd at the bar joining in.

> "Och, Johnny I hardly knew ye!
> With drums and guns and guns and drums
> The enemy nearly slew ye;
> My darling dear you look so queer,
> Och, Johnny I hardly knew ye!"

She looked at Daniel, who smiled and put his hands over his ears to shut out the noise. What if we were here tonight and he'd left Elaine and I'd left Alex and this was the beginning of being together? We would be singing, wouldn't we? And to her own surprise, sitting beside Daniel, she found herself smiling up at the singer, listening with pleasure as he sang his second verse.

> "Where are your eyes that looked so mild?
>   Hurroo! hurroo!
> Where are your eyes that looked so mild?
>   Hurroo! hurroo!
> Where are your eyes that looked so mild
> When my poor heart you first beguiled?
> Why did you skedaddle from me and the child?
> Och, Johnny I hardly knew ye!''

Her smiling attention failed. *Why did you skedaddle from me and the child?* Daniel, hearing that, might feel guilty. She turned to him but he did not seem to be listening to the song. Instead, he was shaking his head at a young woman who had come by with a tray and a notebook, asking for contributions for some Irish cause. The voices at the bar thundered discordantly, joining the singer in his second chorus. The waiter brought their sandwiches and beer.

> "With drums and guns and guns and drums
>   The enemy nearly slew ye;
> My darling dear you look so queer,
> Och, Johnny I hardly knew ye!''

With drums and guns, the enemy, my darling dear you look so queer. The words of the song jumbled in her mind, meaningless, yet filled with menace as if, again, she had been warned that there was no escape, not even here in this seemingly innocent San Francisco pub. And yet those verses are the ordinary verses of that song; they weren't changed or invented to remind me, were they? She watched Daniel, trying to shut out the song. "Where will you stay now in Los Angeles?"

"I'll move into the Crestwood. It's one of those apartment hotels on Wilshire. In a week or two you and I will know a bit more. We'll be able to make plans then, I hope."

"So do I," she said. She drank the rest of her beer.

"You look tired," he said. "Want to go back to the hotel?"

"In a minute. Finish your sandwich."

She leaned back on the banquette. The song went on but the new verses no longer seemed to have a hidden meaning. What if I'm imagining things, what if there is no connection between last year and last week, what if it was a hospital error and those notations he made were just confused, what if his behavior was amnesia caused by his concussion? If I am imagining all this, I am inventing my own hell. I must stop. She turned to Daniel. "Do you want another drink? I'm not tired after all. Let's stay a little while."

"What about you? Do you want something? A Scotch?"

She shook her head and smiled at him. "You go ahead," she said. She saw him signal to the waiter.

"I think I'll have one," he said. "It's been a tough day." She nodded. Let him talk about Elaine, about leaving Elaine, about what was said when he left. He probably needed to talk. But the musicians, having finished their song, started again in a new ballad, its verses taken up by the drinkers at the bar. Talk was impossible. Daniel shrugged and smiled. The waiter brought him a Scotch and they sat, hand in hand, listening to the song, a song called "The Little Beggarman," a song that seemed safe.

Listening, as the bar chorus joined in: "With your rags and your bags and your ould rigadoo," looking up at Daniel, who was smiling. If it *is* just my imagination then I have a chance, all this will pass, Alex will get better and we will be together you and I. The song ended. The musicians put down their instruments and were sent up black glasses of Guinness stout. With the singing ended, the bar erupted in a confused roar of conversations. She sat, holding Daniel's hand, and felt at peace. After a few minutes, he asked, "Will we go now?" She nodded and he called for the bill and they went through the crowd to the front of the restaurant, passing by a cloakroom that she had not noticed when they came in. Just beside the cloakroom was a little vestibule leading to the front door of the restaurant, and in this vestibule, sitting on a campstool, was a black woman, a nun, dressed in a coarse religious habit, a begging bowl in her hands. Marie had seen such women before, usually in the lobbies of department stores, beggars pretending to be members of a religious Order. But now, as she came up to this false black nun, her fear returned. Why was this woman here, begging in this restaurant of all places? And as she approached the false nun, the nun gazed at her with a look that was imploring yet hostile. The false nun shook her begging bowl, the few coins in it jangling like a tiny warning klaxon. When Marie stopped, fearing to pass, Daniel misunderstood and reached in his pocket for some coins.

"Don't." Marie turned to him, whispering so that the woman would not hear. "They're not real nuns, they're frauds."

"What's the difference?" Daniel said. "They're all beggars." He turned to the false nun and put some coins in her bowl. The false nun shook the bowl, thrusting it up toward Marie.

"Charity, please," she said in a cracked voice.

"What charity?" Marie heard her own voice waver, as if in fear.

"It's for a shrine, please. It's to build a shrine."

"I have no change." She went past the outstretched arm, the begging bowl, pushing open the restaurant door, hurrying into the cold damp wind on Stockton Street. Daniel came behind her, taking her arm. There is no escape, she thought. They will have no mercy.

THEIR HOTEL room had twin beds. She went into the bathroom to take off her makeup, and when she came out Daniel was already undressed and in one of the beds. He was not wearing a pajama top. He lay watching as she undressed. She took off her clothes and put on a nightgown. Into her mind came the black nun and the black nun's words. *It's to build a shrine.* She sat on the bed beside Daniel. He opened up the bedclothes to let her in. He was naked underneath the bedclothes and she wanted to make love to him, to forget the black nun, to forget everything else. She began to kiss and fondle him in desperate, clumsy haste, but as she did, she began to weep. He held her. "What's wrong, what's wrong, Marie?" She wept. She could not speak, could not tell him, I love you, you are the reason I have had the strength to resist them. He leaned across her and switched out the light. "It's all right," he said. "It's all right. Try to sleep now."

She lay, sobbing, remembering that tomorrow he would not be here. And as though he knew her thought, he said, "I'll try to get back by Friday. Sleep now. Sleep."

She lay in his arms. She heard again the words of the black beggar nun. *It's to build a shrine.*

"OKAY. Right," Daniel said. She watched him nod as if agreeing with what was being told to him on the telephone. He looked back at her in the morning sunlight, across the crowded delicatessen, and waved, as though to reassure her that his news was good. She listened, trying to catch his words across the hum of breakfast talk. "Who? Moberly. No, I don't know him. Is he good? Yes. And when will that be? This afternoon. Good. What? A myleogram? Do you think? No, no, of course. Okay, thanks very much. Yes, I'll be leaving for Los Angeles at eleven, but his wife will be here. She'll be over to see him. Yes. Listen, Dick, I'll give you a call. What's a good time to reach you? Yes, I'll be in touch with Carter. Thanks a lot."

He put down the phone and came back to the counter at which they had eaten breakfast. "All's well," he said. "He had a good night and they're moving him up to a private room this morning. The neurologist is called Moberly. He'll be looking in on Alex early this afternoon. Dick Watanabe has just been in to see him and he says there's no serious amnesia, although he seems a bit vague about the accident. Of course, you and I know why."

"Yes, of course," she said. This delicatessen was a place where actors ate, as evidenced by the many signed photographs on its walls, and now, as she sat looking across the street she read the sign on a theater marquee opposite. *Another Part of the Forest*. The street outside was cleansed by thin, bright Northern California sunshine. It was a morning world, a world of brisk conversations, of appointments with neurologists, of private rooms and planes to catch and plans for the day. Even the thought of Daniel's leaving did not destroy this morning promise. Alex was being properly cared for, at last. Daniel would be back on Friday, at the latest.

"So," Daniel said. "What would you like to do now?"

"How long do we have?"

He looked at his watch. "Two hours maybe."

"Let's go for a walk," she said. "Let's walk along the Embarcadero and look at the ships."

"Fine," he said. When he came to New York to see her they would go for long walks in Central Park. They would talk and never tire, although, afterward, she would not remember what it was they talked about. When she was with him, the days raced, and, suddenly, when he must leave she would feel despairing and angry, for she wanted to be with him not for those brief illicit days, but every day, every night. She had always been impatient with subterfuge: long ago her school report cards had used words like *willful, outspoken, must learn discipline.* She had never kept silent when she disagreed, had never agreed for the sake of keeping the peace.

He had not been happy with Elaine, but it had been difficult for him to think of hurting her. Now he had made his break. He was here; he was not going back to Elaine. It was quite different from any other morning they had been together and, as he paid the check in the delicatessen and they went out into the morning sunlight to walk down to the Embarcadero, Marie felt that everything was going to be better. Everything that had happened in San Francisco could be read as a good omen. The black nun last night was a meaningless coincidence. She had begun to hope.

"HOPEFUL?" Dr. Moberly said. "Yes, Mrs. Davenport, I'm quite hopeful. Of course, complications can always develop, but there are a number of good signs. He's had some temporary amnesia, but his speech is not impaired, he's able to write; yes, there are a number of positive signs. I'd be very hopeful, if I were you."

"If things go all right," she said, "how long do you think he'll be in the hospital?"

"Hard to say. Probably, he'll be able to go home in a couple of weeks." Dr. Moberly stood up, as though dismissing her.

He had come to speak to her in a hospital waiting room and now seemed in a hurry to leave.

"Thank you, Doctor."

"I'll look in again in the morning," Dr. Moberly said. "By the way, John Carter's been telling me about your husband's work on platelets. Very impressive. Very. Well, nice to meet you." He shook hands and went out. There was a nurse waiting for him in the corridor and they went off together, checking over a list she handed to him. It was four o'clock in the afternoon. Marie had waited two hours for Dr. Moberly. She had waited here, rather than in Alex's room. The nurses had been busy with Alex, bathing him, feeding him, and monitoring his vital signs. Now she took the elevator up to the private patients' floor and walked along the corridor to room 62. The door was shut and there was a No Visitors sign on it. Perhaps he was asleep? She opened it carefully and looked in. At once he sat up in the bed and beckoned to her. "Shut the door," he said.

"What's wrong?"

"Where were you?" he said. "You've been away for hours."

"I was downstairs, waiting to see the neurologist."

"Moberly. What did he say?"

"He said he's very hopeful. If all goes well you'll be out of the hospital in a couple of weeks."

He nodded. "I told him I fell in Carmel. Is that what you told him?"

"Yes."

"All right," he said. "Here's what I've done. I phoned the Institute in New York and told them where I am. I also phoned our apartment and picked up our messages. There was one from Mother, wondering if we were back yet. And one from the immigration service."

"What do they want?"

"They didn't say. They gave a number and asked us to call. I rang Mother and told her I'd had to come out here and that you were with me. As for the immigration people, we'll just let that ride. It must be about France, wouldn't you think?"

"I suppose so."

"Well, to hell with it. I haven't committed any crime. I simply came back to the States without telling anyone. It was that hospital's fault. I could sue them, if I wanted to.''

"I suppose you could."

"Of course I could. But I won't. We'll just forget all that."

"You seem a lot better."

He lay back on the pillows. He turned his head and looked out the window. "There was another message on the service," he said. "It was from some priest."

"A priest?" Alarm rose in her. "What priest?"

"I don't remember. He asked you to call him."

"Call him. Where?"

"I don't know. Do you know any priests?"

"No."

"You were a Catholic, weren't you? I mean, when you were a kid?"

"Not really," she said. "Why are you asking?"

"Nothing. No reason. Just conversation. I've been lying here thinking about a lot of things."

"What things?"

He did not answer. "What's wrong?" she said, again. "Tell me. Please, Alex?"

"Were you asking advice from some priest?"

"About what?"

"About us?"

"Why do you say that? Of course I wouldn't ask a priest for advice. I don't like priests, I'm not a Catholic, I told you that. I hated school and the Mass and prayers and all of it. What was this message? You must remember. What was the priest's name?"

"I don't remember."

"That's not true."

"Why should I lie?" he said. "Would you lie to me?"

She was silent.

"It was a Father Somebody. He wanted you to call him."

She looked at him. "I'll go and phone," she said. "Maybe the message is still on our service."

"I doubt it. Why don't you use this phone?"

"No. Try and get some sleep. I'll be back."

She hurried out into the corridor. What priest would call her

135

in New York? Was it the Monsignor? It had to be. He was the one who had her New York number. What did he want? Was there to be some sort of inquiry? At the nursing station she asked where the nearest pay phone was and was directed to go down to the ground floor. There she dialed her New York service and asked if they had a message for her.

"No, Mrs. Davenport, no message."

"My husband picked up a message that a priest had called me. Could you look and see if it's still around?"

"Sorry, Mrs. Davenport. We have nothing here."

She replaced the receiver. Trembling, she dialed information.

THE PHONE rang in the rectory. Monsignor was watching the Rams game and knew Father Cowan would pick it up. Monsignor heard him come out of his room and hurry downstairs, calling, "It's all right, I'll get it."

Monsignor did not hear the conversation, but a moment later Father Cowan came into the living room. "There's a lady on the phone, she wants to know if you were trying to reach her in New York."

"What lady?"

"A Mrs. Davenport."

"Oh, yes," Monsignor said. "No, I didn't try to reach her. Wait a minute. I wonder if Father Niles called her. He said something about contacting her, but I thought he was kidding. Is he in?"

"No, he's out jogging."

"Well, who knows," Monsignor said. "Maybe he did. Get her number and I'll check with him when he comes back."

"I'll do that," Father Cowan said. He went upstairs again and Monsignor went back to the game. A moment later Father Cowan called down. "I left the number by the phone, Monsignor. It's a San Francisco number, okay?"

"Fine." Monsignor watched as a pass was dropped on the twenty-five-yard line. The miracle lady. Funny thing, the way Ned can't let go of that story. Come to think of it, he's more like a newspaperman than a priest, nowadays. Monsignor wondered about Ned's bishop, who had given permission and funds for his present occupation. Times have changed. Imagine a bishop going for a program of that sort.

The Rams scored. Monsignor was pleased. When Ned came back from his jogging, Monsignor forgot to mention the phone call. It was only after supper that night, when Father Cowan had gone off to attend a Boy Scout meeting and Monsignor and Ned were having a nightcap and watching the ten o'clock news, that he remembered the miracle lady.

"By the way, Ned. Remember the girl I told you about, the one who thought she saw an apparition?"

"Of course. What about her?"

"She called this afternoon. She wanted to know if we'd tried to reach her in New York. I didn't, that's for sure. You didn't call her, by any chance?"

Ned looked a bit sheepish, as well he might. "As a matter of fact, I did. Listen, I charged it to my home number. First, I called the Point Lobos Motor Inn but they said she'd checked out. So I called her in New York. I was thinking that I might go home via New York instead of Boston. You know that article I mentioned to you, the one on superstition and belief?"

"Oh, yes," Monsignor said. He did not remember.

"I thought it might be interesting to talk to someone like her, someone who's not a believer, yet who's been caught up in a religious experience. The Saul of Tarsus analogy. The biblical connection: the prophet, unwilling, chosen by God."

"Is that so," Monsignor said. In his own mind he was not at all pleased by Ned's moving in on this thing. Probably it will just encourage that girl in her delusions. Still, I gave him her number in New York, when he asked for it. *Mea culpa*. "By the way," Monsignor said. "You didn't get her in New York because she's in San Francisco."

"What's she doing there?"

"How would I know? She left a number. It's by the phone upstairs, if you're interested."

The commercial break ended. They both watched an item about inflation, then one about some brush fires. When the news finished and they were putting out the living-room lights, Ned Niles said, "I'll give a ring in the morning, if you don't mind?"

"Ring who?"

"Mrs. Davenport. Okay?"

"Suit yourself," Monsignor said, then hesitated. "No, on second thought I'd rather you didn't. I don't believe we should encourage her."

"Well, okay then," Ned said. "It's up to you."

But he looked so downcast that Monsignor relented. There was no real harm in Ned, after all. And I did tell him the story and he's interested in stories of this sort. "Oh, well," Monsignor said. "Come to think of it, what harm can it do? Just don't let her think we're all set to canonize her within the year."

Ned laughed. "I take your point," he said. "It's silly of me, but for some reason I haven't been able to get that story out of my mind."

"Go ahead then," Monsignor said.

"Thanks, Barney," Ned said. "I appreciate it."

AFTER MARIE had called the service in New York and the refectory in Carmel, she went back to Alex's hospital room. He asked if she'd had any luck. She said no, there were no messages on the service. She did not mention the call to Carmel.

Later that evening, when she was back in her room at the Shropshire Hotel, she again telephoned Carmel. When the priest who answered went off to make inquiries and came back saying that possibly Father Niles had called, she did not ask who Father Niles was. She gave her hotel phone number and went to bed, anxious and uncertain. Was it he who had called or was it some other unknown priest, some priest in New York? She did not know any Father Niles. She did not know any priests in New York. She slept fitfully. At four A.M. she woke, screaming. For the first time since Alex's accident, she had dreamed the apparition dream: the girl figure, its arm outstretched, looking up at her from the rocky shelf of cliff, calling out the words of command. The fact that the dream had returned meant that they were not satisfied. She would have to do something more. Toward dawn she fell back into sleep. Shortly after nine the telephone shrilled loud in the morning stillness.

"Mrs. Davenport?"

"Yes."

"I hope I haven't wakened you."

"No, no. Who's calling?"

"You wouldn't know me, but let me explain. I'm a friend of Monsignor Cassidy's. My name is Father Niles. You called the refectory here in Carmel. You asked if someone had phoned your New York number. That was me. Didn't they give you my message?"

"No, the service gave it to my husband. He didn't make a note of it."

"Well, that explains it. Actually, I rang because of the conversation you had with Monsignor the other day. I was wondering if you and I could get together someplace to discuss that matter."

"Yes, of course," she said. She must do as they asked.

"Well, let's see. The message I left was a suggestion that we meet in New York. But now that I realize you're in San Francisco, that might be even better. Are you going to be there for a few days?"

"Yes."

"That could work out nicely for both of us. You see, I'm here on a vacation. Monsignor is my cousin. And I was planning to come up to San Francisco for a few days before going back east. I was thinking of driving up tomorrow or the day after. Could you see me then?"

The day after is Saturday. Daniel will be here. If Daniel's here, it will be difficult. "Would it be possible tomorrow?" she asked.

"Tomorrow. Yes, okay. It would be in the afternoon, though. Shall we say about four? I'll be staying at the refectory at the parish of St. Benedict Labré. It's right in San Francisco. Hold on a minute, I'll give you directions. Do you have a pencil?"

She sat up in bed, scrabbled in the bedtable drawer, and found a pencil and pad. "Yes."

"All right, then. Here're the instructions I was given myself. You go along O'Connell Street until you come to Garibaldi Square. You look north, right?"

"Yes."

"If you look north on the square you'll see a church dome, a

139

golden Russian dome, it's a sort of local landmark, they tell me. That's the dome of St. Benedict Labré. Go in that direction for two blocks and you'll come to a little dead-end street called Standish Street. Go in. The refectory is the second gate on the left. Ring twice. I'll be waiting. Have you got that?''

"Yes."

"And if by any chance you can't make it, my number there is 415-464-6785. Okay?''

She wrote it down. "Yes."

"Right. I'll look forward," he said.

"I'll be there." She put down the phone, stared at her hastily scribbled notations, then took a clean sheet of paper, wrote them out clearly, and read them over as though memorizing them for an examination. When she had finished she showered and dressed. She felt calm, the calm of one who knows the worst. When the nuns asked me back to their convent the other day, it could have been coincidence. This is no coincidence. I have been contacted. She thought of those others who had been chosen. There had been no special reason for choosing them; the simple Indian shepherd; the half-starved French peasant girl rooting around a riverbank for scraps of food; the illiterate Italian children; the pious postulant in the Paris chapel. And now me, the unbelieving adulteress.

They have made contact. They didn't give Alex back to me as part of a bargain. They don't make bargains. They will use him to prove their case. They will make him into a miracle that will mock his whole career. They will destroy my life with Daniel. I disobeyed them. They will have no mercy.

A BELL TOLLING from the tower of an episcopal church rang out the tones of the half-hour as Marie walked up O'Connell Street, coming to Garibaldi Square, a quiet city place of trees and a green grassy plot surrounded by a concrete walk. Pigeons pecked along the walk as people sat out the afternoon on park benches. In the green center plot two blond long-haired boys sailed a Frisbee in graceful arcs, like discus throwers from another age. The day was hot. She felt again the menace of the sky. In the square, she took out her sheet of directions and stood like an explorer, facing north as she had been told. Ahead, ris-

140

ing from a huddle of more conventional roofs, she saw not one golden Russian dome but three, brightly surreal in the sunlight. She went toward them, beginning to hurry although she was early. After two blocks she came to the little dead-end street named Standish Street. The refectory gate was the second on the left. It bore a wooden sign in gothic script: THE CHURCH OF ST. BENEDICT LABRÉ, and gave the times of Masses and Confessions. To the right of the sign was an electric bell. She pressed the bell button twice, as she had been told, and heard a bell shrill twice inside the building. She looked up at the golden domes. Beneath them was an ornamental clockface that read three forty-five. She was early. For a moment she thought of hurrying away before the door opened and coming back on the stroke of four. But, as she hesitated, the refectory door opened and a priest came down the steps. He wore a black silk shantung clerical suit, a black cotton dickey, and a white Roman collar. He was about forty, thin and wiry, with sandy hair, bright blue eyes, and a long thin nose. His face made her think of a fox. He grinned foxily as he unlatched the gate. "Are you Mrs. Davenport?"

"Yes."

The gate swung open. He offered his hand. "I'm Father Niles."

He shut the gate, preceded her across the dusty courtyard, up the stone steps, and into a dark hallway hung with pictures of saints. He led her into the rectory parlor, its furniture and floor scrubbed to the bright polish of institutional poverty. It was hot and airless in the parlor although an open window looked out into the courtyard. The priest's bright blue eyes moved like a predator's from her calves to her thighs, to her breasts, as, overcoming her repugnance toward this man and this place, she smiled at him and accepted his offer of a chair. He sat opposite her. He took from the side pocket of his jacket a large spiral notebook and a ballpoint pen and placed them on the table in front of him. It was as though her inquisition had begun.

He smiled. "I didn't expect to see you so soon."

"So soon?" She felt confused. Did he mean she had come too early?

"Well, when I left that message on your service, I suggested that we meet in New York. My work is in Worcester, Massachusetts, but I do get to New York from time to time. However, it was lucky that we could meet here. As I told you, I was coming here, anyway, to round off my vacation."

"You're on vacation."

"Yes. It's my first trip to the West Coast, as a matter of fact. Been looking forward to it. Monsignor Cassidy is my cousin, as I told you. And then the parish priest of this church here is an old friend from college days. So, I'm having a nice visit."

"I'm interrupting your vacation?"

His eyebrows lifted. "No, no, why would you say that?"

"I mean this investigation. That must be work for you."

"What investigation?"

She gestured futilely, her gesture taking in herself and the dark, hot, airless parlor. "This," she said. "I mean, me."

He laughed, a thin laugh that she knew to be false. "Investigation? My goodness, no, this isn't an investigation. It's just that I was very interested when my cousin told me your story. I've always taken an interest in appearances of the sort you describe. I write little articles from time to time. My work is in publishing, religious journals and so forth. I just thought I'd like to ask you a few questions about your experience."

"You're not going to write something?" she asked, alarmed.

"Oh, no. I wouldn't write anything until a great deal more had happened than just one apparition. And, in any case, I'd respect your privacy, if that's what you wished."

He was not telling the truth; even that talk of his being a writer was not true. He was an investigator; why else would he want to ask more questions? "You said 'questions,' Father. What sort of questions?"

"Well, let's see." He opened his spiral notebook, flipping through pages of loose spidery handwriting. "There are some interesting features in your story. First of all, the fact that you're not a practicing Catholic. And the fact that you didn't come forward for a whole year and that you told Monsignor you never would have come forward except for something that happened to a friend of yours, an accident which made you think the apparition was forcing you to come forward. Am I right?"

She nodded, her eyes on the floor, not daring to look at him. Why had he come straight to the accident unless that was what he wanted out in public, the miracle, the Lazarus thing?

"And you'll excuse me, but apparently you told Monsignor that you went to Carmel to have an affair with a man and that the apparition appeared to you in the morning after you and this man spent the night together. Right?"

Again, she nodded.

"And while you only saw the apparition once, you've dreamed about it, had nightmares about it, several times since."

"Yes."

"Can you tell me more about these dreams?"

"It's always the same dream," she said. "The figure appears on the rock and calls out to me, telling me to go and tell the priests. It frightens me. I wake up screaming."

She saw him lean forward to consult his notes. Then he looked up. "You said you're not religious. Were you ever religious?"

"No, I wasn't."

"But you were brought up as a Catholic. Surely, at some time in your childhood you must have had religious feelings."

"I didn't," she said. "My mother was a Catholic but she wasn't very religious and my father isn't Catholic and he's not religious at all. I always felt I was like my father. I was sent to a Catholic school when we moved to Montreal. It was a convent school and I found it too strict and I didn't like it. Once I left school, I never again went to church."

"A convent school. What Order was that?"

She felt herself flinch. This was all planned. He knew the answer in advance. "The Sisters of Mary Immaculate," she said.

"The Sisters of Mary Immaculate?" He leaned back in his chair, cracking his knuckles with a loud, unpleasant sound. "Where have I heard of that just recently? Wait. Isn't there—yes. We went driving down to Big Sur the other morning and passed one of their convents. Isn't that an extraordinary coincidence. It must be a small Order of nuns. I'd never heard of it."

"Yes," she said. She was not deceived by his false surprise. "It's a very small Order."

"Did you know they had a convent in Carmel?"

"Yes. Last Monday I went for a walk and came on it. It's quite near the place where I saw the apparition."

"Is it? Well now, that's interesting. Did you go in? Did you talk to the nuns?"

"Yes. They invited me to stay to supper."

"Did you tell them about the apparition, by any chance?"

"I told you," she said. "I told nobody."

"Of course. I forgot. Still, it's odd that their convent is so close to the place where you saw the apparition. What do you think? Do you think that's just coincidence?"

The question was a trap. She looked out of the window. A gust of dry hot air blew across the dusty courtyard, sending a sad confetti of discarded church leaflets sailing up into the yard, to coast, then drift down again like falling leaves. One came to rest on the windowsill. She read its title. *Catholic Truth Society*. She looked back at the priest. "A coincidence?" she said. "What do you think?"

FATHER NILES did not know what to think. He began to think there was a great deal more to this than met the eye. Certainly this case seemed more bizarre than anything in the literature of such apparitions. Yet he must be careful not to seem too interested. He remembered Barney's warning about not letting her think she'd be canonized within the year. This was Barney's turf, after all. Still, it was intriguing. The great question was, what was she up to? Was she really as unbelieving as she pretended to be? "Tell me, Mrs. Davenport," he said. "One of the slight discrepancies in your story is that you say you don't believe in any of this and yet you must believe it, in some way. For instance, you seem to believe in it strongly enough to feel that if you don't come forward and tell what happened, something bad might happen again to this friend of yours. Am I right?"

She hesitated. "Yes."

"Yet you refused to tell Monsignor what it is that happened to your friend. Don't you see that, from Monsignor's point of view, unless you do tell him, he won't be in possession of all the relevant details?"

"So unless I involve my friend, I won't be believed. Is that what you're saying?"

"No, no." Father Niles leaned forward, pulling on his nose with thumb and forefinger, as he pondered her question. "First of all, I'm not in a position to tell you anything. It's not up to me. I'm not conducting the investigation."

"So there is an investigation?"

"I wouldn't say an 'investigation.' Look, there are dozens of such incidents reported almost every year. Obviously, the Church doesn't investigate all of them. Often, it depends on the bishop of a diocese whether or not an investigation is called for. In your case the first step would be for Monsignor Cassidy to bring this to his bishop's attention, if he thought it right to do so. As far as I know, he hasn't done that yet."

"But if he doesn't," she said, "whatever this thing is, this apparition, this force, won't be satisfied, will it?"

"Depends," Father Niles said. "I mean, it depends on whether you saw what you thought you saw, doesn't it? So far, it's a question of one apparition. No other phenomena. Unless what happened to your friend could be described as a phenomenon?"

"So, what you're saying is—" Suddenly she seemed almost hysterical. "You're saying that unless I tell the other part you won't believe me. I have to bring my friend into it, is that what you're telling me?"

"I'm not telling you anything of the kind, Mrs. Davenport. I'm sorry, I didn't mean to upset you. It's very good of you to come and talk to me, but believe me, this isn't my affair. It interests me as a case history, that's all. It's Monsignor's business, not mine."

"It's not my business, either. Why me? Why somebody who doesn't believe? It doesn't make sense. Does it make sense to you?"

Say nothing more, Father Niles counseled himself, but could not take his own counsel, for, of course, not believing was no reason for her not to be chosen. "Look," he said, "there are no givens in these matters. Saul of Tarsus, as you'll remember, was on his way to Damascus to persecute Christians when a miraculous encounter with the Holy Spirit transformed him into a believer. He became St. Paul, the great founder of the Christian Church.''

''But that was the Bible,'' she said, angrily. ''That was just those Bible stories, they're like fairy tales, long ago, we can't check on them. I'm talking about more recent times. I bought certain books and read them. I can't find any case where this Virgin appeared to someone like me. Isn't that true?''

Hold your tongue, he warned himself. But he could not. ''Sorry, no, that's not right. There was a man called Alphonse Toby Ratisbonne, in 1842. He wasn't a believer. In fact, he was an Alsatian Jew.''

''A Jew?''

''Yes, he was a relative of the Rothschilds, as a matter of fact.'' Father Niles smiled, weakly. ''As you see, I'm interested in these things. Anyway, Ratisbonne went into the Church of St. Andrea delle Frate in Rome, purely to admire the architecture, but when he was inside the church he had a vision of the Virgin. And although he was a Jew and an unbeliever, he was completely convinced. He converted at once to Catholicism, became a monk, and when he died he was the head of a religious Order.''

''But what if he hadn't been convinced? Aren't there any cases like that?''

''I wouldn't know, would I?'' Father Niles said. ''I mean, if the cases weren't reported, how would we know about them?''

''But was there ever a case like mine? One where the person saw an apparition but didn't come forward until something else, something abnormal, happened?''

''Well, in biblical times I suppose we *could* find examples. But you don't want to consider biblical cases, you said?''

There was a silence. Again, the hot dry wind swept through the courtyard, but this time it came in at the open window like the breeze from a warm electric fan, ruffling the sheets of the priest's notes. Father Niles shut the notebook and put his ballpoint pen on top of it.

''Tell me,'' she said. ''What am I supposed to do now? What must I do?''

He leaned forward, pulling on his nose with thumb and forefinger. "I don't know," he said. "I suppose it's up to Our Lady."

"What does that mean?"

"Perhaps you have not been chosen. Usually, there is more than one apparition. It's my feeling that if Our Lady wants her message acted on, she will appear again."

"To me?"

"To you, or to someone else. I would guess, though, that in view of the order to build a shrine on that rock, the apparition will appear in the same spot. You're not planning to go back to Carmel, are you?"

"No, I wasn't."

"Are you going back to New York?"

"I don't know."

"But you'll be in San Francisco for a little longer, will you?"

"I don't know. It depends on my husband."

"Oh. Is your husband here with you?"

She did not reply. She looked out of the open window.

"I'm sorry," Father Niles said. "It's just that I'll be staying on in San Francisco for a day or two, in case you want to get in touch with me. I mean, if anything else happens, I'd be very interested to know about it. And I'll speak to my cousin. I'll mention to him what you told me about the Sisters of Mary Immaculate. That might have some relevance."

"Do you have to do that?"

"I thought you'd want that. Surely you want us to do whatever's necessary so that you'll be spared any more things happening to your friend?"

She nodded her head, looking as if he had threatened her.

"On the other hand," he said, "if you don't want me to mention it to my cousin, please say so."

"I'd rather you didn't," she said, miserably.

"Very well, then." He put the notebook and pen in his pocket. "We'll leave it as it is."

He stood and she stood too. "Thank you," she said. He led her out into the dark hallway and opened the refectory door. "Careful of the step. The gate's not locked. Just pull it shut after you."

He stood by the open door, watching her as she went down the steps and across the yard. There was something about her that disturbed him, something almost frightening, something he did not understand. "God bless you," he called after her. He saw her flinch. Why did I say that? She hates God. He watched her open the gate, then shut it and go off alone along the little dead-end street. The sky darkened. Lightning sheeted the heavens, throwing a spectral light on his face. He watched her turn the corner. Thunder broke above him in a cataclysmic clap. He shut the door and took out his breviary. Pacing the rectory corridor, he read his daily office.

THE hospital bed was empty. It had been made up. There was no sign of Alex's dressing gown or slippers. Marie went to the closet, opened it, and saw that his clothes were still there. They must have taken him someplace. Where? X ray? Operating room? She went out and hurried down the corridor to the circular nursing station. The nurse standing at the center of the desk smiled at her. "Yes, can I help you?"

"My husband, Dr. Davenport, in 62. Do you know where he is? He's not in the room."

The nurse looked at a folder in front of her, then called back. "Anyone know about Davenport? Did he go to radiology?"

"No, sorry," a nurse said.

The nurse who had inquired looked up at Marie. "Just a minute, I'll ask."

There was a young man at the rear of the nursing station wearing whites, a stethoscope around his neck. He was typing on a computer terminal. The nurse went up to him and said something. Marie did not hear what it was. He got up and came to the desk. He smiled at Marie. "Hello, there," he said. "Your husband was sent down to intensive care. We moved him about an hour ago."

"Why?"

"He had a little episode. The doctor will tell you about it."

"Aren't you a doctor?"

"No, I'm the charge nurse."

"Well, who can I see, please?" she asked.

"Go down to intensive care, it's on the seventh floor. There'll be someone there who can tell you. Sorry I can't be of more help. I just know he had a little episode about an hour ago

149

and the doctors thought he'd be better off in intensive care. Okay?"

"Thank you." She went with leaden steps toward the bank of elevators. While I was at St. Benedict Labré, he had an episode. What episode? What's an episode? *On the other hand, the priest said, if you don't want me to mention it to my cousin, please say so. And I said: I'd rather you didn't.*

In the elevator there was a sick woman on a stretcher, wheeled by a nurse who held up the woman's saline bottle. The woman's face was yellow and discolored as though by bruises. She looked deathly ill. She said, "Jelly, it was. Jelly with cream whip. That's three days now, it's jelly, green jelly, pink jelly, yellow jelly. You could throw up."

"I'll speak to the dietitian," the nurse said. "We'll get you some custard or a pudding. You like custard?"

"I like ice cream," the woman said. "Why can't I have ice cream?"

"Well, we'll check with the dietitian," the nurse said. The nurse seemed bored by the conversation. She looked at Marie and smiled. Marie tried to smile back but looked down at the woman's discolored face and thought of Alex's cheek bruise, which had been going yellow since yesterday. What was an episode? *Very well then, the priest said. We'll leave it as it is.* She found the intensive-care unit by following a set of green arrows. It had closed doors on which was stenciled Intensive Care Unit. Halfway up the corridor there was a nursing station. She went to it and gave her name. The nurse in charge consulted a terminal, then picked up a telephone. "Dr. Mara, please. Oh, Dr. Mara, we've got Mrs. Davenport here. Okay. Thanks."

She put the phone down. "If you'll just wait in the waiting room, please. The doctor will be with you very soon."

Surely, the priest said, you want us to do whatever's necessary so that you'll be spared any more things happening to your friend? An orderly and a nurse pushed open the doors of the intensive-care unit and wheeled out a stretcher. As the stretcher passed her, Marie looked into the terrified eyes of the patient, a tiny black child with a plastic tube in his left nostril. The doors shut. "The waiting room is over there," the charge nurse said.

Marie went to the waiting room. There were three people there watching television. The noise of the television was unbearable. She turned to leave the waiting room but saw a wall telephone with a notice beside it saying that visitors would be formed by telephone when they could visit intensive care. She stood by the door, trying to shut the television out. She did not at first hear the telephone ring. One of the other people in the waiting room answered it. "Mrs. Davenport?" this person said. Marie went out into the corridor. She saw a young doctor standing talking to the nurses at the nursing station. As she went up to him she read his name tag. *Bernard Mara, M.D.* He turned to her. He had an olive-skinned complexion and an athlete's strong, muscled neck. "Mrs. Davenport?"

"Yes."

"Hi. Your husband had a little setback so we brought him down here. His vital signs became unstable and his temperature dropped. We were expecting him to spike a fever but that hasn't really developed. However, we're keeping an eye on him. All right? I've notified Dr. Carter. I believe Dr. Carter is in charge of his case. His own doctor is a Dr. Bailey, is that right?"

"Yes, thank you. Can I see him?"

He hesitated. "I guess so. But not for long, okay?"

"Thank you."

"See the nurse. Tell her I said it's okay. Good-bye, now."

He turned and went back in. She went to the station and spoke to the nurse, who spoke to a second nurse, who got up and led her into the unit. Alex was in a large room with eight beds in it. Only three of the beds were occupied. There was a team of nurses and orderlies working on a patient who wasn't Alex. She saw Alex lying very still in a bed. She went toward the bed and saw the flickering bouncing light of the monitor screen above it.

"Alex?" she said. "Alex, are you awake?"

"I'm all right," his voice said. It was cracked and hoarse and automatic, as though he were repeating something that had been told to him.

"Alex, it's me."

He looked at her. There was no recognition in his eyes.

151

"They were worried that you were developing a fever," she said. "That's why they brought you here."

"I'm all right," the cracked, hoarse voice said again.

There were no chairs for visitors. She stood, looking down at him, trying to smile, then saw him begin to tremble. The trembling increased alarmingly. She went over to the nurses, who were working on the other patient. "Nurse?" she said. "Could you have a look?" She pointed to Alex. One of the nurses went to Alex, looked at him, then took his pulse. "Call Dr. Mara," the nurse said to another nurse, then said to Marie, "It's all right. But would you just wait outside, please?" Marie nodded. The intensive-care team, abandoning the other patient, surged around Alex's bed. Marie turned and went out of the room and out through the doors of the intensive-care unit. She stopped by the nursing station and said, "I'll be in there, if you need me." She went into the small waiting room and sat as far away as she could from the noisy television set. *I'm all right.* The cracked zombie voice, the eyes that did not know her, the shaking like a terrible ague. *I should get up and telephone Father Niles. Tell him I was wrong. Tell him to tell. Tell him to hurry. But what if they call me back in to see Alex? What if he dies and I'm not here?* She sat for some moments in sick indecision, then got up, asked about public telephones, and was told she would have to go down to the ground floor. The number of the refectory of the Church of St. Benedict Labré was on the sheet of directions she had consulted earlier. She rang and asked if she could speak to Father Niles.

"One moment, please, I'll see if he's in."

Let him be in. Oh, God, please let him be in. She had asked God. It was not just a phrase. She had asked, as if she believed in God. She wondered if this was a lie she told herself, a lie to make Father Niles come to the phone. But if it was a lie, it failed.

"I'm sorry, Father Niles is not here at the moment. But we're expecting him back for supper. Who shall I say called?"

"What time is supper?"

"You could call about seven," the voice said. "Would you care to leave your name?"

"Mrs. Davenport. I'll call at seven."

When she hung up, she decided to call Daniel. She reached his service in Los Angeles. When she gave her name, the service said, "Oh, yes, Mrs. Davenport," and gave her a number at the UCLA Medical Center. She had to wait while Daniel was paged. When he came to the phone she told him what had happened. He said he would call Moffitt Hospital. He took her number and told her to wait by the phone. She waited. A woman came and wanted to use the phone but Marie said it was an emergency, she was waiting for a call from a doctor. The woman went away. The pay phone rang.

"Daniel?"

"Yes. Now, listen, Marie. Didn't you tell me something about Alex having abnormalities, low temperature, pulse, and so on?"

She heard the alarm in his voice. "Yes," she said. "He made notations about it in a notebook, the one that got lost."

"They were very low?"

"Yes," she said. "They seemed impossible to me. I think his heart stopped too."

"What did *he* say about it?"

"He didn't. He was hiding it from me. He did say maybe he wasn't well enough to evaluate his condition."

"It doesn't make any sense," Daniel said. "Apparently something like that happened on the floor when the nurse checked his vital signs. They rushed him down to intensive care but he was all right by then. He's been normal since. The only thing possible is that the nurse made some sort of mistake. I don't know. I wish I could be with you. I'm trying for Saturday. Now don't worry, he's in good hands. They'll keep him in intensive care for a while just to make sure. Oh, by the way, I'm moving to the Crestwood tonight. Elaine's coming home tomorrow. I'll be at the Crestwood from now on. Got a pencil?"

Obedient, she found her purse and the sheet on which she had written down the directions given her by the priest.

"It's 456-3335. And I'll leave word on the service where you can reach me at any time. Listen, if he has a really bad turn, I'll get someone else to take over here. That's a promise."

"You're expecting him to get worse."

"I didn't say that. Frankly, I don't know what's wrong with him. How are you? You must be exhausted."

"I'm all right," she said.

"I love you." The words were like a loyalty oath. She could sense his worry, the worry he was trying to conceal from her. "I'll call you first thing in the morning," he said. "You're still in the same hotel?"

"Yes." She heard voices on the line, someone speaking to Daniel. "Sorry," he said. "Just a minute." She waited. "Marie, I have to go."

"All right." She hung up. She went upstairs to the intensive-care unit in a purgatory of anxiety. At the nursing station she asked if there was any news of her husband. "Wait in the waiting room," she was told. "We'll let you know."

Shortly after seven she went back down to the ground floor and rang the number at St. Benedict Labré.

"Father Niles? One moment, please. Who's calling?"

"Marie Davenport."

"Hello there." His voice sounded friendly. "How are you?"

"I'm all right," she said. "Father, do you remember I said to you not to mention anything to Monsignor Cassidy about the nuns? The Sisters of Mary Immaculate. Do you remember that?"

"Yes, I do. I haven't said anything."

"Well, I was wrong. I want you to tell him. Maybe you could phone him and tell him. It's urgent."

There was a silence on the line, a silence in the refectory of St. Benedict Labré. Then he said, "Something happen to your friend?" It was a question that was not a question, it was a statement. He was their agent. He had been waiting for her call.

"I don't know," she said. "I'm not sure."

"You're not sure? I hope it's nothing serious."

"It's serious," she said. "I wouldn't have called."

"I see." She heard him clear his throat. "Mrs. Davenport, might as well be honest with you. I've become very interested in your story, especially since we spoke today. I don't want to intrude on your private life, but it occurs to me that it might be a good thing if you could tell Monsignor, or even me, what this

154

other element in your story is, the thing you seem to be afraid of. Does that make sense?"

"Is that what I have to do?" she asked. It was an order, wasn't it? This was the way they gave orders; they gave them as suggestions, as ways to help you.

"Well, I'm not sure what you want," his voice said. "On the one hand you say you don't want an investigation, but on the other hand you seem to think that this thing that happened to your friend is not just coincidence. If you do think there's something miraculous—for want of another word—about what's happened, then I think you might be wise to tell the whole story, and not just part of it."

"I see." It was an order. He had said the word, *miraculous*. They had come out in the open. If you don't do this, if you don't tell the whole story, your husband will die. "All right," she said. "I'll do what you want."

"I don't *want* you to do anything. I'll speak to my cousin, as you asked me to. All right?"

"Could you call him now? Please?"

He hesitated. "I was planning to call him tomorrow. All right, I'll call him now. Will you be at your hotel in case he wants to get in touch with you?"

"No. I'll be at the hospital." She said it without thinking.

"What hospital?"

"Moffitt Hospital."

"Can we reach you there?"

The hospital, he knows about the hospital now. But he always knew. They know. "If you ask for the intensive-care unit," she said, "I'll be in the visitors' waiting room."

"I see." Again, there was a moment of silence on the wires. She thought of the dark parlor in the refectory of St. Benedict Labré. "Is your friend in intensive care?"

"Yes," she said.

"I'm sorry. Very sorry. All right, then, I'll ring my cousin right away if that will help set your mind at rest. And try not to worry. It could just be coincidence, you know."

"Yes."

"Good night, then," he said.

"Good night."

"YES, he's better. He's doing fine."

"Can I see him?"

"Well, just for a moment. Come this way."

In the large room, a woman writhed, moaning, in one of the beds. In another bed someone was hooked up to a dialysis machine. Alex was sitting up, pale but relaxed. When Marie went toward him he turned to look at her. "Hi," he said. She knew that he recognized her.

"How are you?"

"Fine. Much better."

She perched awkwardly on the edge of his bed. As she did he looked around the intensive-care room, casually, but furtively. "Are they going to send me upstairs soon?" he whispered.

"I don't know."

"Could you find out?"

"I'll ask."

"Where are you staying?"

"At a hotel called the Shropshire."

"Write down the phone number on a piece of paper, in case I want to call you."

She opened her purse and did as she was asked. He was wearing his wristwatch. He took the slip of paper, folded it, and tucked it under the watchband. "Won't you lose that?" she asked.

He looked at her, resentfully. "No, I won't. Did Daniel go back to L.A.?"

"Yes."

"We never should have left Carmel."

"What do you mean?"

"I was getting better. I told you I didn't want to go to a hospital. Why did Daniel butt in? You tricked me, the pair of you."

"But it's lucky you did go. Do you realize how ill you were, just a few hours ago?"

"I know my condition." His voice rose to a near shout. "We should have stayed in Carmel."

A nurse, hearing his loud voice, came up, looked at him, then nodded meaningfully to Marie. "I'm sorry," she said.

Marie stood up. "Maybe I can come back later?" she asked the nurse.

"We'll see," the nurse said. "He's looking a lot better, isn't he? Yes, of course he is."

Marie went back to the waiting room, which had become her prison. *He's looking a lot better. Yes, of course he is. If I do as they want, he will get better. It's as simple as that. Monsignor Cassidy will call tonight. They want me to tell the whole story. I am waiting for his call.*

She went out and told the nurse at the nursing station that if anyone called for her she would be in the waiting room. "It's an urgent call," she said. She went back to the waiting room and sat, hour after hour, sat until almost midnight. But Monsignor Cassidy did not call. Did that mean that Father Niles had not told him? Or did it mean that they wanted something more? Twice she had gone out to inquire about Alex. She was told that his condition was stable. At midnight she left the hospital. When she got back to the hotel the desk clerk gave her two messages. One was from Daniel, saying he would call tomorrow morning. The second read: *Mother Paul called 9 p.m.* There was a telephone number. Marie looked at the message, confused. Mother Paul? Then she remembered: the Mother Superior of the convent in Carmel.

Did you know they had a convent in Carmel?

Yes, last Monday I went for a walk and came on it. It's quite near the place where I saw the apparition.

Is it? Well now, that's interesting. Did you go in? Did you talk to the nuns?

Yes. They invited me to stay to supper.

Did you tell them about the apparition, by any chance?

I told you. I told nobody.

But *he* told them, he told them tonight. That is why she called me. She's the one who asked me to stay to supper. Then the old nun, Mother St. Jude, gave me that look and I said I would stay. The nuns are part of this. They are part of the plan.

In her room, she undressed and put the message from Mother Paul beside the phone. She would ring the convent first thing in the morning. Just before she fell asleep she saw again the face

157

of Mother St. Jude, saw that look of reverence mixed with overwhelming love.

Next morning she woke to a shrilling telephone.

"Hello?"

"Marie?" It was Alex's voice.

"Oh, Alex. Are you all right?"

"Yes, fine. I'm back in my own room."

"You're back from intensive care. Oh, that's good. When did that happen?"

"They moved me back up here about seven this morning. Listen, I want to see you."

"Of course," she said. "I got to bed very late. But I'll dress now and come over."

"Good. Don't be long, will you. I want to talk to you."

"No, I won't. Has the doctor been in yet?"

"No. See you soon."

"Yes, soon," she said. She got up, showered, and dressed. He was better, of course he was better; they were having it their way now. If she went on doing exactly what was asked of her, he could be out of the hospital in a day or two. She wondered what he wanted to talk about. From his tone of voice she did not think it was about Daniel, or a divorce. She took a taxi across the city, climbing the steep hill that led to the hospital, high above the bay. When she went into the ground-floor reception area, she forgot Alex's room number and had to stop and ask.

"There are no visitors," the reception-desk attendant told her.

"I'm his wife."

"Well, you'd better check when you get up there."

When she reached his floor, the nurse sitting in the nursing station smiled at her. "Good morning."

"I'm Mrs. Davenport. Is it all right if I go in to see my husband?"

The nurse looked at a folder. "Yes, sure. He's back up from intensive care, isn't he? I think there's someone in with him now. A minister."

Marie turned and hurried toward the room. What minister? Ministers went around in hospitals, bothering people, she knew that. Alex would have gotten rid of him by now.

The room door was ajar. She did not knock but pushed it

158

open and went in. Alex was propped up on the pillows, looking wan. Sitting in a chair opposite was a man in a clerical suit, holding a black straw summer hat. When he turned around she saw that it was Father Niles.

"Hello there." His fox mask split in a deceitful grin.

"What are you doing here?"

"Well now, it's an odd story. I came up here today to see a priest I know, who's a patient here. But when I got here, they'd taken him off to the operating room. So, while I was waiting, I remembered our talk. I remembered that the other day, when I phoned the Point Lobos Motor Inn to reach you, they said you'd checked out, you and your husband. So, if you'll forgive me, I put two and two together, a little bit of detective work, so to speak, and it came to me that your husband might be the friend you mentioned. So I went down to the intensive-care unit and asked if they had a Davenport there. And they sent me here. I just got here. Right, Doctor?"

She saw him look to Alex for confirmation, smiling his two-faced smile. It could be true that this was the way he had found out. But it could be—it probably was—a lie. They were all liars, these holy Roman frauds. He had risen now and was offering her the chair. "What do you want?" she said to him. "My husband is very ill. He's in no condition for you to be bothering him."

"I'm sorry. I didn't mean to bother him. Dr. Davenport's been telling me about his accident."

"What accident?"

"Well, he's been telling me about his head injury. How he fell while he was out walking on the cliffs at Carmel."

"That's right," Alex said. "And I'm all right now. I'm much better." He looked warningly at Marie. He turned to the priest. "You know my wife?"

"Yes."

"Are you the person who called her the other day?"

"Perhaps," the priest said, smiling. "Yes, I think I did call her, as a matter of fact."

"What about?"

"Nothing, nothing. Just a religious matter. Nothing important. I'm sorry to have disturbed you, Doctor. I'll go now. Nice meeting you." He stood, waggled his fingers in a gesture of farewell, then moved toward the door. He looked at Marie. "Oh, Mrs. Davenport, could I? Just for a moment?"

"I'll be right back," she said to Alex. Furious, she followed the priest out into the corridor. He turned, almost cringingly. "I'm really sorry for butting in like that. I'm afraid curiosity is my great fault. Listen, I did speak to Monsignor last night. I do think he's much more interested now, as a result of what I told him."

"Never mind that. What were you saying to my husband?"

"Nothing, really. I was very careful. But if your husband is the friend you spoke of, and if he had his accident near the place you saw the apparition, then your whole story becomes really intriguing."

"I told you, I don't want him mixed up in this."

"I understand. You're in a difficult situation. I can see that. In view of this affair you were having."

"I'm doing everything I can to please you. But I can't mix my husband up in this. That's final."

He smiled disingenuously. "To please *me?* I don't understand."

"I think you do. You're the one who's in charge of all this, the investigation, the whole thing. You didn't come here this morning to see some other priest. You came to find out who my 'friend' was."

"That's not true, Mrs. Davenport. On my word of honor."

"How can I believe you? None of this is coincidental and you know it. It's all part of a plan."

"What plan?" he said, smiling to show her she was being foolish.

"You know very well what plan. The plan to involve my husband in this. That's what you're pushing for, isn't it?"

"No one is pushing for anything, Mrs. Davenport. You're a free agent."

"Am I? Does it look like it? I was told to tell the priests to build a shrine. I wasn't asked if I wanted to do it. I was told to do it."

"I take your point. But, you know, Mrs. Davenport, you still have the right to refuse. It's basic to Christian theology that man is free to say no to God. Miracles and miraculous appearances are only signs which solicit belief. That's all they are. Remember, the Church doesn't require anyone to believe in miracles.''

"I don't know what you're talking about," she said. "Signs, miracles, solicitings. This is force. I am being punished.''

"Now wait, let me try to clarify it for you. Once again, a miracle or a miraculous apparition is only a sign and, theologically speaking, it cannot be a sign which *compels* assent. Remember, in the gospels, the Pharisees said no to the signs, but Jesus' disciples said yes. There are no 'punishments' for not coming forward. Your nightmares are probably a result of your guilty feelings about this. You have no proof that your husband's accident is related to this other matter. It could still be a coincidence.''

"But you don't believe it's a coincidence, do you?'' she said. "If you did, you wouldn't have sneaked in here this morning to question him. There are things about his illness that couldn't be coincidence, things I can't tell you about.''

"All right, then." He smiled, uneasily. "It's my fatal curiosity again. I know I shouldn't ask, but what are these things? If we knew them, would they constitute real proof? Or is there some other logical explanation?''

He was lying, he was trying to trick her into speaking out. That was his game. "I'm not going to discuss it," she said. "I have to get back to my husband now.''

"Of course. By the way, I'll be in San Francisco until tomorrow evening and then I'll be going home to Massachusetts. I'd like to keep in touch with you, if you please. Just to know the rest of the story. Here.'' He took a worn black wallet from his hip pocket and handed her a visiting card. She read:

Rev. Edward J. Niles.

TRISPHERE PRESS
29 Auburn Street,
Worcester, Mass.
Phone 466-6276

He held out his hand. She did not want to touch him but she shook hands. "Good luck to you," he said. "I hope everything works out for you. I really do.''

She turned away. As she went toward the door of Alex's room, she heard him say quietly, "Remember, the Church doesn't want you to do anything you don't want to do. But perhaps Our Lady does. That's something else."

She stopped. She sensed a great tension in his voice as though, at last, he was on the verge of telling her the truth. "What do you mean?" she said.

"I was thinking of Catherine Labouré, that young nun who saw the Virgin in a convent chapel in Paris. I was thinking of Our Lady's warning to Catherine. She said, 'You will be tormented until you have told him who is charged with directing you. You will be contradicted, but do not fear. You will have grace.' I think you have been tormented, Mrs. Davenport. I hope that you will be given grace."

"I still don't know what you're talking about," she said. She pushed open the door of Alex's room. She did not look back at the priest.

When she went in, Alex was not in bed. The bathroom door was shut. "Alex?"

"Just a minute," his voice answered. She saw that the closet where his clothes were was ajar. She looked in. The suitcase was still there but his clothes and shoes had been removed. As she shut the closet door he came out of the bathroom, fully dressed, the tennis hat jammed down around his ears.

"What are you doing?"

"Leaving. Come on."

"Wait. You can't just walk out like this. You're not well."

He looked as if he might strike her. "I admitted myself and can discharge myself," he said. "Anyway, I'm not going to bother with all that. We're going to leave, just take the elevator and leave. The doctors will be here soon on their morning rounds. I want to be gone by then. Are you going to help me or not?"

"But where will we go?"

He stopped, seeming puzzled, as though he had not thought of that. "Carmel," he said. "We'll go back to that motel. It's quiet, nobody knows us there, and I was doing fine until Bailey showed up and got me in this mess."

"What mess? You're far better off here."

162

"You don't know what you're talking about," he said. "You don't know the dangers."

"What dangers?"

"Never mind. Are you going to help me or aren't you? We'll go to your hotel and pick up your things. Then we'll rent a car and drive to Carmel. I don't think I'm able to drive. You can drive. All right?" He paused. "Look, we can talk about us later. Right now, I've got to get out of here. Are you coming?"

"Yes," she said. He's a puppet, he's not Alex. Otherwise why would he go back to the Point Lobos Inn?

"All right," he said. "Where are the elevators?"

"To our left as we go out."

"Where are the service stairs?"

"I don't know."

"Hurry. Go and look. I'll be in the bathroom until you come back. And don't come back with a nurse or doctor, do you hear? Don't try to stop me. I want your promise, Marie."

"I promise."

She went out into the corridor. The nurse at the nursing station was talking on the telephone. An old woman in a dressing gown was strolling slowly up and down. A second patient was being walked by a nurse who was pushing the patient's I.V. stand. Marie looked to her right and saw a door marked Exit. She went back into the room. The bathroom door was closed. "Alex? Let's go."

He came out at once. "Which way?" She nodded to him to follow. They went into the corridor and reached the door marked Exit without anyone noticing them. They went through the door and she saw a flight of stairs with an iron stair railing. Alex paused as if he were dizzy. She took his arm and led him down one flight of stairs. "Through there," he said. "We'll take the elevator now."

When the elevator came, it was half filled with people, patients and technicians and an orderly. They went down and she took his arm again as they came out at the ground-floor reception area. It looked perfectly normal: a discharged patient being assisted as he left the hospital. "Get a taxi," he said.

"I know."

She went to the reception desk and asked about a taxi. The woman at the desk said, "What's your name?"

"Johnson," Marie said.

The woman picked up a phone. "Okay, Mrs. Johnson, just wait outside the front door. A taxi will be up right away."

She went back and took Alex's arm. As they went outside some people followed them through the entrance doors, talking among themselves. Then, as Marie moved forward with Alex, she saw a figure disengage itself from the larger group and go past her. He was wearing a black straw summer hat. It was Father Niles. He walked rapidly. He did not seem to have seen them. She watched him cross the street and go toward the parking structure. She felt Alex grow tense. He had seen the priest. "It's all right," she said quietly. They watched as the priest disappeared from view into the entrance to the parking structure. Then a taxi came up the circular driveway. The driver leaned out and called "Johnson?" She led Alex toward the cab. As Alex bent down to get into the cab, his hat fell off. He picked it up and, like a criminal concealing himself, jammed it back on his head. "Shropshire Hotel, it's on Stockton Street," she said. The taxi pulled out. As it paused at the entrance to the street, Marie looked over at the parking structure and saw a small green car drive up the ramp. Its driver reached out to pay the parking fee. It was the priest. As the taxi moved out onto the street, the little green car moved in behind it. She looked over at Alex, but he did not seem to have noticed. He sat, staring ahead, his face with its yellow bruise and puffy eyes, like a clown face in a Rouault painting. Again she thought of that animus they had taken from him. She thought of the driven automatous way he was going back to Carmel. She looked at his clown face in tenderness and fear. "Alex," she said, "do you know what's wrong with you, what's really wrong with you?"

At first, she thought he had not heard her. But as the cab rushed down the switchback streets, he slowly nodded his head, as though her question had been dialed, word by word, into the machine which was his brain. "I'm better," he said. "Fine now. Okay?"

She felt that she would weep. "Okay," she said. "Okay."

She looked back through the rear window. The little green car was still there.

WHEN THEY reached the hotel she paid off the cab and stood, searching the street. Where was the green car? "What are you waiting for?" Alex asked. "Nothing," she said. "Nothing." She led him into the lobby. "Wait here," she said. "I'll go up and get my things." But Alex would not let go of her arm. He steered him toward the elevator and went up with her. In her room he sat, listless, while she hastily packed her suitcase. He went with her to the front desk and stood watching as she paid the bill. "Where's the nearest car-rental place?" he asked the desk clerk.

"Just down the street, two blocks, there's an Avis."

He nodded. He let her carry the bag outside. In the street she looked up and down, searching for the little green car. There was no car. "Call a taxi," Alex said. "I don't want to walk."

"Why don't you wait here and I'll bring the car back?"

He looked at her, his lusterless eyes flickering as if he were trying to think of some answer. But he did not speak. He shook his head.

"You don't trust me, is that it? Is that it, Alex?"

He ignored this. He stepped out into the street, holding his arm up, signaling for a cab, although no cab was in sight, and stood there, waving, until at last a taxi stopped. When they reached the Avis office he went in with her and stood at the counter, watching as the clerk filled out the form and she signed it. A small car was brought up from the garage. When she drove it outside she stopped for a moment in the street, pretending to familiarize herself with the lights and windshield wipers. There was no green car in sight. Perhaps it had just been coincidence that the priest's car had come down the same streets as they had. She started up the car and drove out of San Francisco, climbing up a freeway scramble, moving into a fast stream of traffic on a freeway headed south. Alex had not spoken to her since the journey began. He stared ahead but did not seem to be looking at the road or the movement of the passing cars. About twenty minutes out of San Francisco, as they were slowed by a rush of cars near San Bruno, he turned to her. "Why did that priest come to the hospital? Why did he phone you in New York? He said it was a religious matter. You haven't gotten religion, have you?''

"Of course not.''

"Then what was it about?''

"It wasn't important,'' she said. "It was a mistake. He mistook me for someone else.''

She saw him bow his head as though he were thinking about her reply. "He asked about my accident. Why would he ask about that?''

"It was just conversation,'' she said.

"But why did he come to my room? Was it to see you? Was that why he came?''

"I don't know,'' she said. "Look, it's not important. He knows nothing. He's irrelevant. We won't be seeing him again.''

The road climbed upward into the mountains, moving through a wooded area, passing a beautiful lake that was a reservoir. It was a bright, clean California morning. Sun warmed the interior of the car. "Bailey,'' he said. "Daniel.''

She felt a sudden alarm. "Daniel? What about him?''

"Why did he come to Carmel? Did you call him?''

"Yes.''

"Why?''

"Because I was worried about you. Because he's a doctor.''

"Did you tell him what happened?''

"Yes, I told him.''

"About France, about that hospital there?''

"Yes.''

"Damn it, I told you not to tell anyone!''

"I'm sorry. I don't think you have any idea how ill you were. Or how ill you are now.''

"Of course I do,'' he said. "You're the one who doesn't know anything. You don't understand, you don't know what this is all about.''

"Do you, Alex?''

He did not answer. He said, "Daniel doesn't know where we're going, does he?''

"Of course not. How could he?''

166

"He's not to know. Promise me?"

"Why must I do that?"

"He'll just want to put me back into a hospital. That's what he'll want. I'm not going back into a hospital. Do you hear me, Marie?"

"Yes," she said. "I hear you, but I don't agree with you."

He slumped down in his seat. After a few minutes she looked over at him. He seemed to be asleep. He slept until they reached the outskirts of Monterey and, when he woke, looked about him vacantly, as though he did not know her, or where he was.

"Alex?" she said. "Alex, are you all right?"

"Watsonville," he said, reading a road sign. "So we're near Monterey?"

"Yes."

A large semi, loaded with Japanese cars, moved up to overtake her on the right. She swerved, caught in the wind of the semi's passing and as she braked to let the big vehicle move into her lane up ahead, she checked her rearview mirror. As she did she saw a small green car, three cars back. She slowed to forty miles an hour, letting the cars behind her move up and overtake her. But the third car, the green car, slowed down, falling back until, as she rounded a bend, it disappeared from sight. Alex put his hand on her bare arm. She felt her flesh crawl. His hand was ice-cold and clammy. "Marie," he said, "listen, I have to trust you. I have no choice."

"What do you mean?"

"Listen. I may have bad spells in the next day or two. But I'm getting better. I know it."

"How do you know? How could you know?"

"Trust me," he said. "Just this once, trust me. Can't you do that? Look, we won't talk about us. I don't want to talk about it now, do you?"

"Not particularly," she said. She looked in the rearview mirror. The green car was in sight again.

"I'm only asking you to help me for a few days," he said. "Once I'm better we can talk about the rest of it."

He knows. She looked straight ahead at the reeling ribbon of road. He heard us. I don't have to tell him.

"I don't want you to call Daniel or anyone else. I want to be left alone. I know it will be all right, if I'm left alone. If you'll help me. Will you help me? Will you do what I tell you?"

"How can I make promises? Anything might happen to you."

"Listen," he said. "Give me four days, a week, okay? Keep an eye on me. Keep people away. And if I have a bad turn, don't worry. I'll come out of it. Just take it on faith, okay?"

On faith. She looked in the rearview mirror. The green car was a little closer now. She could not be sure if the driver was the priest, for the driver was not wearing the black straw hat the priest had been wearing earlier. But he must be the priest, the priest who pretends that Alex's illness is just coincidence, the priest who is following us now to see the end of it.

"Please?" Alex said. "Please, Marie?"

She put her hand on his death-cold hand. "All right."

"Nobody. Promise?"

"I promise."

MONSIGNOR Cassidy moved purposefully in the water, joining his hands in front of him as in an attitude of prayer, then parting the waters to permit his passage in a stately breast-stroke. The pool was a very fine one, twenty-five yards long, heated to a temperature of eighty degrees, with adjacent Jacuzzi, shower, and sauna facilities. It was on the property of Ed Hofstra, a building contractor and a parishioner. A month ago, when Dr. Da Silva told Monsignor that golf as he played it was not exercise, Monsignor took up swimming. Now he swam fifteen laps, most days.

Today, as usual, he had the pool to himself. He swam between four and five in the afternoon at a time when no one was at home in the Hofstra residence excepting Mrs. Evans, the housekeeper. It was his custom to use this part of his day to review current projects and future plans. But today, moving steadily in the water under a cloudy sky, Monsignor's thoughts darkened. He recalled his cousin Ned phoning last evening from San Francisco, trying to enlist his aid. He now regretted making that inquiry on Ned's behalf. Ned had wanted him to find out if the Davenport girl had said anything to the nuns about the apparition. Monsignor had put the question more discreetly, simply asking Mother Paul if the girl had mentioned anything at all to her, anything out of the ordinary. And Mother Paul said no. Mother Paul is a sensible sort, not the sort of person I want to be talking to about apparitions. Ned would never understand that. No wonder his bishop didn't give him a parish. He has no sense of proportion, Ned.

As he swam, he thought he saw a few drops of water pinging in the pool. He looked up at the sky. Rain? At any rate, Ned will be going back east on Sunday or Monday. And the Davenport girl lives in New York, not here. Let the whole thing die a natural death. Six more laps? This is my ninth, isn't it?

The sliding glass doors of the Hofstra living room opened and Mrs. Evans came out. Mrs. Evans was a large black woman who wore a white uniform and rubber-soled nurse's shoes that squeaked on the tile bricks around the pool as she came toward him bearing a large bath towel. "Monsignor," she called. "Wanted on the telephone. Father Cowan."

Monsignor swam to the pool steps and climbed out, accepting the bath towel with thanks. While he dried himself Mrs. Evans carried out a phone and plugged it into a jack on the sun deck. Monsignor settled himself on a lounge and picked up the receiver. "Kevin?"

"Sorry to bother you like this," Father Cowan said. "But I wonder, would you like me to sub for you this evening at the Holy Cross Dinner?"

"Why so?" Monsignor was puzzled. The Holy Cross Dinner was an annual event and the society expected him, not his curate.

"Well, your cousin came back today and Mrs. Peters wants me to find out if that means you'll want dinner in the refectory. So I thought maybe you'd like me to take over the Holy Cross do."

"My cousin? Father Niles?"

"Yes, he's come back from San Francisco. I haven't seen him but he told Mrs. Peters he'd probably stay on for the weekend."

Did he indeed, Monsignor thought, but knew when to hold his tongue. "Well, that's unexpected, Kevin. I thought he was leaving from San Francisco. At any rate, it's very good of you to offer to sub for me, but I mustn't disappoint them. They're expecting me. Will you be in, yourself, for dinner?"

"Yes. In that case, I will."

"Well, that's all right, then. I wouldn't want Mrs. Peters having to get dinner just for Father Niles. You don't know where I could reach him, do you? Is he there, by any chance?"

"I don't think so, Monsignor."

"Well, if you or Mrs. Peters see him, tell him I'll be home in about half an hour and I'd like to have a word with him. All right?''

"Okay, Monsignor. Listen, it would be no sweat for me to take on the Holy Cross do.''

"No, Kevin. Thanks, but duty calls. Thanks, again.''

When Monsignor put the phone down he did not linger at the pool but showered in the Hofstras' facility, got in his old Cadillac, and drove straight to the rectory. When he arrived he went down to the kitchen, but Mrs. Peters was not there. He looked in the parking lot and saw that her Volkswagen bug was missing. She must have gone into town to do the shopping. He saw a green rental car in the lot. That must be Ned Niles's. Monsignor went out of the kitchen, calling, "Ned, Ned?'' but heard no answer. He went to the sitting room and there was Ned on the telephone. He waggled his fingers at Monsignor and went on talking.

"Yes, of course, whatever time is convenient. What? The community hour, yes. What time is that? Five-thirty to six-thirty. Very good, then. See you soon. Thank you.''

He hung up. "Hello, Barney. I'm like bad news. I won't go away.''

Monsignor forced a smile. "Well. Surprise,'' he said. "Didn't you like San Francisco?''

"Oh, it's quite a story,'' Ned said. "First of all, will it be inconvenient for you if I stay on here for a couple more days? Be honest with me. I can easily make other arrangements.''

"No, no,'' Monsignor said. "Stay and welcome. But, what's all this about?''

"Take a seat,'' Ned said. "Let me see if I can explain. Remember, last night after I called you back, you said you hadn't asked Mother Paul directly if Mrs. Davenport had mentioned an apparition to her.''

Monsignor sat in his usual chair. "Right.''

"Well, I'm afraid I was so curious on that point that I rang Mother Paul from San Francisco and put the question to her straight up.''

"Did you now?'' Monsignor said. He could feel his adrenaline level rise. Keep your cool, as the kids say, he told himself. Keep your cool.

"And I had the most extraordinary response. Would you believe it, Barney, that while Mrs. Davenport never mentioned such an apparition, one of the old nuns there has been having dreams of an apparition standing on a cliff."

"Mother Paul told you this?"

"Yes, in fact she got quite excited. She wanted to get in touch with Mrs. Davenport and talk to her. Or have her talk to this old nun. Well, to cut a long story short, I gave her Mrs. Davenport's phone number. And this morning Mrs. Davenport came back to Carmel. Now, this is the interesting part. I thought she was coming back to see the nuns. But I've just been talking to Mother Paul. And the thing is, Mother Paul never reached her. So, she's come back for some other reason. There's something really strange going on here, Barney. Do you know that Mrs. Davenport took her husband out of the hospital in San Francisco, a very sick man who's been in intensive care, and drove him down here today? Why, for God's sake?"

"But how do you know all of this?" Monsignor asked. "Did you talk to Mrs. Davenport since she came back?"

"No, no," Ned Niles said. "Let me explain." As he listened to Ned's explanation, Monsignor could not believe his ears. Going up to the hospital like that, sleuthing around like a private eye, following them all the way back here, phoning Mother Paul, butting in, taking over as if he were in charge, Monsignor no longer pretended to smile as he listened to Ned's explanations. And when Ned had finished, he asked, brusquely, "Does Mrs. Davenport know you followed her back here?"

"No, no."

"That was Mother Paul you were speaking to just now. Did I hear you say something about seeing her between five-thirty and six-thirty?"

"Yes, I'm going over there, later on. I hope you don't mind."

"Tell me, Ned," Monsignor said. "What exactly do you expect to get out of this?"

"It's not a matter of getting something out of it. I've always had an interest in apparitions of the Virgin, as you know. And this is an extraordinary case. I know you'll laugh, but it crossed my mind this morning that perhaps God intended me to play

172

some part in it. I mean, imagine one of those nuns having the same sort of dream.''

"Dreams," Monsignor said. "That's what we're talking about, isn't it? Dreams. And one supposed apparition which this girl claims took place but which was never repeated to her except in the form of nightmares. I'm no expert on these things but I don't see how you can be so sure there's something supernatural going on here."

"I think there is. After all, this girl isn't some religious nut who wanted to see an apparition. She told you herself she was in the middle of an adulterous affair at the time."

Monsignor tilted his chair back and looked at the ceiling, a habit he had when annoyed. "Yes, indeed. But don't you think she shows all the signs of a delusional type? Hates religion, hates priests, feels we're hounding her, feels God is her enemy. And all this running around, from New York out here, then to San Francisco and back, it fits that sort of pattern."

"Yes," Ned Niles said. "Yes, I see what you mean. But I believe there's a missing element in her story. There's something else, something she doesn't want to tell us. And I think I know what it is. Something happened to her husband when he fell and injured himself on the cliffs at Carmel. Don't you think that's more than a coincidence, Barney, his falling and being injured in the same place where she saw the apparition?''

"Frankly, I don't," Monsignor said. "I still think she's a delusional type. Especially, now that I hear she's come back here. Look, Ned, I hate to say this, but this is my parish and my responsibility. So, do me a favor, will you? Stay for the weekend, by all means. Delighted to have you. But I'd prefer that you don't see or talk to Mrs. Davenport while you're here. And, by the same token, I'd be obliged if you'll give Mother Paul a call now and tell her that, on my recommendation, you won't be visiting her and won't discuss this matter any further. And that I'd prefer that for the present she doesn't discuss it either, not with the other nuns, not with anyone."

There was a silence in the sitting room. Ned Niles got up and went to the window. He looked out at the long adobe schoolhouse, at the mission-style church, surrounded by the graves of early parishioners, at the courtyard with its great wooden cross

and its windbreak of molting eucalyptus trees. Above the tree
the sky had clouded over. Spits of rain fell on the dusty flag
stones of the yard. He turned back to Monsignor. "Can I mak
a deal with you, Barney?"

Monsignor said nothing.

"Let me ask *you* a favor. Supposing you let me do one mor
thing. Let me go over now and see Mother Paul and hear wha
sort of dream this old nun had. If it doesn't match Marie Daven
port's dream, then, right, I'll drop it. But if it matches the appa
rition Marie Davenport saw, then I'll report back and let yo
know. I feel it's my duty, in a way, to follow up on this. Bu
I'll tell you what. Even if the dream and the apparition are simi
lar, I'll leave it up to you as to what, if anything, is to be ou
next move. Is that fair?"

It is not fair and he knows it, Monsignor decided. I am unde
no obligation to him, no obligation whatsoever. But if I don
let him do this, then he will be under no obligation to me. H
can tell this story to anyone he meets, he can write it up an
publish it. He's not a priest anymore, he's a writer; and writer
want to make a name for themselves. He could write this up a
his investigation, not mine; how he tracked down the story de
spite the indifference of a certain Monsignor. He could mak
me look stupid, or worse. Indeed, he could. "All right, Ned,"
Monsignor said. "But on one condition. I want to make it clea
to you, as I'll make it clear to these nuns. Unless somethin
else happens, another apparition, something we can verify i
some way, then this matter goes on the back burner as of to
night. Dreams are not apparitions, apparitions are not necessar
ily apparitions of Our Lady: you know all of that as well as I do
You can go and see the nuns and check out this report, bu
that's it. I don't want you seeing Mrs. Davenport. I don't wan
you talking to her. Understood?"

"That sounds like an order."

"It's not an order," Monsignor said. "You asked for a deal
I'm offering you a deal. Okay?"

"Fair enough," Ned Niles said. "Thanks, Barney." But he
did not sound thankful. He turned away from the window,
cracking his knuckles.

"So, I'll see you at suppertime," Monsignor said, rising. "You're going over there at five-thirty?"

"Five-thirty. Right."

Monsignor nodded. He turned his back on Ned Niles and went along the corridor to his study. Keep your cool, he warned himself. But he did not feel cool.

"WE CAN let you have the same room," the desk clerk told her. "It's the one your husband had, the one with a view of the beach."

Not the beach, the headland, she thought. It faces the headland. She looked out of the doorway of the motel office. Alex was waiting for her in the car. "Yes, that will be fine," she told the clerk. She registered, took the key, and went outside again. As she did she saw that Alex was no longer in the car. She looked about, alarmed, and saw him walking along the gravel driveway, going in the direction of the cliff walk. She did not take the car, but hurried after him on foot. "Where are you going?"

"I'm going to the room."

"Wait. I'll drive us over."

"No. I want to walk." He walked on. She went back to get the car. As she turned the key in the ignition she looked to see where Alex was and she saw him turn in at the unit that faced the headland. Yet he didn't know that the desk clerk assigned us that unit. She watched him begin to walk up the stairs, going toward the room he had been in before. Was it just chance, or was it something else? Did he go there automatically, without thinking? Is it chance that the clerk assigned us this particular unit? She felt a sudden chill. Isn't this the way mad people think; they see a purpose in things, a plot, a scheme that doesn't exist? She put the car in gear and drove down toward the last unit, the one facing the headland. Alex was standing at the top of the steps, waiting for her. She had the key. She parked and went up to join him. "How did you know this is our room?" she asked him.

He looked at her strangely. "Have you got the key?" he said.

She let them in. He went at once and sat on the bed. He

175

looked drained. "Let's put you to bed," she said. He nodded and allowed her to help him undress. When he was between the sheets, she brought the suitcases up from the car and unpacked his pajamas. He lay with his head turned toward the window. She had him sit up and helped him put on his pajamas. He said, "I'm hungry. I want some soup."

"I'll get some," she told him. "If you're hungry, that's a good sign, isn't it?"

"Yes," he said. "It's a good sign. Don't be long."

"I won't."

She went out, leaving the door unlocked. As she walked toward the dining room she thought of the last time she had seen the green car. It was when they passed the Point Lobos State Reserve, just south of Carmel. A few minutes later, she had pulled in at a vista point, pretending to check the tires. She had waited there but the green car did not appear. Perhaps the priest turned off at Carmel? She remembered that Daniel was going to try to meet her today in San Francisco. What would he think when he found out that she was no longer there and that Alex was no longer in the hospital? He would be sick with worry. She would have to phone him later, when Alex was asleep.

She got two bowls of soup from the dining room and went back to the unit. As she went up the wooden steps, it began to rain. Alex was no longer in bed, but sitting at the table. "Better to eat sitting up," he told her. He stared at his bowl of soup as though it were a puzzle he must solve, then began to drink it very carefully, sipping small spoonfuls. He did not speak to her and she did not speak to him. After he had drunk about half of the soup, he stood up and got back into bed. She watched him check his pulse and make a notation on the pad by the phone. Then he lay down and pulled the covers up to his chin. "I'm going to sleep, now. You don't have to stay here. Go for a walk, if you like."

"It's raining," she said. She sat by the window. It was just after three. If she phoned Daniel at UCLA he might be in his office. But what would she tell him? How would she explain their coming here? The easiest thing would be not to call him. But if she did not call him he might think she had changed her mind about coming away with him. He might.

176

She saw that Alex had turned toward the wall. She got up and went to look at him. He was asleep. Suddenly, she felt she must get in touch with Daniel now, even if she had to tell him some lie. The rain had stopped. She took the key and went out to the motel office, where there was a pay telephone. She rang the UCLA number but the nurse said he had not come in this afternoon and was not expected. She rang the Crestwood but got no answer from his room. Perhaps he had already gone up to San Francisco to look for her. Anxious and indecisive, she came out of the motel office and as she did found herself face to face with the sign that said Cliff Walk. As she looked at it she became convinced that it was a signal: it was a warning about the convent, about the thing she had left undone, about the nun, Mother Paul, who had telephoned last night. Why didn't I call her back? That must be what they want. Cliff Walk. I could go along the cliff walk to the convent now, down through the fields to the coast road. It's not far.

At once she set off, hurrying, following the path, the path of the butterflies. She did not think to take her car and drive to the convent. She did not think of anything except that the sign was a signal and she obeyed the sign. She walked quickly, under skies filled with the presence of rain, going along the path that forked, taking the upward fork, leading to the headland. As she began the climb to the top of the headland she felt the tension of nearing that hated place. Perhaps she was not meant to go to the convent, but to come here. What did they want of her? A dread of them filled her as she walked on. She saw again the trolley in that hospital room in Nice, she saw the dead face as the French doctor drew back the sheet. *I am the resurrection and the life.* They give and they take away. They kill and resurrect and kill again.

She walked toward the place. When she came to it she stopped and looked down at the great shelf of cliff, thrusting into the seas. She then looked directly below her at the jumble of rocks, the twisted Monterey cypresses outside that dark cavelike place where the apparition had shown itself. Above her, gulls wheeled and cried, warning of storm. She stood very still, tense, as though a fusillade of bullets would ring out, tearing into her body.

177

Below her, the twisted trees stirred in the wind. She watched their branches part, then come together again. She was sure that it would happen: it was the same movement of tree branches she remembered from her nightmare. The sky darkened almost to blackness, an absence of light that must surely precede the other unearthly light that would surround the figure of the girl child. The gulls no longer cried. All was still. She waited. But, within seconds, the darkness lifted. There was nothing supernatural here. It was, again, a normal cloudy afternoon. This was a cliff on the coast of California, a meeting of land and water, the natural confrontation of elements in a serene, familiar world. She turned away, continuing to walk along the cliff path toward the convent, when, beneath her, there started a familiar trembling, as though the ground were shaken by an explosion. There was a rumbling that was not thunder. Within seconds, it passed. She had felt this before in the years she lived in California. It was an earthquake tremor, a minor movement on the Richter scale. She turned, looked out to sea, then down at the cliff below, looked, and, shocked, looked again. The great shelf of rock had cracked. A thin straight line ran down its entire length, a fissure less than six inches wide, intersected by a second narrow fissure, also straight, the whole forming a great cross that ran the length and breadth of the rock. She looked back to the spot where the twisted trees guarded the cavelike place. But all was normal. Gulls wheeled in from the ocean, crying like banshees. She looked again at the great cruciform design, an accident of nature, caused by earthquake, by a fault in the earth's crust. Turning, she hurried away from that sight, along the path and around the headland, coming to the sloping field that led down to the coastal road. She began to run down through the dry grasses of the field, toward the twin towers of the mission chapel, the red tiled roofs of the convent building. She reached the road and ran up it, up to the convent gates, up the long avenue of tall eucalyptus trees, past the painted sign.

SISTERS OF MARY IMMACULATE
Gift Shop

There were no tourist cars in the parking lot. She went through the small side entrance marked Gift Shop. Welcome. Inside the gift shop, old Sister Catherine was on her knees with a dustpan, sweeping up small shards of broken glass. On the display shelves, teddy bears and dolls were sprawled in abandoned disarray. Some had fallen on the floor. The broken glass was from the special display case, now empty, jagged fragments sticking out of its frame. The large Virgin doll that had been in the display case had been taken out and lay, with its Infant, on the shop counter. Sister Catherine looked up from her labors. "Marie," she said, and smiled in welcome. "Nice to see you again, Marie."

"Hello, Sister."

"Did you ever see such a mess? It gave us a good shaking here. Do you think it was a big one?"

Marie bent down, picking up teddy bears and placing them on the counter. "I don't know."

"It was an earthquake, a real one," the old nun said. "That was no sonic boom." She swept the last shards of glass into her dustpan and carried the dustpan to a wastepaper basket already filled with broken glass. "Just put the teddys anywhere," she said. "I'll fit them back in their cases later." She pointed to the big Virgin doll. "It's a pity about that," she said. "That's a replica of the real statue of Our Lady of Monterey that's in our chapel. When the earthquake hit us, the first thing I saw was this come crashing out of its case, right through the glass. I thought it would hit me." She turned the big doll over. The doll's bisque face was cracked. A piece of the cheek had broken off, revealing the mechanism of the doll's eyes, weighted in the center of the head by a leaded pendulum. In addition, one of the arms was dangling. "I'll have to see what I can do with epoxy," Sister Catherine said. "Where were you when the earthquake came?"

"I was outside. Up on the headland."

Did the old nun look at her strangely, when she said that, or did she imagine it? "On the headland," Sister Catherine said. "You could have been killed. I wonder if there's much damage in the convent. I'm not supposed to close up here for another hour." She paused, then laughed a surprisingly mischievous, girlish laugh. "Tell you what. Let's go over for a minute and see. Will we do that?"

"Yes," Marie said. "I want to see Reverend Mother."

"She'll be up in the gardens, I'd say."

Sister Catherine locked the gift shop and led the way across to the convent's main door. The door was locked. Sister Catherine took out a key and admitted them. Inside, all was still. Sister Catherine led the way to the community room. There was no sign of breakage there. "No windows gone, thanks be to God. We'll go and have a look at the kitchens."

The kitchens were similarly undisturbed. As they came out, Sister Catherine turned left into another corridor. "Oh, dear," she said. Marie, coming behind her, saw that a plaster statue had fallen from its niche in the wall and lay shattered on the floor. Opposite, a statue of St. Joseph remained in its niche, unharmed. The broken statue that Sister Catherine picked up was a statue of the Virgin in blue and white robes. "I wonder, is there damage in the chapel?" Sister Catherine said. Behind them, they heard the rustle of habits. Two nuns had entered at the main door and were coming toward them. Both wore aprons made of potato sacks over their skirts. "Is there damage?" one of the nuns asked. It was Sister Placidus.

"Just this," Sister Catherine said, holding up the statue. "I wonder about the chapel, though."

"No, all's well there," Sister Placidus said. "Gonzaga, you go and see about the rooms at the end." She smiled at Marie. "Hello, how are you? Mother sent us to have a quick look. But we have to get back to work right away."

"Is Mother Paul up in the gardens?" Marie asked. "Could I see her? I know she wanted to speak to me."

She saw the two nuns hesitate. "It would be better at five when the work is done," Sister Placidus said. "Could you come back then, do you think?"

Sister Gonzaga, with a rattling of the wooden rosary beads around her waist, came bustling though a door at the other end of the corridor. "All's well back there," she said. "We're lucky it was only a small quake."

"Not so small," Sister Catherine said. "It broke some things in my shop."

"If you can come back at five?" Sister Placidus said to Marie. "Mother doesn't see visitors until after five."

It was an order, Marie decided. What will I do till then? I am afraid to walk back by the cliff path. I will have to go home by the road. "Yes," she said, hearing her voice speak out as though some other person answered. "Yes, I'll come at five."

"Good." Sister Placidus and Sister Gonzaga bobbed their heads in farewell, and hurried off toward the main door. Sister Catherine took out her keys. "Well, I'll clear up in the shop now. We'll not have many tourists a rainy afternoon like this. Come, Marie."

She led Marie out and locked the door behind them. Marie said good-bye to her in the parking lot and walked down the avenue of eucalyptus trees to the road. Ahead of her a rainbow appeared, arcing over the peaks of the Los Padres Mountains to bury itself in a green hill near the roadside. She looked at the rainbow. Was it some sort of sign? I am now in a world where nature is no longer natural. Why was there an earthquake at the very moment I walked away from the cliff? Why did it split the rock in the shape of a crucifix? She thought of the doll statue crashing down from its case, of the other statue of the Virgin shattered in the convent corridor. What was it the priest said? *A miracle is only a sign; it does not compel belief.* But they are trying to compel me, they are trying to frighten me. Ahead the rainbow seemed to shimmer, then dissolve. It began to rain. She did not seek shelter, but kept on walking. By the time she reached the inn, her hair was limp, her dress and shoes were wet and wilting. As she went up the steps of the unit, she saw two small pug dogs on the landing above her. The pugs turned to face her, yapping excitedly, running around her in little waddling circles as though about to nip at her ankles. Alex's door was not locked. When she opened it the dogs followed her in. Inside, she saw a very fat man wearing a peaked red and white baseball cap, an electric blue track suit, and multicolored running shoes. The stranger was sitting at the foot of Alex's bed. Alex lay on the bed. He was dressed in jeans and sweater and he was weeping.

The pugs waddled past her, yapping, frisking around the fat man's shoes. The fat man rose, admonishing the dogs in a high snappish voice. "Down, boys, down there, lads! Enough of that." The pugs slunk under the table as though miming a fear they did not feel. The fat man turned to her. He had light blue eyes in a coarse alderman's face. "Hi, how are you? Are you Marie?"

"Yes." She looked past him at Alex, who did not look at her. "What happened?" she said.

"You felt the quake?"

"Yes."

"Well, the boys there, they get really nervous if we have a little quake, so I always take them out right away and give them a run. So we went up that cliff walk there—oh, I'm in 36, just across the way, my name's Herb Luddington, how are you?" He stopped to offer a pudgy hand. "Anyway," he said, "he was standing right at the edge of the cliff, weeping, calling for Marie. He didn't want to leave, at first, but I got him to come back with me. I found out this was his room and came up here with him. Frankly, I didn't think I should leave him alone." He lowered his voice to a whisper. "Has he had a breakdown or something?"

She nodded. "Thank you very much. Thank you," she said, turning toward the door, trying to get rid of him. But to her consternation the fat man sat down again on the edge of Alex's bed. He put his soft fat hand out and stroked the back of Alex's hand. "All right now, good buddy," he said. "We found Marie. Marie's here, okay? We're going to look after you."

He looked up at Marie. "I'm a therapist," he whispered. "I was just going to try a little massage to relax him. I think it would help."

"No, thank you," she said. "Alex? Alex? I'm here."

Alex looked at her. He continued to weep.

"He'll be all right," she told the intruder. "If you'll just leave us now, I think I'll pull the blinds and let him rest. That's what he needs, a rest."

"True thing," the fat man said. "True thing." He had an irritating habit of using emphatic pauses between each word. "Let me tell you something," he said. "He needs rest but he needs more than rest. You know what I mean?"

"No, I don't. Anyway, thank you very much for all your help."

But the fat man showed no signs of leaving. "What's the head bandage for? Did he have an accident?"

"He fell. Excuse me." She sat on the bed beside him. She put her arms around Alex. "Alex," she said, "it's all right. I'm here."

Reluctantly, the fat man stood up. "Is he using any type of sedative? I have some pills in my room, got them from a good friend of mine, a terrific doctor. I know what Alex's going through. I've been there myself. True thing."

She tried not to listen. She held Alex. She held his head against her breasts. He wept, inconsolable. The fat man came up behind her and tapped her on the shoulder. "Can I speak to you for just a minute?" he said, beckoning. Unwillingly, she let go of Alex and followed the fat man to the far end of the room. He leaned toward her. He smelled strongly of disinfectant. "I don't want to make a big deal of this," he said in a confidential voice, "but you know what I think?" He paused, his dermanic face round, serious, histrionic. She waited. "I think," he said, spacing each word as though it were a separate sentence, "I think that Alex was up there getting ready to . . ." He joined his hands, then spread them. "Jump."

Suddenly, she was filled with apprehension. "You do?"

"I do. That's why I stayed with him. I don't think he should be alone. That's why I recommend massage, or sedation. But something. Some . . . thing."

"I'll stay with him," she said. "Thank you again."

"Okay," he said, sounding angry. He looked at the pug dogs. "Hey, Chu! Hey, Chin!" The pugs came frisking out from underneath the table, waddling up to him. "Come on, boys. Guess we're not wanted here."

"I'm sorry," she said. "I didn't mean that."

"Never mind. Never mind. When I said we're not wanted here I was on the money, wasn't I? Oh, yes, I was. Well, that's fine. I'm going back now to 36 and make the boys a little dinner. Then we'll watch TV. So, if you need help, help is just a phone call away. Extension 36. Come on, boys."

"Thank you," she said, again. She watched the pugs waddle

after him as, garish in his multicolored clothes, he went toward the door in a strange pigeon strut, his chest puffed out, his head held high. "Dee-pressive," he suddenly sang out. "Dee-pressive. Remember, when he says he's feeling better, that's the time to watch him. True thing."

The door shut. She turned back to Alex. "Alex," she said, going to the bed, sitting beside him again. "Alex, can't you tell me why?"

He shook his head. She held him in her arms. She sat for a long time, listening to his sobs. When at last he fell asleep, she moved to the chair by the window. A little after six-thirty, the telephone rang. "Hello," she said, in a whisper.

"Mrs. Davenport? Is that Marie?"

"Yes."

"Mother Paul here. We were expecting you, weren't we?"

"I'm sorry. My husband is ill. I can't come."

"Oh, I'm so sorry. I hope it's nothing serious. Father Niles has just left. He's been telling me about your experiences. I mean, it's interesting to me because one of our nuns has been having a dream that sounds very like what you described to Father Niles. Of course, this was just a dream, not a vision. I really would like to talk to you about it, though."

"Yes," she said. "I was going to come."

"Well, I was wondering. Of course, I don't want to bother you while your husband is ill. We'll mention him in our prayers tonight, by the way. But perhaps if it's inconvenient for you to come to me, I could come to you. Sometime tomorrow, whenever it suits you."

"Yes," she said. She saw Alex stir. Was he awake? Was he listening?

"Shall we fix a time, then? What about the morning, say at ten, would that be convenient? I may bring this other nun, or I may not. Perhaps you'd prefer I didn't bring her until we've talked?"

"Whatever you say."

"Well, I'll decide on that tomorrow. Is ten all right?"

"Yes."

"Good. I'll see you at ten. I hope your husband will be feeling better. I'm sure he will."

She heard Mother Paul hang up. *I hope your husband will be feeling better. I'm sure he will.* Was that a promise? She switched on the light and went to look at Alex. He had moved, but he was still asleep. She touched his brow. His skin felt cold and clammy. She went to the closet and got a blanket, which she laid over him. As she did, she heard a knock on the door. She went to open it, switching on the porch light. Outside, on the landing, was the fat man in his track suit, his pug dogs at his heels.

"Hi, there. I saw your light go on. How's he doing?"

"He's asleep."

"Good. Good thing. Anything we can do for you?"

"No, thank you."

"Sure?"

She looked into his light blue eyes and was afraid. Was he just an outsider, a passerby, or was he part of their plan, someone sent to frighten her with his story of Alex on the cliff, ready to jump? Since he had told her that, she could not leave Alex, not for a minute. "No, thanks," she said, again.

"Maybe you want to get something to eat? I could stay with him. It would be a pleasure. Right, boys?" He looked down at the pugs, who responded by pawing his running shoes.

"Thanks, but I'm not hungry."

"Maybe later on then. We'll be in all evening. Right, boys?" The pugs frisked. One barked. The fat man turned to leave, then hesitated. "Who's Daniel?" he asked.

"Who?"

"Daniel. He's worried about someone called Daniel."

"What?" she said. "What did he say?"

"When I found him out there about to jump off the cliff, he was calling your name. He turned to me. Did I tell you he was crying? Well, he was. He said to me, 'She told Daniel. She's gone to tell Daniel. They're going to come for me.' That's what he said. Make any sense to you?"

"Yes, it does. Thank you for telling me."

"Listen, let me get you a sandwich and some coffee, right? What kind of sandwich would you care for?"

She felt her eyes fill with tears. "What do you want?" she asked him. "Who sent you?"

"Who sent me?" He threw his head back and laughed, his fat breasts jiggling in the track suit. "Who . . . sent . . . me? Who knows? Fate, Chance—maybe the Good Lord. Anyway, Marie, if I can call you by your lovely name, the Good Lord or whoever sent me out on my run with the boys this afternoon sent me at the right moment for your husband. I don't want to frighten you. No way. But you'd be a widow now. That's the bottom line, Marie. You'd be a widow."

"I'm sorry," she said. She wiped her eyes.

"So trust us. We're friends, me and my boys, aren't we, lads?" The pug dogs looked up at him expectantly. "Right, lads? Remember, we're just across the way. Just pick up the phone."

"Was my husband really going to jump? Are you sure of that or did you just suspect it?"

"How can we be sure of anything?" the fat man said. "People pull back. They go to the brink, then they change their minds. How can we know what anyone else is thinking? No, Marie, I can't say for certain. But I wouldn't turn my back on him, if I were you." He smiled. "Friendly advice," he said. "Come on, Chu." He bent down and patted one of the pugs which was nosing at Marie's ankles. "Let's go, lads."

She watched him, light as a dancer despite his bulk, as he ran easily down the wooden steps. In the driveway he waved to her, then ran on to his own unit. The pugs had trouble keeping up. She went back in, closing the door. Alex was sitting on the edge of the bed, his head in his hands.

"Who was that?"

"It was that man who found you on the cliff this afternoon."

He stood up, as though he had not heard her answer. "I'm thirsty," he said. He went into the bathroom, ran the tap, came out with a glass of water, and went to sit on the chair by the window.

"Alex," she said. "Why were you up on that cliff?"

"I was looking for you."

"Why were you looking for me there?"

"I saw you going up there, earlier."

"And why were you crying?"

He shrugged.

186

"That man thought you were about to kill yourself."

He looked at her then, strange, with his discolored cheek, the shaven patch in his skull. "Did you believe him?" he asked. "If you believe that, you're a fool. The last thing I want to do is kill myself. Don't you understand anything?"

"I'm sorry."

"Who is that man, anyway? The fat man. He's spying on us. I know it."

"Why do you think that?"

"I just know it. There's something about him, he's too interested. Like that priest who came to my room in the hospital, the one who followed us here."

She stared at him, surprised. "How do you know he followed us here?"

"His car was behind us when we left Moffitt Hospital. You kept looking at it. You saw it near Monterey and then you pulled in at that vista point below Carmel, trying to see if he was still behind us. Right?"

She sat silent, unable to think of a reply. His lackluster eyes examined her, without hatred, without affection. "You lie to me," he said. It was a statement, not a question.

"I'm trying to help you."

"How? By running to priests and saying prayers? I don't understand you. I never would have guessed you were foolish enough to believe in that sort of nonsense."

"I don't believe in it," she said. "I've never believed in it."

"You're lying. You lie all the time now. Lying is part of your nature. I see a lot of things I didn't see before." He stood up and started to undress, taking off his sweater, then his jeans. "Can you find my pajamas? I'm going back to bed."

"Don't you want something to eat?"

"No, I want to sleep. Tomorrow I'm going to be better, much better. What I need now is rest."

She watched him put on his pajamas, then get into bed and pull the blanket up to his chin. "Should I put the light out?" she said. "I'm going to bed myself."

"Do what you want."

She undressed and got into the twin bed next to his. He took his temperature. He checked his pulse, then made a notation on

187

the pad, put the pad under the pillow, and closed his eyes. She switched off the light and lay in the dark, listening to the sound of his breathing.

"Why were you crying?" she said. "Alex, please? Why were you crying?"

He did not answer. She listened, trying to determine if he was awake or asleep but could not be sure. After a time, exhausted, she slept.

SOMETIMES when Mother Paul put the gear of the convent pickup truck in neutral, it slipped into reverse. This happened at the turn of the road leading to the Point Lobos Motor Inn. Mother Paul was waiting for an oncoming car to pass before taking a left into the motel driveway and, when it happened, the pickup truck backed across the road and almost went into the ditch. It was something that had to be fixed but where was the money to fix it? The convent's official car, an old Chrysler sedan, had been out of action for more than a year, ever since Mullen's Garage had given an estimate of four hundred dollars to put it in working order. So the pickup truck was what Mother Paul used for all her errands and jobs. When driving it she sometimes wore a straw sun hat over her veil because in that way she looked less like a nun at the wheel of a pickup truck. This morning she was not wearing the sun hat. As she got the truck back into gear and turned in at the motor inn, she thought of the way Father Niles had invited himself here. He was certainly the opposite of Monsignor in his manner of doing things. Monsignor would never have phoned her, as Father Niles had done.

"Mother Paul, Father Niles. Did she show up after I left last night? I'm very curious."

"No, she didn't come," Mother Paul informed him.

"I wonder what's wrong. Did she call you?"

"No."

"Perhaps it would be a good idea if you gave her a call. I do think it would be interesting for you to hear what she says first-hand."

"I did call her," Mother Paul said. "Last night. I'm going

189

over to see her this morning. Her husband was ill, that's wh
she didn't come."

"Interesting. When are you going there?"

"At ten."

"Would you like me to drive you over?"

"I think I'd better go alone," Mother said. "If that's righ
with you, Father?"

"Of course, of course. Listen. There's a dining room in tha
motel. Perhaps you and I could meet for a coffee after you tal
to her."

"Well, if you like," Mother Paul said. She was not at al
pleased.

"Should we say ten-thirty, a quarter of eleven? I'll be in th
dining room from ten-thirty on. If your talk takes longer, don'
worry. I'll wait. Will that be all right?"

"Yes," she said. But now as she drove into the motel drive
way she wondered if it was all right. Did Monsignor know
about this or was Father Niles acting on his own? Perhaps sh
should speak to Monsignor himself, before saying anythin
else to Father Niles. After all, Monsignor doesn't really know
any of this. When poor Mother St. Jude told me about thos
dreams of hers I recommended that she mention them to Fathe
Cowan or to Monsignor. But I don't think she did. She's told n
one except me. Poor St. Jude. If only Monsignor and Mothe
Provincial could know the way we all feel about her. Monsi
gnor never will. He sees our contemplative nuns as drones, ex
tra mouths for us to feed. Of course, he has to be practical. An
Mother Provincial is very practical. I sometimes wonder
though, if all of us in religion haven't become too practical.

As she drove the truck in low gear along the driveway, sh
was reading the numbers of units. From the way the number
ran, the one she was looking for must be at the far end of th
driveway. When she reached the last two units, she saw she ha
been right. As she parked and got out of the truck, a man sittin
on a deck chair outside the opposite unit looked up from hi
newspaper and nodded to her. He was a stout fellow wearin
running shoes and some sort of gym clothes. He had two of th
dearest little dogs with him, fat little fellows who, when the
saw her get out of the truck, ran up, barking. She bent to tickl

190

their ears. One of the things she missed in the religious life was animals. She had always loved dogs, had had them at home when she was a girl. "There now, there now," she said. The dogs stopped barking and licked her fingers. She stood up, smiling, in the happy humor she always felt after seeing dogs or cats. The stout fellow, their owner, folded his newspaper and smiled at her. "They like you," he said. "Yes, indeedy."

"I'm very fond of dogs," Mother Paul said. "What are their names?"

"Chu and Chin. I had three boys once upon a time, but I lost the third. He was called Chow. Chu, Chin, Chow. It was the name of a musical."

"Yes, I think I remember that name," Mother Paul said. "They're lovely little fellows."

Smiling at him, then at the dogs, she turned and went toward number 62. As she began to go up the steps, the stout man called out, "Going to visit the sick?"

"What?"

"Up there." He pointed to the door. "Dee-pressing. Poor guy."

Mother Paul was not sure she understood. "Are you a friend of the Davenports?"

"Just a neighbor," the stout fellow said. "He's not well, poor guy. No . . . not . . . well," he repeated, spacing his words for emphasis.

"Oh, really," Mother Paul said. She now regretted having patted his dogs. She went on up the steps. As she did, she saw that the venetian blinds were drawn in the upper unit. Surely they were not still asleep? Mother Paul habitually rose at five for morning prayer. She hesitated before knocking. As she did she saw the stout man go inside his unit, followed by his dogs. And then, as she finally decided to knock, the door opened. Marie Davenport was in the doorway, her finger to her lips, warning her to silence. Behind her, Mother Paul saw a bedroom in darkness, and a light from a bathroom door. From inside the bathroom, a man's voice called, "Who is it?"

"Just the maid," Marie Davenport said. She slipped out of the door to join Mother Paul on the landing, calling: "I'm going for coffee. Be back in a minute." She shut the door and

took Mother Paul's arm, going down the steps with her. "I'
sorry," she said. "I'll explain later. Let's go to the dini
room. We can talk there."

"Yes, as you wish," Mother Paul said. After all these yea
in America she still used phrases that were translations from h
native French. When she was younger she had believed th
Americans were not much different from the English Canac
ans she had known in Montreal. But she no longer believe
this. Americans appeared open but were introverted. Their su
face friendliness was a mask to conceal their true feelings. Th
young woman was no exception. When she showed up at tl
community hour the other day, Mother Paul had thought h
very ordinary, someone who had dropped in by chance becau
she had once been a student in the Order's school in Montre;
There had been nothing to indicate that she had a special pt
pose in her visit. It had taken a mystic like Mother St. Jude
detect that she was not a casual caller. Mother Paul remen
bered that Mother St. Jude had willed the girl to stay for suppe
And who would guess, even now, that this politely spoken g
told Monsignor and Father Niles that she hates religion and
it stands for? Mother Paul looked surreptitiously at the girl a
noticed for the first time that her dark hair, with its center pa
ing, fell on either side of her face, rather like a nun's veil. B
her face did not look like the face of any nun Mother Paul h
known. Rather, it was the face of a nun as it might be depict
in a religious painting: pale, beautiful, suffering—a holy fac

"And how is your husband today?" Mother Paul asked.

"Oh, he's better. Much better. I'm sorry I didn't introdu
you, but, because he's been so ill, I didn't want to bother h
with all of this. I mean, he wouldn't understand."

They went into the motel dining room. The waitress pick
up menus and led them to an imitation-leather booth with
view of the ocean. She gave them the menus and asked if th
would like to order breakfast.

"What would you like?" Marie Davenport asked. Mot!
Paul said she would like just a cup of tea with milk.

"And a coffee," Marie Davenport said. The waitress we
off. There was an awkward moment of silence before Mot!
Paul decided to start.

"Father Niles has been telling me about what happened to ou. It really is extraordinary, isn't it?"

"Yes."

"Now, I must tell you my side of it," Mother Paul said. About six months ago Mother St. Jude, you remember her, e tall older nun?"

"Yes, I do."

"Well, Mother St. Jude is a very special person to all of us in e convent. She's very retiring, as you may have noticed. In ct, she hardly ever speaks. And I would say she's the person I ould think of at once, if you were to ask me do I know anyone ho is truly holy. At any rate, about six months ago, she came me and told me she'd been having a very disturbing dream. he dreamed she was walking on a cliff and, below her, there as a big flat shelf of rock and some trees—she's not sure about at part—but she thinks the trees were growing out of the rock. nd in this dream a figure appears to her, a figure dressed in hite, but she can't really make the figure out and it's calling ut to her, but she can't distinguish the words it says. Yet, in e dream, although the figure is very indistinct, Mother says e knows it is Our Lady. And because she can't hear what it is ying to tell her she is filled with a feeling of despair. And so, ach time she has the dream, she wakens in panic, as if she's aking from a nightmare. Well, we talked about it and I sug- ested that she mention it to Monsignor Cassidy, or to Father owan, who is confessor to most of our nuns. But I think she as too shy to do that. Anyway, she continues to have these reams and they're causing her great suffering. I didn't tell the ther nuns about it because Mother St. Jude didn't want me to. he thinks of it as a penance Our Lord has given her to remind er of some lack of devotion on her part. Of course, I can't be- eve that. She's the most devout person I know. But, anyway, arie, I've been worried for her for months now, so when Fa- er Niles told me that you've been having similar dreams, I as greatly interested, for Mother St. Jude's sake. And that's hy I've come to see you. Father Niles says that in addition to aving the dreams, you actually saw an apparition."

"I saw something. I saw a girl, a young girl. I mean, I think I id. For a long time I wanted to belive it was a hallucination."

"But you no longer believe that, do you?" Mother Paul sa[w]
the girl avoid her eyes, when she asked this, bowing her head [as]
though she were a humble postulant before her Mother Sup[e]-
rior. But this girl was no nun. Father Niles had said she was [a]
married woman having an adulterous affair at the time O[ur]
Lady appeared to her. "Father Niles tells me you've change[d]
your mind recently," Mother Paul said. "He says somethi[ng]
happened to your husband which made you decide to come fo[r]-
ward."

"My husband? I never said anything to him about my hu[s]-
band. What did he say about my husband?"

"I'm sorry," Mother Paul said. "Father Niles said your hu[s]-
band had an accident which had some connection with your v[i]-
sion of Our Lady."

"He told you that?" Mother Paul felt the girl's sudden a[n]-
ger. "Why did he say that, I didn't tell him that, I didn't te[ll]
him anything of the kind. What sort of games do you peop[le]
play, pretending that you know nothing about what's ha[p]-
pened, when the truth is you know all about it; you helped
make it happen, Father Niles, you, all of you."

At that moment, while Mother Paul wondered what on ea[rth]
to say—indeed, wondered if this girl was quite sane—the wa[it]-
ress arrived with a cup of coffee and Mother Paul's cup of te[a.]
"Thank you," Mother Paul said to the waitress. The waitre[ss]
went away. Mother Paul put milk in her tea, then said, "Mar[ie,]
I want to tell you something, and I hope you'll believe it's t[he]
truth. I didn't know anything at all about you and what's ha[p]-
pened to you until Father Niles called me the other night. T[he]
reason I didn't bring Mother St. Jude here this morning is si[m]-
ple. I came here to try to help her get over these terrible drea[ms]
of hers. I haven't told her anything about you or what you sa[y]
because she's an old woman and she's frail and I didn't want [to]
upset her any further, until I had a talk with you and could ma[ke]
up my mind as to whether this is a coincidence, or somethi[ng]
else, something supernatural. That's why I'm here this mor[n]-
ing. I came here on my own to talk to you honestly and openl[y,]
to try to find out what sort of person you are and what I shou[ld]
do now. There's no conspiracy, believe me. Unless it's Go[d's]
will and Our Lady's wish that we do, indeed, try to have[.]

shrine here. And that's one of the things I thought I'd ask you. Mother St. Jude has always worried and wondered about where this place is that she sees in her dreams. She doesn't have any idea where it can be. You say the place where you saw the apparition is near here. If I tell Mother St. Jude about this, would you be prepared to go with her and show it to her?"

"I don't have any choice, do I?"

Mother Paul looked at the girl's troubled face, at eyes filled with anger and suspicion. "I don't understand," Mother Paul said. "What do you mean?"

"I have to do it. For my husband's sake. Because you force me."

"I'm not forcing you," Mother Paul said. "You must do what you think is best."

"I'll go with her."

Mother Paul bowed her head. "Thank you," she said. "I'll tell Mother St. Jude. She'll want to see you, I'm sure. When would you like to meet her?"

"Today. As soon as possible. Wait." The girl hesitated. "How can I leave my husband? Supposing he takes a bad turn?"

"We could, perhaps, get someone to stay with him. Two of our sisters have nursing experience."

"No. No nuns. He wouldn't stand for that. I'll go back now and she how he is. If he seems all right, maybe I can go with you for an hour or two. What am I worrying about? He'll be all right. As long as I'm doing what you want, he'll be fine, won't he?"

"Maybe we can find some lay person to stay with him," Mother Paul said. "I might be able to arrange it through St. Bonaventura's; that's our local school."

"He'll be all right," the girl said. She stood up. "I'll just go and check on him."

"Are you sure?"

"Yes, I'm sure. Let's stop playing games. Look. Meet me outside in five minutes. We can leave then."

"Well, as you wish," Mother Paul said, uncomfortably. If the husband was ill, he should not be left alone in a motel room. It was very wrong. But Marie Davenport had already gone out of the dining room. Mother Paul picked up her cup of tea and tasted it. The tea was cold.

AS MARIE went back toward the unit she looked up and saw that the venetian blinds had been opened and that Alex was standing at the window, looking out. She wondered if he had seen her go to the dining room with Mother Paul. When she started up the wooden steps he turned and looked at her, and when she reached the door she heard him unlock it. As she went in, she stared at him in surprise. He seemed quite different from the man she had left not half an hour ago. His cheek bruise was less noticeable, his color was normal, the skin rosy, his eyes bright and alert. Even his walk had changed. He moved impatiently in a manner familiar to her from before the accident. "Where were you?" he asked.

"I went for coffee."

"Why didn't you wait for me?"

"Sorry," she said. "Are you hungry? Do you want breakfast?"

"Yes."

"I'll get some for you," she said. "What do you want?"

"I'll get it myself." She noticed he was wearing a jacket and tie.

"How are you?" she said. "You look a lot better."

"I'm fine. I feel completely normal. It's amazing. I feel as if I could go right back to work today."

"But you mustn't. You were very ill. You couldn't possibly be well enough to go back to work."

"Why not?" He looked at her and shrugged. "This whole illness has been a mystery. I feel as if I'd had some sort of fever and now it's gone." He laughed. "Aren't you pleased?"

"Of course I'm pleased. What do you mean?"

"Nothing. Look, I'm going over to the dining room and have some breakfast. What are you going to do?"

"I don't know. Maybe I'll go for a walk. Is that all right?"

"Go ahead. I'll see you later." He picked up the tennis hat and put it on, positioning it to hide his wound. "See you back here," he said. "Then we'll decide what to do." He went out. She watched him go down the steps with a quick, normal walk

This is the most astonishing of his transformations. Of course it is. They're showing me what they can really do. They're showing me that they're ready to make a deal. She stood at the window, watching him as he went toward the dining room. She saw Mother Paul standing in the driveway outside the dining-room entrance. Alex looked strangely at Mother Paul as he passed her and went inside. When she saw him go in, Marie came out of the unit and walked quickly toward Mother Paul, who started to meet her. They met halfway along the drive.

"How is your husband?"

"He's much better. We can go now."

"If you're sure he's all right?" Mother Paul said.

Marie looked at her. Could it be possible that she knew nothing, that she was an unconscious agent of the forces she served? "Yes, he's fine," Marie said. "He just passed you a minute ago, going to get breakfast. The tall man wearing a tennis hat."

"Oh? I didn't notice. That's our old truck over there."

She followed Mother Paul to the pickup truck, watched her hike her long skirts as she climbed into the driver's seat. "It's very untidy, I'm afraid," the nun said as Marie got in beside her. As they drove out, Marie looked back toward the dining room. Had Alex seen her? Was he watching her now? Or did it matter anymore? It was as though they were all of them actors, going through set moves. And now, with the precise timing of a theatrical event, as the old truck drove through the gates of the motor inn, a small green car approached the gates, sounding its horn. Truck and car drew parallel to each other and stopped. The car's driver was Father Niles.

"Good morning, Mother. Hello there, Marie."

"Hello, Father," Mother Paul said.

"Where are you off to?"

"We're going over to the convent to see Mother St. Jude."

"Oh," Father Niles said. His fox mask peered up at Marie. "That should be interesting for you."

Lines in a play, lines they have rehearsed. She heard the priest say, "I wonder if you'd mind if I came along, Mother Paul. Only if it's convenient, of course."

Mother Paul's coif made a starchy sound as she turned her head toward Marie. "I don't think that would be suitable, do you?'' Mother Paul said in a low voice, as though concealing her question from the priest.

"Whatever you like," Marie told her. What was this charade of asking her opinion?

Mother Paul's head jerked back toward the priest, her headdress now askew. "I'm afraid it might make it too much of a delegation, Father," she said. "Mother St. Jude is terribly shy."

Marie saw the priest nod his head, unwillingly. "All right then," he said. "Could I come over later, sometime this afternoon, perhaps? I'm very interested, as you know."

"If you wish." Mother Paul fiddled with the truck's gears as though dismissing him.

"See you later," he called.

As the truck drove onto the highway, Marie, looking through the rearview mirror, saw the green car circle and follow them out, then turn off in the opposite direction, going toward Carmel. The truck was very noisy, its tailboards rattling, its engine coughing as it went off down the coastal road. On its worn wooden instrument panel Marie saw a battered silver medal, representing a tall man leaning on a staff, walking through kneedeep waters. On his shoulders was an infant and the infant held the globe of the world. Marie remembered this image from her school days: St. Christopher, the patron saint of travelers, carrying the Christ Child across a river. She looked surreptitiously at Mother Paul. The Superior's face was serene as she watched the road ahead, the road that led to the windbreak of tall eucalyptus trees surrounding the red convent roofs. As the truck turned in at the convent gates, the Superior said, "Mother St. Jude will be in the chapel now. I think it's best if I go and tell her what's happened, then bring her to you. She had a bad heart attack last year, so we usually send one of the younger nuns with her if she has to go out of the convent grounds. Sister Anna, one of our younger contemplatives, is very devoted to her. So, if you go with Mother St. Jude to look at this place, I think Sister Anna should go along too. Is that all right?"

Marie nodded. "Whatever you say."

The truck drove past the gift shop and the parking lot and parked in a little yard at the rear of the convent. Mother Paul got down and waited for Marie to follow. "Come," she said. "I'll put you in the visitors' parlor. If you'll just wait there until we come for you?"

She followed the Superior into the cool stone corridor, saw her open a heavy wooden door to the left of the entrance. "This is our parlor. I won't be long."

Marie went in. She heard the Superior shut the door behind her. The room was dark, its wooden shutters closed against the sunlight. It was furnished with a narrow couch under the window, a pine table, two shabby armchairs, and a sideboard, on which, as though left there by accident, there were several bottles of vinegar marked by handwritten labels. Marie thought of a nun's cell. She thought of that life which might have been hers if she had been a devout Catholic who had seen the apparition, believed in it, and gone at once to proclaim it. Like similar witnesses she might have been forced to hide from publicity, taking up the life of a nun in a convent as some had done. *Solus ad solum,* the old nun had called it. To shut oneself away from the world, alone with God. She felt a panicky impulse to open the door and run out of the convent, run down the driveway to the road, to hitchhike a lift south to Big Sur, to run and keep on running.

But I cannot run away. Whatever has forced me each step of the way will force me to speak. And that will be the end of my life with Daniel. I am a victim. I wait here, a victim.

Somewhere, far away in the convent, she heard a door open, then close. She waited for footsteps to come and fetch her, but no footsteps came. She went to the shuttered windows and unlatched them, pulling them open. Sunlight goldened the room, casting long shadows. She felt a tension enter her body, a tension so great she trembled. She was in their power, was in their prison; they would come to claim her. She would go with the old and holy nun, would show the old nun those rocks, those twisted cypresses, the great shelf of cliff jutting out into the ocean, its surface newly seared by a cruciform scar. And this time the theater of God would be ready. All that had happened until now was a rehearsal for what must happen next. She would see the girl figure, not in a dream, but, as she had seen it that first time, in daylight, amid the sounds of gulls and sea, would hear again that anxious, childish voice calling out its instructions. She would be vouchsafed a second vision, and this time, perhaps, there would be witnesses to testify that the Virgin had spoken to her, commanding her to tell the priests to make this place a place of pilgrimage. *And that will be the end of the life I knew, the defeat of my will.*

Her tension grew. It was as if a current had entered her body. She waited for footsteps, as though those footsteps were the sound of her jailers. She heard the main door of the convent make a sound as if someone had turned an old-fashioned key in the lock. There was a creaking noise as the door opened, then a dull slam as it shut. Footsteps approached, the brisk step of the Superior, followed by a halting tread, a sound of age, of infirmity. She turned toward the door as a bride turns to the altar. She waited for the door to open, saw the handle turn, felt faint. The door swung slowly inward. Reverend Mother Paul. And, behind her, the tall uncertain figure of the old nun, her skin Indian-brown, her face seamed with wrinkles, her eyes cast down. "Come in, Mother," Reverend Mother Paul said, turning to take the old woman's hand and lead her forward. "Marie, you remember Mother St. Jude."

"Yes," Marie said. The old nun raised her eyes and again, as in that first meeting, Marie felt herself enveloped by a look of love mixed with reverence, a look she had never known from any other human being. The old nun came forward, holding out her arms as to embrace her and as she touched her, holding her lightly, the tension left Marie's body. In that moment, mysteriously, her fear of this place and these people was subsumed in a larger feeling, a feeling of peace.

"Come, Marie," Mother St. Jude said. "Let us sit for a minute. Reverend Mother has told me your news." Slowly, she went with Marie and sat with her on the narrow couch. The Superior remained by the door. "Mother St. Jude would like to talk with you, Marie. And then, I think, she'd like to see this place. Wouldn't you, Mother?"

"If Marie will show it to me, yes." The old nun looked again into Marie's eyes. "It was good of you to come back, Marie."

"Is it far away?" the Superior asked.

"Half a mile, maybe less," Marie said. "We would have to

go up through the field opposite the convent. Once you reach the top of the field, there is a path. I wonder if Mother St. Jude will be able to walk that far.''

Mother St. Jude smiled. "Yes, yes. I am a good walker.''

"Well, we'll send Sister Anna to help you,'' Mother Paul said. She looked at Marie. "I would rather you didn't say anything to Sister Anna about why you're going there. Until we're sure, I think it's better not to get the other nuns excited.''

"Where is Sister Anna?'' the old nun asked. "Is she in chapel?''

"No, she's working in the kitchen today,'' Mother Paul said. "I'll go and fetch her.''

When the Superior left the room, the old nun leaned toward Marie and touch her lightly on the arm. "Marie? Marie, I want to tell you something. I am not worthy to talk of such things. Indeed, I do not talk about them. But I am telling you because you are very special to me. I believe you are special to me because you are special to Our Lord. What I want to say is this. There have been times in my life when God has denied me His presence. These absences happen without warning. Yet, without Him, I do not exist. Do you understand me, Marie? Yes, yes, you do. His absence is my despair, it is my death in life. Of course, I continue to pray, but I pray in a different way, prayers of loss, prayers which beseech Him. I am small and weak and alone at such times because I do not have the shelter of His love. An absence came on me last Easter. And it remained. I told no one, not even my confessor. I told no one because I have never been able to speak of these things. But I began to have this dream, the dream I told to Mother Paul. I continued to have it until the day you walked into this convent. Let me tell you about that dream. It was so indistinct that it seemed my eyes had failed and I could no longer see clearly. I knew that my dream was of a place by the sea. I could hear the sound of waves. It was dark as though a storm moved overhead. I was on some sort of cliff and a figure would appear below me, clothed in white, surrounded by a bright light. I knew, I always knew, that it was Our Lady, although I could not see its face. It would raise its arms and call to me, but the sound of the waves prevented me from hearing what it said. It would call and call and I would strain to hear until, suddenly, it would fade from sight. And I would wake in anguish, the anguish of knowing that, somehow, I had failed God. And because of my failure, God was absent.''

Mother St. Jude bowed her head. The coif of her headdress slipped forward awkwardly, revealing the hairline of her brow, the hair shorn, astonishingly dark, the hair of a young woman. ''And then you came to see us that day,'' Mother St. Jude said in a voice that was barely above a whisper. ''And the moment I saw you, God came back into my soul. It was true happiness, that happiness that the saints have spoken of—St. John of the Cross and St. Teresa. Not that I am a saint, Marie. I am nothing. But when Our Lord showed Himself to me again, I knew it was because you had come to see us. And now you have come back and I am to go with you and see the place I dreamed of. You are, indeed, God's messenger. I hope that when you show me this place I may know what Our Lord wants of me. I thank you for coming.''

Marie looked into those dark eyes, filled mysteriously with love for her, and felt a great sadness. ''I didn't want to come back,'' she said. ''I came back to save my husband's life. I have been forced to come here and tell what I saw. If not, my husband will die.''

Again, Mother St. Jude bowed her head. ''Do you believe that God would harm your husband?''

''I don't believe in God. I am your opposite,'' Marie said. ''Happiness, for me, is knowing that I am in charge of my own life, that I can do as I choose. Don't you see that you're a victim, as I am a victim? What sort of love is it that's withdrawn from someone as good as you, sending you into despair? What sort of love could I possibly feel for a force which has done these things to me and to my husband?''

The room was still. The question hung in the air. Then Mother St. Jude said, ''I know nothing of God's intentions. But I can tell you what St. John of the Cross has written. 'I am not made or unmade by the things which happen to me but by my reaction to them. That is all God cares about.' Do you understand, Marie?''

''No,'' Marie said. ''No, I don't.''

The old nun took Marie's hand in hers. "If Reverend Mother orders me to do something, I do it, not because I want to, or because I think it is right. I do it because she represents Christ in our community. It is Christ who commands me. St. John tells us that to do things because you want to do them or because you think they are right are simply human considerations. He tells us that obedience influenced by human considerations is almost worthless in the eyes of God. I obey—always—because God commands me." She smiled. "So, I am not a victim, Marie. And thanks to you, God is again present within me. Let us go now, shall we? I am sure that Reverend Mother is waiting for us."

They went out of the parlor. Outside, in the sun and shadow of the convent corridor, Mother Paul waited with another nun. They came forward. "Marie, this is Sister Anna," Reverend Mother said. "I think you met on your last visit."

Marie did not remember this nun. She was young, probably in her early twenties, and stout, with a white pudgy face and incurious pale blue eyes. She bobbed in a sort of curtsy, saying in a flat midwestern accent, "Oh, yes. Pleased to meet you."

"Sister Anna is going to go with you on your walk," Reverend Mother said. "Are you ready, Mother St. Jude?"

"Yes, Mother," the old nun said. She allowed Sister Anna to take her arm. Mother Paul went to unlock the convent's main door. "I'll see you later," she said, standing aside to let them pass. As Marie went down the steps, following the two nuns, she heard Reverend Mother lock the door behind her. Ahead, as they began to walk down the convent driveway, the tall eucalyptus trees groaned and swayed in a sudden wind. Dusty leaves swirled in circles around the nuns' long skirts. Marie, hurrying, caught up with Mother St. Jude, walking on her left side. "Where are we going, then?" stout Sister Anna asked.

"Up to the headland," Marie said.

"It will be good to have a long walk," Mother St. Jude said. "Do you know I have not walked this far outside the convent in years? Oh, yes, I was twice to the hospital but we went in a car. I feel nervous outside."

They crossed the road, climbing into the field that led up to the headland. The grass was summer-brown and dead and dry to the tread. The old nun settled into a slow but steady pace, bending over like a hooded figure in a medieval painting as she made her way up the slope, the fat young nun scrambling awkwardly beside her.

"Yes," Mother St. Jude said, turning to Marie as though there had been no interruption in their talk. "I remember the first time I ever had to go out of a convent. It was long ago, in Chicago, when we were cloistered. During the war we had to register for something, some government regulation. Six of us were put on a bus and sent downtown. I had not been out of that convent since I went in as a postulant back in 1924. I remember when we went out into the streets it seemed to me that I had come into a great desert. The space, and the people hurrying about, and the noise of the traffic. I remember I felt as if I would faint."

Sister Anna, holding the old nun's arm, giggled. "Oh, Mother, I never heard you tell that."

"It's the memory of that time," Mother St. Jude said. Her fingers gripped Marie's arm. "I am nervous again. Are you nervous, Marie?"

"Yes," Marie said. She looked up at the headland. The sky above it was clean of clouds. A hot dry wind whipped the grasses with a faint crackling sound as though the brush had already caught fire. Sister Anna panted short-windedly, as though she ran a race. They went on, moving more slowly as the incline grew steeper. Occasionally, Mother St. Jude would pause, less, Marie guessed, for her own sake, as for the sake of her overweight companion. And so, in this way, slowly, they came to the top of the field and the narrow path of the cliff walk that wound around past the headland to the Point Lobos Motor Inn.

"Which way do we go now?" Sister Anna asked.

"To the right," Marie said.

"Are we going someplace in particular?"

"It's just a walk," Mother St. Jude said. "Take my arm, Anna."

Marie went ahead, the two nuns following. The path ran along the cliff's edge, giving them a clear view of the precipitous drop and, far below, the lonely small coves where breakers rolled in, in long white sleeves. And as Marie approached the fateful place she began to walk slowly, as though she went toward danger. Ahead, she saw something coming up over the curve of the headland. It was one of the little pug dogs. It ran toward her and, in a moment, its twin came into sight, following it along the path. Where the dogs were, their master must also be; and soon she saw him come up over the rise, this time wearing a bright yellow track suit and red running shoes, running lightly, coming toward her and the nuns at a fast speed. The pug dogs ran past her to Mother St. Jude, who stopped and smiled at their antics. "Funny little dogs," Sister Anna said. The pug dogs waddled forward cautiously, sniffing at the old nun's skirt. The fat man came up, stopping as he reached Marie. "Oh, hi," he said, as though surprised to see her. She looked at him, afraid. Of course he was not surprised. He had come here on purpose. He was part of some plan.

"Hello," she said. She made to move on, but he blocked her path.

"I thought you'd gone," he said.

"What?"

"I saw your husband a little while back. He said you were taking off for New York."

"He said what? Where did you see him?"

"He was loading up your car. I told him he was sure looking a lot better. Fan-tastic. That's some recovery, I'll say."

"When did you talk to him?" she asked. She felt her heart pound.

"Just now. About ten minutes ago." The fat man looked past her at the nuns. Marie saw that, despite his easy running style, his face and neck were slathered in sweat. "Morning," he said to the nuns. "Two nuns are good luck. If you meet two nuns. Or is it bad luck? I don't remember. What do you say, Sisters? Have you ever heard of that? Good luck or bad luck?"

Mother St. Jude bowed her head. Sister Anna, also shy, shrugged and smiled uneasily. "This way, Mother," Marie said, gesturing for them to come forward and pass the fat man. "Excuse us," she said to him.

"Oh, excuse me. Go right ahead," the fat man said. "Yes, I

thought you'd be going to New York with your husband. You staying on here, then?''

"Yes," she said, moving past him, dismissing him. What did he mean he saw Alex loading up the car? Alex must have said something, must have told him he was leaving. New York? Is he going without me, does he know about me and Daniel, is that it, is he walking out on me before I walk out on him?

"Bye now," the fat man called after her. As the nuns passed him, he chuckled, suddenly. "I think it's bad luck. Sorry about that, Sisters.''

Sister Anna gave him a shy nod as she passed. The old nun kept her head down. He turned and whistled to the pugs. "Come on, boys. Let's go, boys.''

Marie and the two nuns continued on, not speaking. When she looked back, the fat man and his dogs, diminished by distance, were already climbing up the adjoining headland. A hot inland wind blew toward the ocean, furling the nuns' long skirts. Mother St. Jude's hand sought Marie's and held it. Hand in hand, like children, the three of them went along the narrow path. Marie glanced at the old nun's seamed brown face. Did Mother St. Jude know how close she was to the frightening seascape of her troubled dreams? Marie sensed that she did and sensed too that in this moment of approaching crisis Mother St. Jude had retreated behind her lifelong barrier: a wall of silent, intense prayer.

Marie, leading the others, moved carefully along the cliff's edge. As the hot wind flattened the grasses bordering the path, she noticed a cluster of dried leaves caught in the interstices of those grasses. She looked again, and with a strange sense of premonition, realized that the leaves were not leaves but a cluster of monarch butterflies, their wings pressed shut, their tiny bodies rocking in the hot buffeting breeze as they struggled to stay on the ground. Were they, who had once gaily led her to this rendezvous, now in grim pantomime, warning her to go no further?

But, already, as she drew level with the shut-winged struggling creatures, she had reached a point where, just ahead, she could see the tip of that great lower shelf of rock that jutted into the ocean. The tide was out. No waves spilled over the prow of the cliff's great deck. Holding the old nun's hand tightly, Marie went forward and turned left, leaving the path, going to the cliff's edge. She stopped. Sister Anna, moving past the old nun, came to the rim of the cliff, looking down at the sea. Mother St. Jude turned to Marie, and now those dark luminous eyes were filled with uncertainty. "Is it here, Marie?"

"Yes, here."

The old nun turned to the sea. Marie saw her peer forward, looking this way and that, first at the flat shelf of rock fissured by yesterday's earthquake in a great cruciform scar, then at the jumble of rocks directly below her, the cavelike entrance guarded by twisted cypress trees. The young nun, Sister Anna, walked up and down the cliff's edge. "What a lovely view," she said. Below, two squabbling gulls called out in anger, hunting each other in and out of crevices in the lower reaches of the cliffs—then, silent, rose like ghosts, their slow powerful wingbeats carrying them high above Marie and the nuns. The hot wind from the desert suddenly stilled, a cathedral stillness broken only by the distant sighing of the tide. Marie remembered the inscription in the convent chapel. *An invocation produced a sudden total calming of the elements during which the vessels were enabled to come about and the crews and vessels were saved.* She turned to look at Mother St. Jude and saw that the old nun had gone down on her knees, facing the jumble of rocks and the cypress trees. Beside Marie, the flat voice of Sister Anna said, "It's so quiet, all of a sudden. So quiet. Do you think there'll be a storm?"

Marie looked up at the sky. All was still. The sky was a blue, cold silence. She looked back at Mother St. Jude and saw that her eyes were closed and her lips moved in prayer. It was the hush before some great happening. "It's so quiet," the flat voice said again. Marie watched the cypresses, watched for that mysterious movement to begin, watched for the strange theatrical light to glow beneath the cavelike entrance. It had all been planned: the kneeling nun, the sudden hush. This time they have made sure. They have arranged my witnesses. And if I deny them now? She saw the doctor lift the white sheet. *I am the resurrection and the life.* The drained corpse face, the eyes closed. No! She watched the cypresses. She felt herself tremble, tense as though bullets would tear into her body. And then, although there were no clouds, the sky changed, growing darker as if something had passed before the sun. Marie watched the cypresses. The cypresses moved. Although there was no wind, the cypresses moved.

It is going to happen. It is happening now as it happened then, and now they will force me to speak and my life will be changed. The cypresses are moving. I will see the apparition. In fear, in rage, in despair, Marie waited. The cypresses parted. The theatrical light glowed around the entrance to the cave. In revolt, she shut her eyes and put her hands over her ears. I will not be forced. She heard a cry behind her: was it one of the nuns? The apparition was here. She knew it was here. She kept her eyes shut and pressed her palms tight against her ears. But, even as she did, she heard, in her mind, the childish voice calling out, "Marie, I am your Mother. I am the Virgin Immaculate."

No, no, Marie screamed silently. Go away. She turned back from the cliff, holding her ears, her eyes shut, running blindly down from the path into the field, stumbling in the dry grasses, falling flat. She lay in the grass, her back to the cliff and the sea. Thunder rumbled far away. In the silence that followed she lay trembling, her body wet with sweat. I have refused. I have refused.

She heard a cry. Was it the same cry she had heard before, the voice of one of the nuns? She listened. "Mother of God," the voice cried. "Mother of God." She recognized the voice now: it was the flat midwestern voice of Sister Anna. She opened her eyes and squirmed around in the long grass, to look back at the cliff path. The sky was a blazonry of blue. She saw both nuns kneeling, facing the cliff's edge, both bent in an attitude of prayer. Again, the thunder rumbled. She stood up. Slowly, she walked toward the cliff, coming first on Mother St. Jude, who looked up at her, her old face filled with doubt, her dark eyes afraid. "Marie, did you see anything?" the old nun asked in a weak, frightened voice.

"No," Marie said. "I saw nothing."

"You didn't hear, you didn't see?" It was Sister Anna, rising from her knees, her fat pale face a moon of wonder, her blue eyes saucers of amazement. "She called to me. Our Lady called to me," Sister Anna said in a shaking, excited voice.

"Yes, it called," said Mother St. Jude. "I heard it call, but I couldn't hear what it said. What did it call, Anna?"

"She called to me, 'Anna, I am your Mother,' she said. 'I am the Virgin Immaculate.' And then she said, 'A shrine must be built on this rock. You will tell the priests, Anna.' Did you not hear her, Marie?"

"No," Marie said. "I heard nothing."

"It was like my dream, yet not like my dream." Mother St. Jude remained kneeling as she spoke. "It was even more unclear. I didn't see a figure, I saw only a light. I heard a voice but I could not hear the words. But it doesn't matter. Anna heard. It called to Anna, not to me. We were brought here so that Anna could be told of Our Lady's wishes."

Marie looked at Sister Anna, who was pacing the cliff's edge, in wild excitement. "Down there on that rock, that's where she wants it built," Anna called, in her flat, monotonous voice. "A shrine to be built there. That's what Our Lady wants. 'The Virgin Immaculate,' she said. Oh, God be praised. I have seen Our Lady. I have seen Our Lady. And Mother, you saw something. You will both be my witnesses. That must be Our Lady's wish."

"I saw nothing," Marie said. "I heard nothing."

"Come, Anna," Mother St. Jude said. "Come, let us pray. Let us give thanks to Our Lady."

"Yes, Mother." Obedient, the young nun went to kneel beside Mother St. Jude. Both bowed their heads. And then as Marie watched them begin to pray, lightning came down like a sword, seeming to flash all around them, striking at the great shelf of rock beneath them, near that point where, yesterday, the earthquake had split the rock in a cruciform scar. The old nun and the young nun both shivered as in shock. Thunder rolled overhead. Sister Anna jumped up and ran to the cliff's edge, pointing. "Look! Look! She has given us a sign."

Stiffly, Mother St. Jude rose from her kneeling position and went forward as though fearful of what she might find. "Look, Mother; look, Marie," Sister Anna cried. "The rock has split. It has split in the shape of a cross."

"So it has," the old nun whispered, herself making the Sign of the Cross as she spoke.

"Marie, come and look." Excitedly, Sister Anna turned back, caught Marie by the arm, and led her to the cliff's edge. "See it, look there. It cracked. It split when the lightning struck it. It's Our Lady's sign. There was no crack there, before, was there?"

Marie looked at the rock, then at Sister Anna's credulous face. Will I tell her she is wrong, that it was yesterday's earthquake, a natural cause, that the lightning had nothing to do with it. But if I deny that the lightning caused it, then I must tell about the earthquake. Silent, she turned and looked down at the fissures. She sensed that Mother St. Jude had come up beside her. "Was it split before, Marie?" the old nun asked. "My eyes are poor. But I don't think it was, do you?"

"I don't know," Marie said. "I don't remember."

"Of course it wasn't," Sister Anna cried. She clasped her hands together, excited as a child. "I saw Our Lady. Our Lady spoke to me. Imagine, she spoke to me. She looked so young, so very young. Oh, Marie, didn't you see anything? Didn't you even hear her? Her voice was so young."

Mother St. Jude took hold of Marie's hand. The old nun bent her head and faced the sea. "Marie did not see Our Lady," Mother St. Jude said. "That's right, isn't it, Marie?"

"That's right," Marie said.

"But you saw her, Mother," the credulous excited voice insisted, and now it had in it a hint of anger. "You saw something, you said you saw something."

"I saw, but not clearly. You are the one who saw, Anna. Our Lady spoke to you. Our Lady of Monterey spoke to you."

"Our Lady of Monterey!" Sister Anna cried. "Why didn't I think of that. It's the same, it's Our Lady who appeared to the Spanish sailors two hundred years ago. And the shrine that must be built will be her shrine. Mother, what will we do now?"

"We must go back to the convent," Mother St. Jude said. "We must tell Reverend Mother what you saw and let Reverend Mother decide what should be done. Marie, will you come with us?"

"Yes, we need you, Marie," Sister Anna said. "We need you to tell them that I saw Our Lady and about the lightning. Please, Marie?"

But Marie, looking past Sister Anna, saw, on the far headland, a figure clad in yellow, coming her way, the pug dogs behind him, dejected as they tried to keep up. He said Alex is going to New York. Perhaps he has already gone. But what will they do, now that I have refused them again? She looked at Mother St. Jude. "I think I had better go to my husband. He's ill."

"But will you come down later?" Sister Anna said. "I'm sure Mother Paul will want to talk to you."

"I'll see." Marie looked at the old nun. "Mother, will you be all right? Can you go back on your own with Sister Anna?"

"Of course. Go to your husband, Marie. And God bless you."

She stared at the old nun. Tears blurred her eyes. She is the willing victim, I the unwilling. And then, unable to speak, Marie turned and ran back along the cliff path, going toward the Point Lobos Motor Inn. She ran so that the fat man would not catch up with her. She ran to find out if the fat man had lied, or if he had spoken the truth, if Alex had packed and gone to New York, or was now, because of her, again in that state between life and death. And so, running in the dry hot wind, she rounded the headland and saw ahead of her the units and the path that divided, one fork going down to the beach, one climbing up to the headland. A woman and two small children were strolling on the beach, the children running barefoot in and out of the edge of the waves. Marie looked back and saw the fat man gaining on her. She was no match for his practiced speed. As she came up the last hill, which culminated in the graveled driveway bordering the units, the fat man was just behind her. She could hear his heavy, whistling runner's breathing and then saw him, on her left, going past. He did not acknowledge her presence. His face glistened with sweat and there was a wet track down the small of his back. The pug dogs, weary, ran alongside her, too tired to bark, falling back further as their master drew ahead in a final spurt. Marie watched him sprint along the driveway and run up to his own unit, where he began a series of loosening-up exercises, ignoring her as she passed by. Outside the last unit she saw her rental car.

When she saw the car, Marie stopped running. Sick, dreading what she would find, she went up the wooden steps. The motel door was ajar and, when she went in, there was no one in the room. She went to the bathroom and, as she reached the doorway, felt as though she would faint. She saw his naked shoulders, his head lolling as he lay in the bath, eyes closed. She went toward him, stumbling on the bath mat, falling to her knees beside the tub. And then, in sudden grateful joy, she saw that he was not dead. He turned his head and looked at her. "Where were you?"

"I went for a walk, remember?"

He sat up straight in the bath. Steam rose from the bath water. "You went off with some nun," he said. "I saw you." He smiled. "What were you doing, praying for me?"

"No. Are you all right?"

"Yes. Get me a towel, will you?"

She stood and took two towels off a rail. He rose, dripping from the bath, and began to dry himself. "What's this story about you going to New York?" she asked him.

"Oh, the fat guy, whats-his-name, did he tell you? I was putting bags in the car when he came by. He's a pain, isn't he? Actually, I was thinking it would be nice if we left today, but after I'd packed I changed my mind."

She looked at him. His eyes were clear, his manner brisk. "Why?"

"Well, it's been rough. I think it might be wise if I took it easy for another day or two before we go home. Okay?"

"Of course," she said. He can't have heard what I said about leaving him. He's planning our life as he always did. She looked at him again. It was as though, apart from the bruise on his cheek and the cut on his head, he had suffered no injury. He was no longer that person in limbo between life and death, but the Alex she had known before his accident. She felt a strange euphoria. Does that mean I've won, does it mean they've given up on me? Sister Anna saw the apparition, Sister Anna will be the witness. Perhaps that's what they want now, perhaps it's over for me. But the moment she thought it she felt superstitiously afraid. She looked at him as he toweled himself. At any moment they could change him back. And, as though he knew her thought, he said, "After all, I did have a severe concussion and a fracture."

She followed him into the bedroom, watched as he began to dress himself. "I've been thinking about Dan Bailey," he said.

She went to the window. She did not want to let him see her face. "Oh?" she said.

"I'd better call him."

She looked down at the beach. The woman and her two children were still there. The children were now playing with a ball. Their mother sat in an ungainly position, staring at the waves, her legs stuck out in front of her on the sand.

"I don't want him getting suspicious," Alex said. "God knows, he's probably suspicious already."

"Suspicious?" she said, watching the woman on the beach.

"You know what I mean. This business of our disappearing from Moffitt after he helped check me in. After all, you told him what happened in France."

"Some. Not all of it," she said.

"Anyway, I'll call him and thank him and say I feel so much better, I'm planning to go back to New York in a day or so. I don't want him calling Moffitt and getting them all in an uproar, do I?"

"I suppose not." She looked at him. He was sitting in the chair, putting on his socks.

"Jesus Christ," he said. "Do you realize this couldn't have happened at a worse time for me? I'm going to have ten people starting work on that new series of tests next week. I've spent a year setting up funding for it. That's what I'll do. I'll call Dan now."

"Go ahead," she said. "Call him. I've got to go down and get something from the car."

She saw him pick up the phone as she went out. He will call Daniel and if he gets him he will be friendly and he'll tell him we're going back to New York in a day or two. Daniel will be out of his mind, he won't know what to think. I'll have to call him back. I'll call him from the motel office."

She went down the steps and got into the rental car. She sat in the driver's seat, facing the headland. She felt herself begin to tremble, remembering the strange girlish voice, "Marie, I am your Mother. I am the Virgin Immaculate." I ignored that voice. Yet Alex is better, he's better than at any time since France. Perhaps they have some new plan to make me give in. Daniel? At once, a headache pain caught her in an iron clamp. An aura rose like a level in her left eye. In panic, she dragged herself out of the car and went toward the steps. Alex was ringing Daniel. She did not care anymore, she would not hide it from Alex any longer. He isn't the one in danger, now. Daniel is the one in danger. Dizzy with pain and blindness she went into the motel unit. Alex was sitting at the table, writing something in his notebook.

"Did you call Daniel?"

He looked up. "What's the matter with you, are you all right?"

"It's just a headache. Did you reach Daniel?"

"No, I had no luck."

"What do you mean, you had no luck?"

"He's not in his office. He didn't come in today. I tried his home number, but there's no answer."

"Oh, God, where is he?" she said. She sat down heavily on the bed.

"What's wrong, what's the matter?"

"Nothing," she said. "Maybe he went to San Francisco."

"Why would he do that?"

"Maybe he went to see how you were."

"Why would he do that? He wouldn't do that. He'd phone the hospital if he wanted to know how I was, wouldn't he?"

She did not answer. She got up and went into the bathroom. In her toilet kit she found the migraine pills and took two. "I mean, wouldn't he?" His voice, irritating, called out to her again.

"I don't know." She had the number of the apartment hotel where Daniel was staying. She came out of the bathroom. "I'm going down to the motel office," she said. "I forgot something."

"What did you forget?"

"It's nothing."

214

"I'll come with you. Let's go for a walk. It might clear your headache."

"No, you go." She no longer cared what he thought. She must reach Daniel.

"Do you want some aspirin?"

"No, I have some."

She saw him stand up. The aura level rose until she was blind in the left eye. "Don't come with me," she said. "I'm just going down to the office, I'll be back in a minute."

"What's the matter, are you mad at me, or something?"

"Of course not," she said. She went out. At the top of the steps she paused, like a blind person. She felt she could not make it to the motel office. She thought of going back into the room and phoning Daniel in front of Alex. But, at that moment, a voice called out, below her, "Leaving?"

The fat man was standing at the door of his unit. He was wearing a gray business suit, a vest, and tie. The vest stuck out from his body, its peak too short, revealing a bulging expanse of white-shirted belly. "I said, are you leaving now?"

"You tell me."

"What do you mean?" His face mooned up at her. "I don't get it."

Slowly, she walked down the steps. *I will ask him what I must do. They mustn't hurt Daniel.* She drew level with him. She felt she would scream.

"I'm leaving myself," he said. "Just checking out, as a matter of fact. I've finished my business here."

"Have you?" She stared at him out of her good eye. "What's the next move?" she said.

He pretended to be puzzled. "What? Oh, you mean me," he said. "I'm going back to L.A. You're from New York, right?"

She nodded painfully. "Los Angeles," she said. "Is that it?"

"That's the place," he said. "You know L.A.?"

She nodded.

"I live in Brentwood," he said. "Me and my boys run every morning on San Vicente. It's real nice, running there. Coral trees. Do you know it, by any chance?"

Daniel's hotel is in Brentwood. "I know it."

He bent and picked up a large aluminum suitcase. "Well, have a good trip," he said. "You *are* leaving today, aren't you?"

"If you say so."

"What?" he said, then laughed. "Oh, I get it. Joke." He opened the trunk of his car and put the suitcase in. He nodded to her and went back to his unit. When he opened the unit door his pug dogs ran out. She turned away, walking toward the motel office. Daniel, please be there. Behind her, she heard the pug dogs bark, then the slam of a car door. She felt the aura diminish. Sight returned to her left eye. Her headache was gone, as suddenly as it had begun. The headache and the aura were like little electroshocks. They apply them, as threats, as warnings. Now they have withdrawn them. Why? Daniel, please be there.

ON the infrequent occasions when he said Sunday Mass in the chapel of the Sisters of Mary Immaculate, Monsignor Cassidy did not take breakfast in the convent. For one thing he was only too aware of the dismal state of these nuns' finances. They were almost as poor as the medieval Poor Clares, he sometimes thought. And, of course, he always had a good breakfast waiting for him later in his own refectory. But this morning was different. Sister Beata, the nun who was their cook, smiled in triumph as she brought in glasses of fresh orange juice, a dish of scrambled eggs, and a pile of pancakes with pats of butter and maple syrup on the side. Trying to butter us up, Monsignor thought, sadly. "Look at this," he said to Ned Niles. "I think they're trying to sell us something."

"They're very excited," Father Niles said. "I could feel it here this morning. The responses at Mass. Especially from those contemplative nuns on the other side of the altar. I could hear them clearly, even though I was at the back of the chapel."

Monsignor put butter and maple syrup on the two pancakes he had selected. I mustn't get irritated, he warned himself. But, my God, Ned would try the patience of a saint. "The cloistered nuns have always been very devout in their responses," he said. "Nothing special about that."

"I don't know," Father Niles said. "I must say I felt something special. I mean, ever since yesterday when I talked with Sister Anna, I've felt privileged to be here."

"Privileged?" Monsignor said. "Why so?"

"I have a strong feeling that this is the real thing. Something ordained. For instance, this business about there being a local tradition of devotion to Our Lady of Monterey. Although, it would be more appropriate, I think, if we were to call this appa rition the apparition of Our Lady of Carmel."

"Carmel?" Monsignor said. "Why Carmel? What's wrong with Monterey?"

"Well, first of all it was Carmelite friars who landed here in 1602 and named this place, the Bay of Carmel. And then the Carmelite Order, as you know, is the Order which is linked to the tradition of mysticism and the great mystic saints, St Teresa and St. John of the Cross. And then, in modern times, Saint Thérèse of Lisieux, was of course, a Carmelite nun. You see the link?"

"Not exactly," Monsignor said. "In the first place, these nuns are not Carmelites. Or mystics."

"True enough," Father Niles agreed. "Although in my view Mother St. Jude has a touch of the mystic about her. Not to mention the third in this interesting triumvirate, Marie Daven port. The sinner pursued by God, so to speak."

Monsignor lost all taste for his pancakes. Was Ned ever going to learn? Monsignor looked around the room. They were alone, but still. Convent walls have ears. "Ned," he said. "I thought I told you. The only nuns who know about her part in this are Mother Paul and Mother St. Jude. The other nuns don't, and that's the way I want it, for now. I'd appreciate it if you don't mention her, even to me. Do you follow?" He nodded toward the door that Sister Beata had used to bring their breakfast in.

"Oh. Sorry," Father Niles said.

"And another thing," Monsignor said. "I believe you told Mother Paul that this place might well become a place of pil grimage. Do you think that was wise?"

"I'm sorry," Father Niles said, again. "I was just trying to warn her of what they might be in for. In all my reading about these types of events, one thing is for sure. Once people hear about a thing like this they come from far and near. And they don't wait until the apparition has been given the official seal of approval, either."

"Exactly," Monsignor said. "Visitors of that sort are just what we don't want."

"I know. But these things do get around. And it is such

lovely spot, isn't it? It would make a natural place of pilgrimage."

"And was that all you told her?" Monsignor asked, although he knew it was not. He had questioned Mother Paul himself before Mass this morning. A sensible woman, thanks be to God.

"Well, I also mentioned the possible advantages to the convent. I mean, if this place becomes a shrine, if a church were built and so on, it could be like St. Anne de Beaupré in Quebec. There would be offerings, donations. The convent would benefit."

"I'd think Mother Paul would be smart enough to figure that out for herself," Monsignor said. "Don't you?"

"I'm sorry. Are you mad at me again, Barney?"

"Oh, Ned," Monsignor said. He looked at the scrambled eggs, which were on a little warmer dish over a candle brazier. Perhaps some eggs? The cook would be hurt if he didn't partake. He spooned a small helping onto his plate. "I'll be honest with you," he told Father Niles. "I have no stomach for going down in the history books as the parish priest of some famous shrine. Besides, it just doesn't seem the right moment in time for this sort of thing. But, on the other hand, if there *is* something here, I want to be sure that it's handled properly, that it doesn't deteriorate into hearsay and exaggerations and conflicting testimony. If Our Lady really did appear to those nuns yesterday, then this may be the most important thing I have to deal with in my entire life as a priest. I don't intend to make a mess of it."

He saw the look Ned gave him when he said that. The thing about people like Ned was they thought they had a patent on the pure-of-heart routine. Ned sees me as all wrapped up in building fund politics, rich parishioners, and the Crosby Pro-Am. And who can blame him, the way I've talked the past few days?

"Well, exactly," Father Niles said. "I know how you feel. I understand completely."

Monsignor watched Ned sip his coffee. If only you did, Monsignor thought. If only you did.

WHEN Mother Paul went to the kitchen to see if the priests had finished, she found herself wishing that it was not a Sunday. If

219

it were a weekday the garden nuns, as she called them, woul
have been out of doors. As it was a Sunday, and a day of res
and prayer, everyone was underfoot. Gonzaga was lurking i
the corridors. Innocenta was with Beata in the kitchen, an
Placidus, Marguerite, and Annunciata were holed up in th
community room. So, where to find privacy to talk with he
visitors? It would have to be her study.

"Have they finished yet?"

Sister Beata pointed to a tray on which Mother saw th
remains of the priests' breakfast. "They didn't eat much
Mother."

"Are they still in the parlor?"

"Yes, Mother."

She knocked before entering. Monsignor was standing at th
parlor window and Father Niles was at the table, reading his o
fice. Obviously, she should have come sooner. They wer
waiting for her.

"Did you have enough breakfast?" she asked, for polite
ness' sake.

"Yes. Very nice. You're spoiling us," Monsignor said
"Are we ready then?"

"Yes, of course. I thought you might use my study. It's a
the back of the house and quite private."

"Good," Monsignor said. He and Father Niles followed he
out into the corridor. One of the contemplatives coming out c
the laundry room averted her eyes and made to pass withou
looking at the priests, but Mother Paul stopped her. "Sister
will you tell Mother St. Jude that Monsignor would like to se
her now, in my study?"

Mother Paul went ahead of the priests, opening the stud
door, apologizing. "It's terribly cluttered in here, I'm afraid.
She had tidied it last night when she heard they were coming
but it needed more than a tidying, now that she saw it as
stranger must. However, Monsignor was very polite, as al
ways. He asked permission before sitting down at her desk. Fa
ther Niles discreetly took a chair in a corner of the room.

"Will I leave you, then?" Mother Paul asked.

"No, no," Monsignor said. "This is as much your inquir
as it is mine. I'd appreciate it if you sat in on it."

"Whatever you say, Monsignor. Will I see if Mother St. Jude is here?"

As she expected, Mother St. Jude was already waiting in the boot room next to her office. Mother St. Jude was never late. Mother Paul smiled at her and put her hand on the old nun's sleeve. "Come along. They won't eat you, you know," she said.

Monsignor did not remember Mother St. Jude. The Superior had told him this morning about her holiness, her simplicity, and about the strange dream she had been having. He looked at the folder prepared for him by Ned and decided not to run through the testimony about her dreams. Ned has written that up. Let's move on to what happened out there on the headland. Monsignor rose and gestured to Mother St. Jude to sit opposite him. "Good morning, Mother," he said, cheerfully. "Sorry to drag you back like this, especially when we asked you so many questions yesterday. I mean, Father Niles asked you." He smiled. She seemed very nervous, this old soul. "The thing I want to clear up is this. Is it true that, to the best of your knowledge, Sister Anna knew nothing about any dreams or apparitions when she went out with you yesterday?"

"Yes, Monsignor."

"Why not?"

The old nun turned to look at her Superior as if for confirmation. "Because Mother Paul instructed me to say nothing whatsoever. So, naturally, nothing was said."

"Do you think Mrs. Davenport said anything to her?"

"No, Father. I don't believe she did."

"Had Mrs. Davenport met Sister Anna before yesterday?"

The old nun turned again to her Superior. Mother Paul said, "Not really, not to speak to, Monsignor. They met in the convent on one occasion but I and the other nuns were present. I don't think they had any conversation."

"So then, you and Mother St. Jude are the only nuns Mrs. Davenport has talked to about what she says she saw, is that right?"

"Yes, Monsignor."

Monsignor looked again at Mother St. Jude. "Now, when

you were out on the headland yesterday, you yourself didn't se an apparition?''

"I saw something," the old nun said. "I mean, I heard voice and I saw a light. I'm not sure that I saw a figure. And couldn't hear what the voice was saying. My sight is poo Monsignor.''

"So you couldn't testify that you saw the Virgin?''

"No, Monsignor.''

"Is it possible that this place reminded you of the place ye saw in your dream and that you confused what happened yeste day with what had happened in your dream?''

The old nun bowed her head. "Yes, it's possible," she sai in a whisper.

"So you could be mistaken?''

He saw her hesitate. Then she raised her head and looked him. "Yes," she said. "But I felt the presence of God.''

"Can you explain that?''

"I have felt it before. Sometimes, in the chapel. Sometime when I pray.''

"I see." He looked at Ned Niles but Ned avoided his ey "Tell me, Mother," Monsignor said. "Since you were the o who had the dream, why do you think Sister Anna saw the a parition and you did not?''

"There is no answer to that question," the old nun sai "We don't know God's wishes, do we? Why did He choo Marie Davenport?''

"Yes, but this time Mrs. Davenport didn't see the appa tion, did she?''

He saw the old nun hesitate. "I don't know, Monsignor.'

"What do you mean?''

"I saw her put her hands over her ears. Then she ran awa from the cliff and lay facedown in the field, holding her ears.

Monsignor looked at Ned and then at the Superior. "What this? Did you know this?''

"No," Ned said. Mother Paul shook her head.

"She told you that she saw nothing and heard nothing, Monsignor said to the old nun. "That's what you reported Father Niles yesterday.''

"Yes, Monsignor. That's what she said.''

"But you think she *did* see the apparition?"

"I don't know."

"She didn't want to see it. Is that what you mean?"

"I don't know," the old nun said, again.

"It *is* possible," Mother Paul said. "You know her attitude, Monsignor."

"Indeed I do," Monsignor said. He rose and, obediently, Mother St. Jude rose also. "Well, thank you, Mother St. Jude," he said. "I don't think I have any more questions for the moment."

"Thank you, Monsignor." The old nun turned to Mother Paul. "What shall I do now, Mother?"

"Go to the chapel," Mother Paul said. "Wait for me there. And remember . . ." She put her finger to her lips. The old nun nodded and noiselessly left the room. Monsignor took out a pack of cigarettes. "I'm sorry to impose my bad habits on you, Mother," he said. "But I have a terrible desire to have a smoke."

"I'll get you an ashtray," Mother Paul said. From a drawer in her desk she took a small Doulton plate, swept the pins which were on it into her hand, and put the plate in front of Monsignor Cassidy.

"Is Sister Anna around?"

"Yes, Monsignor. I'll go and fetch her."

"Thank you." When Mother Paul went out of the room, Monsignor looked at Father Niles. "Curiouser and curiouser," he said. "Did you know about Mrs. Davenport running away from the place?"

"It's news to me," Father Niles said. "Interesting, isn't it?"

Mother Paul knocked on the study door before reentering with Sister Anna. The stout young nun made a sort of halfcurtsy to Monsignor and Father Niles. "Sit down, Sister," Monsignor said. His tone was relaxed and genial. "Well, now. How are you bearing up under all of this excitement?"

"Oh, I'm okay," the young nun said. She reminded Monsignor of the sort of plain uneducated girl who in the old days would enter an Order as a lay sister. But then he remembered that in the history of such matters it was usually some plain, lowly person who was at the center of events. Still, Sister Anna

did not inspire respect. "Tell me, Sister," he said, "what
you know about Mrs. Davenport?"

"Mrs. Davenport?" Sister Anna looked surprised. "Oh,
she married? I wasn't sure. I don't know much about her. S
visited our convent once or twice, I think. She was a pupil
our Order's school in Montreal."

"Did she talk to you about having seen an apparition?"

"Mrs. Davenport?" Sister Anna looked almost indignar
"No, she didn't see anything. She said she didn't see an
thing."

"You're sure about that, are you? Where was she when y
saw the apparition?"

"I don't know, Monsignor. When I looked down at the ro
and saw the light and then this beautiful young girl came c
from behind the trees, I knew it was Our Lady. I didn't think
look where the others were. I just went down on my knees. A
then Our Lady spoke to me."

"So you didn't see Mrs. Davenport at all until afterwards"

"That's right."

"And where was she when you did see her?"

"Where was she?" The young nun twisted in her chair a
looked back at Reverend Mother, as though she were afraid
failing an examination. "I don't know. She was behind n
someplace. I turned and called to her and to Mother St. Jud
Then Mrs. Davenport came up and said she didn't see ar
thing. And then we knelt down to pray again, Mother and I, a
the lightning struck the rock and cracked it in the shape of a l
crucifix. And when I saw that, I knew it was Our Lady's sign
us. I was thinking of Our Lady. I wasn't thinking of M
Davenport."

Monsignor looked at the file. He checked Father Niles's r
ord of the testimony. "Now, after the figure appeared,"
said, "Mrs. Davenport told you she saw nothing and hea
nothing. And Mother St. Jude said that it was like her dream l
not as clear as her dream. What dream was she talking about

The young nun looked confused. "I don't know, Monsign
Did she say that? I don't remember her saying that."

"That's what she told Father Niles. Mother St. Jude told I
ther Niles that she said it was like her dream."

"Oh, if Mother said it, then it's true, it's true," the young nun said vehemently. "Mother is a saint, Monsignor. I just don't remember. I'm sorry."

Monsignor looked at Father Niles and then at Reverend Mother before turning again to Sister Anna. "You must tell me the truth now," he said. "Did Mother St. Jude ever talk to you before this happened? I mean did she ever tell you about a dream she had, a dream about something similar to what happened yesterday?"

"Mother had?" Sister Anna's surprise was genuine, he decided. She could not be that great an actress.

"Well, never mind," he said. "Let's go on to what you saw and heard yourself. One of the things you say this apparition told you was that a shrine must be built at that place. Are you sure it meant the shelf of rock below the cliff?"

"Yes, Monsignor. The rock which was struck by lighting."

"You're quite sure of that, are you? Father Niles tells me it would be very difficult to build there."

"But that was the place Our Lady meant."

"You keep talking about Our Lady, Sister. Do you think she will appear to you again?"

"Yes, I think she might."

"Why do you think that?"

"I don't know."

"Could it be because you've read accounts of these things happening at Lourdes and so on? Is that why you think the same thing will happen to you?"

He saw a hint of anger in her face. But she bowed her head and was silent.

"Do you think people will believe you?" he asked.

"They must. It *was* Our Lady. She will find a way. She's already shown a proof. The crucifix in the rock. It wasn't there until the lightning struck."

Monsignor looked into that stubborn face, into those almost colorless eyes. Faith is a form of stupidity. No wonder they call it blind faith. He looked at Ned's notes and Ned's transcript of the testimony. Suddenly, he noticed they were Xerox copies. Ned has the originals. Someday Ned will publish an account of all this. So, in a way, I am also under investigation. "Thank you, Sister," Monsignor said. "I think that will be all, for now." He shut the file and stood up. "I'd better go and have look at this place," he said. He looked at Ned Niles. "Will we walk, or what?"

"The quickest thing," Ned Niles said, "would be to drive up to the motor inn and go out along the cliff walk."

"Would you like Sister to go with you?" Mother Paul asked.

Monsignor looked at the young nun. He felt as though he stood on the edge of a precipice, looking into some distant menacing future. "Yes," he said. "Yes, I think that might be helpful, if you can spare her?"

"Of course."

He looked at Ned and then at Mother Paul. It seemed to him that the pleasant, rather dull days of his stewardship here were gone forever. "I'd better have Sister Anna go over this again for me on the spot," he said. Then paused. "I have decided to make a report to the bishop."

There was a moment of silence. Mother Paul said, "Very good, Monsignor."

"We'll bring Sister Anna back afterwards, in the car," Monsignor told her. He looked at Ned Niles. "Ready?"

Ned gave what Monsignor could only interpret as a triumphant smirk. I must not lose my temper with him, Monsignor thought. Not with Ned. Ned has become the Recording Angel

WHEN Daniel Bailey woke on Sunday morning in his new room in the Crestwood Apartments he called his service and was given several messages, including one from Gretta Gelson, his receptionist, which the service said was urgent. There were three calls from Marie. She had left no number. He had come back here very late last night and had not checked for messages because it had been an exhausting time with Elaine, tears, recriminations, and some unpleasant discussions about what he would take from the house and what he would leave for her. He had ended up by saying that he wanted only his clothes and books. Yesterday, just before going back to the house to meet with Elaine, he had called Moffitt Hospital twice and been told that Dr. Davenport was not available. What in hell was going on there, he wondered. That crazy report about a temperature of 2 and a pulse rate of 15. He called Marie at the Shropshire Hotel but was not able to reach her. Now, looking over all the messages, he decided to call his receptionist first.

"Gretta, it's Dr. Bailey."

"Oh, Dr. Bailey, I'm glad you called."

"I'm sorry," he said. "Disturbing you on a Sunday."

"No, that's fine. Have you been in touch with Mrs. Davenport?"

"No. I have some messages from her but I was tied up last evening."

"Well, she seems to be in quite a state, Doctor, she wondered if you'd had an accident or were ill. It seems she and her husband tried to reach you several places and couldn't find you anywhere."

"Did she leave a number?" he asked.

He took the number, which he recognized as the inn at Point Lobos. He thanked Gretta, then rang the number. The voice that answered was Alex Davenport's. "Hello," it said. "Who's that?"

"This is Daniel, Alex. Where are you? How are you?"

"Oh, Dan. Yes, we've been trying to reach you. I'm better. In fact I've checked out of the hospital."

"You what?"

"No, honestly, everything's great. Temperature, pulse, everything's great. I'm feeling great and we're back in Carmel."

"But why?" What the hell were they doing in Carmel, what was going on?

"No reason, I simply like it here. Anyway, we're going back to New York tomorrow. Did you speak to the hospital? I bet they were confused."

"I rang them but they said you weren't available. Are you sure you're okay, Alex?"

"I'm fine," Alex said. He sounded angry at the question.

"How's Marie?" He could hear his voice become unsteady as he said her name. From the way Alex talked, she hadn't told him anything. Alex still had no idea of what was going on.

"Marie's fine."

"Is she there? Could I say hello to her?"

"You're checking up on me, is that it?" Alex's voice said. "You don't have to check with her. I'm okay, I tell you."

"No, honestly, I just wanted to say hello."

"Well, she's having a shower right now. Oh, here she is." He could hear Alex's voice whispering in the background. Then Marie came on. She sounded nearly hysterical. "Daniel? Are you all right?"

"Of course. But how are you?"

"I'm all right now," she said. "We tried to get you."

"I know. I got your messages. Listen, how is he? What are you doing in Carmel? What on earth's going on?"

"Everything's fine. Where are you?"

"At the Crestwood."

"Are you going to be there for a while?"

"Yes. Can you call me?"

228

"Yes," she said. "Wait, Alex wants to talk to you again."

Alex Davenport came on. "Dan? Look, I'd appreciate it if ou keep all this stuff about my accident and so on, I mean, just eep it to yourself, will you? There's a reason. I have to get ack to New York at once, it's really urgent, there's a hell of a ot going on, a program I have that's due to start next week and don't want anyone at the Institute thinking I'm sick or some-ing and not able to see this thing through. I've waited two ears to get the funding and start this experiment. I don't want o blow it. Okay?"

"All right, sure," Bailey said. Same old Alex, he thought. alk about self-centered.

"And thanks for all your help with Moffitt, and so on, I ap-reciate it."

"It's nothing," Bailey said.

"I'll call you from New York, all right?"

"Fine."

"Thanks again, Dan." The receiver clicked. Bailey sat star-ig at the phone. What in hell is going on? Doesn't she know I ove her, doesn't she know I've changed my whole life for her? Vhat are they up to, running out of hospitals and crazy temper-ures and Alex like a zombie? And now he says they're going ack to New York. What's she doing, isn't she going to tell im? For God's sake, sick or not, he's got to be told.

HEN SHE handed the receiver back to her husband and atched him talk again to Daniel, Marie looked at him in mazement. She knew she had revealed nothing in her brief ex-ange with Daniel, but surely Alex must have noticed the way e ran naked out of the shower, dripping a trail of water across e carpet, grabbing at the receiver, shaking when, at last, she ard Daniel's voice. Surely anyone who knew anything at all out her must have seen that she was like a demented person nce that moment yesterday when she became convinced that aniel would be their next victim. And yet, listening to Alex as talked with Daniel about his plans, could she doubt that he d no idea of her state of mind or of what was going on be-veen her and Daniel? But he must be told. I should have told m that morning in France before the accident. Daniel is wait-

ing for me. Daniel, who's wondering if I've gone back on m'
promise to him. If they are going to punish me again, they wil'
punish me through Daniel, not Alex. I'm leaving. I'm going t'
Daniel. Now.

She turned to Alex, naked, wet, her hair dripping rivulets o'
water down her back. Stood on the frontier of saying what
once said, could not be unsaid. But as she hesitated, he wen'
across the room and lay down on the bed. He was still ill, sti'
the victim of her decision to defy that other world.

"Better get dried," he said. "You look cold."

I am leaving you today. You can go to New York on you'
own. I'm going to live with Daniel. The sentences moved in he'
mind but she could not speak them. He would be insulted an'
angry, he would be cold and ask questions. This would be a te'
rible interference with his plans. I am afraid of him, she said t'
herself. I have always been afraid of him. This admission, ne'
to her, seemed, suddenly, the alarm bell of truth.

"Go on," he said. "Go and get dressed. Look at the carpe'
You're soaking."

She went into the bathroom. I must tell him. I'll ring Dani'
first and then I'll come back and speak to him. She dried herse'
quickly, toweled her hair, and went back into the bedroom. Sh'
did not look at him until she had dressed. "I'm going down t'
the motel office," she said. "I need some shampoo. They hav'
a vending machine."

"Okay," he said. "I'm going to make reservations back t'
New York tomorrow. I'll try for a noon flight from San Fran'
cisco. That should give us time to drive up there."

She nodded. Let him make reservations. Mine can be can'
celed. When I speak to Daniel, I'll make plans to go to Los An'
geles at once. Then I'll come back here and tell Alex.

She went out, closing the door behind her. She stood at th'
top of the flight of steps, and as she did, a mist, coming in fro'
the ocean, tinted the morning with an ethereal silvery light. Sh'
felt ill and excited, afraid, yet released. Since yesterday, wi'
the unreasoning certainty of someone in a bad dream, she ha'
been convinced that Daniel would be their new victim. Perhap'
her punishment was over. The fat young nun believed that sh'
had seen the apparition. The fat young nun would offer as ev'

dence the false miracle of the crucifix etched in the rock. That must be the reason they had restored Alex's health and why they had not harmed Daniel. A new witness has been chosen.

In the lobby of the inn she stood with her head inside a plastic telephone bubble and dialed the Crestwood in Los Angeles. A moment later, she heard Daniel's voice.

"It's me," she said.

"Can you talk?"

"Yes."

"How are you? Why did you leave San Francisco? And he says you're both going to New York?"

She could hear the worry in his voice: Daniel, reasonable Daniel, who could not begin to know what was happening. "Daniel," she said. "Please, you've got to trust me."

"I do trust you. But he should be in a hospital."

"He's better," she said. "He really is better. He wants to go to New York tomorrow. But don't worry, I'm not going with him. I'm coming to you."

"So you've told him." She could hear the relief in his voice.

"Wait," she said. "I'm going to tell him right after this call. I'm going to drive him to San Francisco and put him on a plane for New York and then fly down to L.A. to join you. I'll be with you tomorrow night."

"You will? God, we'll celebrate. Tell you what. Ring me from San Francisco and give me your flight number. I'll meet your plane."

"All right," she said. "Listen, do you think it's safe to let him go to New York on his own?"

"He should be in a hospital. But if he gets sick on the plane they'll take care of him. Look, I don't know what's the matter with him, whether it's really serious or whether it's some freak thing. All I know is he's going to do things his way, no matter whether you're with him or not. Isn't that right?"

"That's true. But if he gets sick again, I mean if he takes another bad turn when I tell him, what will I do then?"

"If he gets sick again, call an ambulance. Don't let him talk you out of it. He's not going to get sick. You said yourself he's better."

"All right."

231

"Listen, Marie. Call me back after you've spoken to him. I'll be here waiting by the phone. Call me, afterwards. Promise?"

"Promise."

She put the receiver back on its cradle. Standing there in the plastic bubble of the phone booth she thought: They have found another witness. I am going back to my real life, the life I had before this began. I am going to tell Alex that I am leaving him. I am going to live with Daniel. It is Sister Anna's miracle now. I am the only one who knows the truth about the crucifix in the rock. If they are going to make this place a new Lourdes, they need my silence. That must be it. That is why they have released me.

Outside, the mist coming in from the sea moved on a brisk following wind, consuming cars and buildings in a blanket of invisibility as it rolled toward the headland. She watched it pass over her, leaving a clear blue sky above. She looked up at the sky and felt no fear. It is over.

She turned toward the unit. Her tension was now the ordinary tension of telling the truth. How would she tell him? He knows something has been wrong between us. He said so. She thought of his bruised face, of the way they had used him. Can I leave him like this if he is still sick?

A car passed her on the driveway, coming through the mist. It was a large Cadillac with its lights on. It drove up ahead of her and parked by the sign that said Cliff Walk. As she went toward it she saw the doors open and people getting out, two men in dark suits, and then, with a shock, she saw a third person, a stout nun in the habit of the Sisters of Mary Immaculate. She heard the doors slam, saw the driver lock the door with his key. He was Monsignor Cassidy. The other man was Father Niles; the nun, Sister Anna. All three of them saw her just at the time she saw them. They turned to her, three of the enemy, their faces pretending surprise.

"Well, hello," the one called Monsignor said. "How are you?"

"Isn't this a coincidence," the one called Niles said. She stood silent as they surrounded her with their Judas smiles, their falsely cheerful voices. It was not over. They had come for her.

"How is your husband?" said the one called Niles. "He's feeling better, isn't he?"

"Yes," she said. Of course, they knew he was better. This was their way of warning her.

"That's good news," said the white-haired one, the Monsignor. "When are you going back to New York, then?"

"Tomorrow, I think."

"So this is your last day here?"

She looked at his pink round face; his eyes with their false gleam of friendliness, his smile which showed white capped teeth. "I think so," she said. "It depends on my husband. On how he is."

"I imagine you'll be glad to get home," the Monsignor said.

"Yes," she said. "I'll be glad to leave."

"You were with Sister Anna yesterday, weren't you?"

"Yes." *You know I was.*

"Did *you* see anything out of the ordinary, yesterday? I mean when you were out on the headland?"

"I saw nothing."

She saw the Monsignor look at the other priest, a look she did not understand. Then the Monsignor said, "Mother St. Jude had the impression that you ran away from the place. That you covered your ears."

"I had a migraine," she said. "Sometimes I get migraine headaches."

"A migraine headache," the Monsignor said. He turned to the other priest. "That would explain it."

"Strange, though, that she'd get it at that very moment," Father Niles said. Mist swirled around him. In his dark suit, his fox mask twisted in disbelief, he reminded her of a stage devil.

"What moment?" the Monsignor asked. It was as though in the thrust and parry of their discussion they had forgotten her. "Don't forget, for her there *was* no moment. She didn't see anything out of the ordinary. Sister Anna was the only one who did."

She looked at Sister Anna, who stood deferentially in the background, her eyes cast down, like a child waiting for the grown-up talk to end.

"But Mother St. Jude saw something," Father Niles said. "And all three saw the lightning."

"Ah, the lightning." The Monsignor turned to her, smiling. "As a matter of fact, Mrs. Davenport, we came up here this morning so that Sister Anna could show us the cracks which she says the lightning made in the rock. I've never been out there myself. I was wondering, if you're leaving today, perhaps you wouldn't mind coming along with us now for a few minutes. It might be my last chance to have a word with you."

He was not asking her: he was ordering her. They had not forgiven her latest disobedience. This man, Monsignor, was the ringleader. He smiled again, in cheerful deceit. "I really would appreciate it," he said. "I won't keep you long."

And so she went with them along the cliff walk path, the cold marine mist rolling in again to confuse the route. They were, she thought, like people walking toward a grave, a small funeral procession: the nun, the priests, herself. Father Niles went first with Sister Anna and, as she followed, the Monsignor came alongside her. She felt his soft hand grip her elbow. "Careful there," he said. "This fog's getting thick. Tell me," he said. "Between ourselves now. Do you think Sister Anna knew anything about what happened to you, I mean what you saw last year? That's a point which interests me very much. Did you say anything at all to her about it?"

She looked at him: what answer did he want? "No," she said. "I told Mother Paul and Mother St. Jude. I didn't tell Sister Anna."

He let go of her arm, motioning her to move ahead. "We'll have to go single file," he said. "Is it far?"

She shook her head. They had come to the fork in the path and already Sister Anna and Father Niles had taken the upward route and were climbing toward the top of the headland. The mist moved more swiftly now, as a stronger sea wind made it race. The Monsignor's calm, genial voice inquired, behind her, "Do you remember when you came to see me in the refectory?"

He wanted her to answer. She said, "Yes." She did not look back at him.

"Do you remember I said to you that it was possible this apparition might appear to someone else at a later date?"

"Yes," she said. "I remember."

"I think I told you then, that, in that case, you might be asked to come forward and testify about what you'd seen."

There was no escape. That was what he was saying. They needed her. They would make her part of it, no matter what.

"I was wondering," he said. "How would you feel about that? Would you mind very much?"

Tears came, sudden and surprising. She walked ahead of him, weeping. She came around the headland. She could see the priest and the nun in front of her, talking to each other, the nun gesticulating. She wept, her shoulders shaking. She felt the Monsignor's soft warm fingers again grip her elbow. "I'm sorry," he said. "I suppose you would mind. Yes, of course you would. You don't believe any of this. You have your own life. You don't want publicity, isn't that it?"

She nodded, weeping. There was no sense in appealing to him: he was that other world, remorseless, implacable. His air of concern was pure acting. His head shook in condolence but his every action was calculated. She looked ahead and saw the shelf of the rock below the cliff. The mist spilled over it, half obscuring it. She pointed to it. "There it is," she said.

He hurried past her, as though he could not belive what he saw. "That's it?" he said, incredulously. The other priest turned back to join them. "Here we are," Father Niles said. He pointed at the great shelf of rock. "See the cracks there. A perfect cruciform shape. Amazing, isn't it?"

She watched the Monsignor go forward to the very edge of the cliff. He peered down. The mist rolled on, leaving the rock momentarily exposed. She saw the cruciform cracks, the twisted cypresses. She heard the Monsignor say, "You mean this is the place? My God, Ned, it's crazy." He laughed. "It would have to be a sort of Mont St. Michel."

"A difficult site, all right," Father Niles said. "It could be done, though. The only thing that worries me is if we build on that rock how would we be able to see that the rock is split in that shape? If you could leave the rock as a natural floor, the cracks would be there as a miraculous sign."

"Hold on, hold on," the Monsignor said. "We're not starting up a building fund yet, not by a long shot. Where's Sister Anna? Let's just run over what she claims to have seen."

Marie wiped her eyes. She did not see the young nun. She saw the priests stare about in the mist. "Oh, there she is," Father Niles said, pointing.

And then, in the drifting fog, Marie saw Sister Anna at the edge of the cliff, kneeling at the very spot above the jumble of rocks, above the entrance to the cavelike place. Kneeling there, her arms outstretched as in devotion and on her face a look of indescribable adoration. Monsignor and Father Niles moved toward her. Marie followed. Marie looked down at the jumbled rocks, the cypresses. All was normal. The sea sluiced over the edges of the rock. Mist drifted in and out of the dark cavelike opening. She heard Sister Anna cry: "Mother, I have told them. Mother. They are here."

Marie saw thin Father Niles and the heavy Monsignor run to the cliff's edge. She saw the Monsignor go to the kneeling nun. "What do you see, Sister?" she heard him call out. "Tell us, what do you see?"

"Our Lady," Sister Anna cried. "I see Our Lady. The Virgin Immaculate, there she is, she's smiling. She's smiling at me. Mother, see, I have told the priests. The priests are here, Mother."

"What does she say?" Father Niles whispered, leaning down toward the kneeling nun. "Where do you see her?"

"There! There by the rocks. See the light, the light around her? The light. It's fading now."

"Go on, tell me," Marie heard Father Niles say. "Describe it to me."

"It's fading," Sister Anna whispered. "She's gone." She bowed her head and clasped her hands together in prayer. Marie saw the Monsignor pacing at the cliff's edge, peering down, disconsolate. She saw Father Niles kneel beside the stout young nun and join his hands in a gesture of prayer. Marie walked to the cliff's edge and looked down at the place. There was no unearthly light, no movement of the cypresses. There was nothing. She felt the Monsignor come up beside her. "Did

236

you see anything?'' he asked. His voice was quiet, confidential.

"I saw nothing," Marie said. "Nothing. I heard nothing."

"Me neither," the Monsignor said. "Of course, that's the way of these things, isn't it? It's not given to everyone to see them."

She looked at him. She no longer felt afraid. Could it be that he was just an ordinary man, an ordinary priest who knew nothing, who had no plan. She saw him look back at the two kneeling figures. Then, as though irritated, he walked briskly toward them. "Ned," he called.

Father Niles made the Sign of the Cross and stood, brushing grass from the kneecaps of his trousers. "Yes, Barney?"

"Did you see anything? I didn't."

"I didn't either," Father Niles said. "But that's usual in such apparitions. Our Lady has appeared to Sister Anna, not to the rest of us." He looked at Marie. "Unless Mrs. Davenport saw something."

"Mrs. Davenport saw nothing," the Monsignor said. His voice was angry. "I think I can vouch for that. Sister Anna, if you please?"

The young nun made the Sign of the Cross, then stood, submissively. "Yes, Monsignor?"

"Tell us what happened."

"It was just like the last time, Monsignor. The trees moved and there was this bright light and then Our Lady appeared down there. She's very young, younger than me. Her skin is dark, like a Mexican's or something. She is very kind. She smiled at me. She said the same as she said yesterday. 'Anna, I am your Mother. I am the Virgin Immaculate.' And then she said that a shrine must be built here. And I told her I had brought the priests. And then she said something else, something she didn't say yesterday."

Father Niles's fox mask excited. "What was that?"

"She said, 'People will come. This will be a place of reverence.' "

"People will come," Father Niles said, repeating it. "This will be a place of reverence."

"And what happened then?" the Monsignor asked. Marie

237

saw him walk back to the cliff's edge and look down like a detective searching for some hidden clue.

"The light faded around her. Then her figure faded. And then she was gone."

"You see," Father Niles said to the Monsignor. "It's the same vision she had yesterday, and interestingly, it's very similar to Mrs. Davenport's vision of last year."

"But today I saw nothing." Marie heard her own voice, anxious and pleading. "Nothing. I don't believe in these things. I don't want to believe in them. I have a right not to. A person has a right not to believe."

She knew she had angered them, but she could not help it. She was weeping. Now they will try to force me. They will kill Alex, they will kill Daniel, anything to make me; but I am not going to help them, I am not going to be a part of this. "I have a right not to believe," she said again, then covered her weeping face with her hands. She felt someone touch her shoulder. It was the nun. "Marie." Sister Anna said, "I will pray for you."

"No, don't," Marie cried. "I don't want your prayers. Leave me alone."

There was a silence in which the only sound was the sound of her sobbing. She wiped her eyes and saw that the Monsignor had drawn the nun and Father Niles aside and was whispering to them. What were they plotting now? I saw nothing, she told herself. Today, I saw nothing. It's over for me, it's over for me, but they don't believe me, they think I'm still lying. But it's over, it's over. It's Sister Anna's vision now. Sister Anna is the one.

"All right, then," she heard the Monsignor say loudly, as though for her benefit. "I'll see you both at the car." She watched as Father Niles and Sister Anna set off along the walk going toward the motor inn. She stood alone at the cliff's edge. The Monsignor came to join her. "Come now," he said. "Let's just walk back together, Marie. You don't mind if I call you Marie?"

She found her handkerchief and blew her nose. She let him take her by the arm. He did not speak until they had come down from the headland. The sea mists, gusting in, moved across the fields like great spinnaker sails. She heard his heavy breathing as the path wound upward again. "I didn't see anything today," she said. "You don't believe me, do you? You think I'm lying."

He shook his head. "No, no."

"It's Sister Anna's vision now," she said. "Don't you see what's happened? I refused it, and now it has gone on to Sister Anna. She's a nun, she's the right person. I'm the wrong person. There was some mistake."

She saw him take a wad of Kleenex from the side pocket of his black silk shantung jacket and wipe his perspiring cheeks and brow. "Let's just take a minute's rest," he said. "I'm not as young as I used to be." He stopped. She saw that he was very out of breath. He patted his brow with the Kleenex, then looked back toward the headland. "If they ever build a shrine out there, it won't be an easy place to get to."

"So you're going to build a shrine," she said, bitterly. "That's what this is all about, isn't it?"

"I don't know," he said. "All I know is Sister Anna claims to have seen Our Lady on two occasions. I think she's sincere. And I think you're sincere."

"But I saw nothing today," she cried. "Honestly, I saw nothing."

"And yesterday, Marie?"

She did not answer. Suddenly, he was the enemy again. They will not let me go.

"All right," he said. "Let's forget about yesterday."

She stared at him. What did he mean?

"The important thing to me," he said, "is that you *say* you saw nothing. That's what you want to say, isn't it?"

"Yes."

"Well then, you saw nothing. You have that right. I told you before. Nobody's going to force you."

Was it some last trick to trap her into obedience? But as she stared at his round pink face, his thick, neatly brushed white hair, his smile, which was half apology, half reassurance, she could not believe that it was a trick. He was just an ordinary man, an ordinary priest. He knew no more than she did. "Is that true?" she said.

239

"It's true. Mind you, I'll have to make a report to my bishop about what's happened here. Then it will be up to the bishop to decide if he wants to go any further with it—an inquiry, a report to Rome, or whatever. But this is *my* report, Marie. It's not Father Niles's report, it's my report and I decide what goes into it. What you told us, you told us in confidence. If you don't want to go public, that's your right. I'm not a very holy man, but I do believe in God. And I believe that God doesn't reveal Himself to us in an unmistakable way. And the Church teaches that we're none of us obliged to believe in miracles or miraculous apparitions. You've chosen not to. So I'm going to leave you out of my report altogether. Remember, if you say you saw nothing, nobody can prove otherwise. Except, of course, God. And I think God has let you go. I think you're right. It's Sister Anna's vision now."

He held out his hand. "I'll say good-bye to you here. If you just let me go on ahead, I'll have a word with Father Niles and Sister and tell them what I've just told you, tell them we're going to leave you out of this. Good luck to you, Marie. And thank you for coming today."

He turned away. She watched him walk laboriously up the steep path, his heavy black shoes picking a slow careful route toward the Point Lobos Motor Inn. Suddenly she felt ashamed that she had not believed him, earlier. She called out, "Monsignor?"

He stopped, looked back, mopping his brow. "Yes, Marie?"

"Thank you."

He looked at her, then, suddenly, laughed. "Have a nice day," he said and, turning away, went on. She watched until he reached the driveway at the edge of the semicircle of motel units, watched him walk past Alex's unit, the unit facing the headland. In a few minutes he would reach the black Cadillac and drive off with Father Niles and Sister Anna. She might never see him, or Father Niles, or those nuns, again. She had refused and she had won.

She looked up at the sky. No guns were trained from on high ready to shoot her down. There were only dull gray clouds. Like an old battlefield, once cacophonous with the clash of steel, the roar of cannon, the screams of wounded and dying,

240

men, the headland, grassy and quiet, gave no hint of what had happened here. Like a battlefield it had become its history, its truths altered to fit the legend of those who had survived. She thought of Daniel, who would never know about this, of Alex, who had been a part of it without knowing the part he played. She and she alone would remember. She would remember it in silence for the rest of her life.

She thought of that life, that ordinary, muddled life of falling in love and leaving her husband and starting over again: that known and imperfect existence that she had fought to regain against ineluctable forces, inexplicable odds. The priests were gone. It was over. She had been returned to ordinary life, to its burdens, its consequences. She looked up toward the Point Lobos Motor Inn. She began to walk toward Alex's unit, rehearsing what she would say to him.

ABOUT THE AUTHOR

Brian Moore has written many fine novels. Among them
are THE LONELY PASSION OF JUDITH HEARNE,
THE LUCK OF GINGER COFFEY, and CATHO-
LICS. He lives with his wife in Malibu, California.